Mistaken Identity

By Donna Jay

Copyright © 2018 Donna Jay

Cover Image – shutterstock 352461434

All rights reserved. Except for the use of brief quotations in any review or critical article, the reproduction or utilisation of this work in whole or in part in any form by any electronic, mechanical, or other means, is forbidden without prior written permission from the author, Donna Jay.

This is a work of fiction. Names, characters, places and incidents either are products of the author's imagination or are used fictitiously. Any resemblance to actual events or locales or persons, living or dead, is entirely coincidental.

Acknowledgements

Heartfelt thanks go to my beta readers for whipping this story into shape.

Kim, thank you for being my constant champion. Although on the other side of the world, you were always only a message away.

Robert, thank you for catching those pesky misused words, especially when you weren't sure if they were kiwi-isms or just flat out wrong.

Linda, thank you for your eagle eye, and giving this story a final lick of polish.

Chapter 1

Excited about the night ahead, Kelly stared at her reflection in the bedroom mirror, giving herself the once over with a critical eye. Thanks to genetics and a smooth complexion, she didn't need much makeup; a touch of lippy to darken her pale pink lips, a flick of blue-black mascara to highlight the blue of her eyes, and she was good to go.

The beep of her hair straightener made Kelly curse herself. It wasn't the first time she'd almost left the damn thing on. Most of the time, she wore her hair pulled back in a ponytail.

Tonight though, she intended to use every asset she had to seduce Paula. The mere thought of dragging the long, silky locks across Paula's naked flesh made her lick her lips.

Anxious to get a move along, because God knew Paula hated to be kept waiting, Kelly smoothed down her dress and stepped into the living room.

The small flat she shared with her best friend, Nicole, was compact and homely. Kitchen, bathroom, toilet, two bedrooms, no hallway.

From her seat on the sofa, Nicole let out a shrill whistle. "Check you out, girlfriend. Paula won't be able to resist you in that little black dress."

"Glad you approve." Silky locks of long, brown hair fanned out and tickled Kelly's shoulders as she spun in a circle.

"What're you doing tonight?" she asked, coming to a stop.

Nicole leapt to her feet. "Not what, but who, baby." She shot Kelly a saucy wink. "Steve and I have the flat to ourselves so we're going to get busy."

The excited tone of her voice was infectious. With a little bit of luck, and some liquid courage, before the night was out Kelly would be getting her kink on too.

The angry blare of a car horn had her tossing her house key into her clutch purse and cutting a fast track to the front door. Spotting her summer jacket on the arm of the chair, she snagged it as she dashed past.

Temperatures were seasonably warm for February, but nights often cooled off quickly and Kelly was far from a fan of the cold.

Nicole clapped her hands like a drill sergeant. "Chop, chop. Don't keep madam waiting."

Although the words were accompanied by a smile, Kelly didn't miss the contempt lurking in Nicole's eyes. It was no secret Nicole barely tolerated Paula. But being the best friend that she was, most of the time, she played nice.

"Behave." Kelly blew a kiss over her shoulder and hightailed it down the driveway.

The passenger door flew open at the same time as she reached the roadside.

"Hi." Kelly climbed in and buckled up, the leather seats cool against the back of her legs. "Thanks for the lift."

"Any time. I'd rather pick you up than have you riding around on that death trap." Paula squeezed Kelly's thigh before putting the car in gear. "This way I get to admire your gorgeous legs."

Choosing to ignore the dig about her motorcycle,

something that tended to piss Kelly off, she fiddled with the air vent trying to angle the air freshener away from her. The citrusy sweet scent made her feel sick. Another reason she preferred her motorcycle over Paula's shiny red sports car.

"So, who'll be there tonight?"

Coming to a stop at an intersection, Paula turned to Kelly. "The usual, friends and a few work colleagues."

A beat-up sedan whizzed by, then the road was clear, but Paula's foot remained on the brake.

She turned to Kelly, eyes alive with excitement. "I wanted to surprise you. Remember my friend, Ashleigh?"

"Sure."

Kelly had heard all about Paula's best friend, and how much Paula had missed her since she'd moved away with her fiancé. Greg was it?

A car toot-tooted behind them.

Paula glared in the rear-view mirror. "Hold your horses, mister." She let her foot off the brake and coasted forward.

The urge to chuckle bubbled up inside Kelly. Paula

acted so hoity-toity. Most of the time it was comical. Other times, Kelly wanted to tell her to lighten up.

Surely giving over control would help to mellow her out. It's not like anyone else needed to know. Paula could keep up appearances outside the bedroom.

"As I was saying before I was rudely interrupted, Ashleigh and Craig are..."

"I thought it was Greg," Kelly blurted out.

Paula's perfectly shaped eyebrows drew together. "Craig, Greg, who cares? Ashleigh's in town."

The scowl gave way to a grin. "I'm so excited you'll finally get to meet her. I just know she's going to love you. Oh, and please try not to swear, dear."

And here we go again.

Kelly resisted the urge to groan. How the hell Paula managed to add a cutting comment to any compliment was beyond her. Just because Kelly was only twenty-five didn't mean she swore like a trooper. Even though right then she felt like letting loose with a few choice words.

Kelly drew a cross over her heart. "I promise to be on my best behaviour…in front of your friends."

Knowing exactly how to soften Paula up, she ran her hand under Paula's knee length skirt. "But all bets are off behind closed doors."

Goose bumps broke out on Paula's skin. Kelly revelled in her reaction.

"A lady on the streets, a tiger between the sheets." Paula winked as she pulled up the driveway and parked in the garage adjoining her expansive three-bedroom house.

Her boarder, Grace, who was making her name as a sought-after photographer, would probably be out shooting a wedding. With any luck, Paula's other boarder, Lucy, would be home. She was one of those people others tended to gravitate toward, and Kelly was no exception.

Not for the first time, Kelly wondered if Paula couldn't afford to pay the mortgage on her income alone. Something Kelly doubted considering Paula was the CEO of a large retail chain. Perhaps she didn't like her own company, which seemed more likely considering it wasn't often Kelly got to spend time alone with Paula.

Either way, Kelly wasn't rude enough to ask. If her parents had taught her one thing, inquiring about someone's income was the epitome of bad manners.

"Come on, you can help me finish getting the finger food ready before the guests arrive."

Kelly suppressed a groan. As much as she loved working in a busy café, the thought of spending her night off doing more of the same wasn't what she'd anticipated.

Injecting some enthusiasm into her voice, Kelly smiled sweetly. "Sure. What can I do to help?"

***

Later that night, Kelly stood in the kitchen chatting to Lucy, watching Paula drag her friend from one person to another.

Lucy nudged Kelly's shoulder, nodding in Paula's direction. "You been ditched?"

Kelly pegged Lucy to be in her late twenties. She was a stunning woman; dark complexion, jet black hair, and piercing green eyes.

"Nah, not ditched, just shelved for a while. I don't

mind, her friend seems nice."

At least from what Kelly could gather from their interaction before Paula whisked her away.

After taking a swig of her beer, Kelly bumped shoulders with Lucy, returning a not so subtle nudge.

"What about you? Why haven't you been swept off your feet?"

Looking totally relaxed, and not at all offended by the question, Lucy crossed her ankles and leaned against the fridge. "I haven't met the right guy or..."

Without thought, Kelly blurted out, "Or girl?"

Lucy waggled her eyebrows. "Are you coming onto me?"

Heat flared in Kelly's cheeks. "Oh, God, no. I meant…" What the hell had she meant? She could always count on good old booze to loosen her tongue. Kelly shut her mouth before she could put her other foot in it.

"Lighten up, Kelly. I was only teasing. Paula would kick me out on my arse if I even looked at you sideways. Besides, I'm not sure you have the equipment I like."

"Hey, there are toys for…"

The amused expression on Lucy's face stopped Kelly mid-sentence.

Lucy lifted an eyebrow as if to say, "do tell."

Kelly shook her head and they both burst out laughing.

A clunk echoed around the kitchen as Lucy's empty bottle landed in the recycling bin.

"I need to use the loo. Do you think anyone will miss me if I sneak off to bed?"

Before Kelly could respond, Lucy's eyes went wide, her focus on something over Kelly's shoulder.

"Don't look now…"

Of course, the minute Lucy said that, Kelly whipped her head around. Paula was heading in their direction, hips swaying, bleach blonde hair bouncing around her shoulders, and a sexy gleam in her eye. "There you are, darling."

The scent of wine and perfume wrapped around Kelly when Paula leaned in for a kiss. It wasn't often she made public displays of affection, so Kelly made the most of it.

Returning the kiss, she entwined her fingers with Paula's. The feel of her icy cold fingers made Kelly shiver. "You're freezing."

"I've been standing outside clutching a cold glass. What do you expect?"

The remaining few guests had gathered on the deck, huddled around the brazier.

Paula hiccupped and giggled. "But you're right, it is getting chilly."

She twirled a lock of Kelly's long hair around her finger and leaned in close. The feel of her warm breath on Kelly's neck sent a tingle of anticipation racing up Kelly's spine.

"I need to warm up. Got any ideas?"

Delighted, Kelly's mind raced south. "I could think of a thing or two." She pushed her leg between Paula's thighs, as much as Paula's knee length skirt would allow. "I'm sure your guests won't miss you for a few minutes if you disappear for a quickie. I mean to get a jacket from your room."

The mere thought of a half-drunken fling, inhibitions lowered, made Kelly pulse with desire.

"I like your way of thinking." Paula licked her ruby-red lips. "Give me a second to make my excuses and I'll meet you there."

Once again, Kelly was reminded of their age difference. Ten years wasn't much in the grand scheme of things, but the women Kelly had dated closer to her own age wouldn't think twice about keeping up appearances. In fact, her twenty-something year old friends would probably cheer them on as they sauntered out of the room.

Not wanting to blow her chances of getting laid, Kelly discretely swatted Paula on the backside, delighted when she let out a little squeal. "Go make your excuses. I'll meet you there in a couple of minutes."

Needing no further encouragement, Paula blew her an air kiss and trotted off wobbling slightly on her high-heels.

A few minutes later, Kelly added her bottle to the pile in the recycling bin, slipped past a couple in a lip lock on the sofa, and made a beeline for Paula's bedroom. Her pulse quickened with each step she took, images of dominating Paula overriding every other thought.

The room was pitch-black when she stepped inside. While waiting for her vision to adjust, she leaned back against the door. As if of its own accord, her hand sought out the terry robe dangling from a hook on the door, and pulled the belt through the loops.

Once she could make out the shape of her lover, flat on her back in the middle of the bed, Kelly slowly approached. Like an animal stalking its prey, her heart raced.

The fact that Paula remained deathly still added to the intoxicating game of cat and mouse. Sliding onto the bed beside Paula, Kelly gently guided her lover's arms up to the headboard. Once there, she loosely tied them together with the soft belt.

Elated when Paula didn't resist, and taking Paula's non-resistance as silent approval to continue, Kelly slid down the bed and buried her head between Paula's legs.

The second she pulled Paula's panties to the side, and blew on her centre, Paula's hips twitched. Kelly's clit reacted in kind.

Determined to show her how enjoyable it could be to give up control, Kelly spread Paula's labia with her thumb and forefinger, and focused her attention on licking, sucking, and caressing every inch of her exposed flesh.

Within seconds, Paula bucked her hips and thrashed about. The headboard banged against the wall as though she was pulling against the ties. A response that pleased Kelly immensely.

"What are you…?" Paula's voice was barely above a whisper.

In her beer fuddled mind, Kelly decided to turn things up a notch. "Shh, I'm in charge. Lie back and enjoy."

On a whim, she pulled Paula's underwear off and pushed them into Paula's mouth.

Back between Paula's legs, Kelly flung them over her shoulders. With each swipe of her tongue, Paula writhed beneath her. Her muffled moans spurred Kelly on.

The second Kelly entered her, Paula's back arched, her muscles clamped down on Kelly's fingers, and her sweet release washed over Kelly's tongue.

Ignoring her own arousal, knowing Paula would be in a hurry to get back to her party the minute she came down from her orgasmic high, Kelly slid up Paula's body and reached for the headboard.

Surprise and delight shot through Kelly when she discovered the belt had come loose. Paula could've easily taken back control, but she hadn't. If Kelly had been standing she would've done a happy dance. Deep down, she'd always suspected, hoped at least, Paula was a submissive at heart.

"I need to go to the bathroom." She pulled the panties out of Paula's mouth, kissed her on the lips, and headed for the bedroom door.

"Wow. Am I dreaming?" Paula asked, her husky voice barely recognizable.

On the other side of the bedroom door, Kelly felt like she'd stepped out of a dream and into a nightmare.

Horrified, she stood frozen to the spot, mouth open.

"Hey, you look like you've seen a ghost." Paula eyed her curiously.

Paula? Kelly's head spun. Her vision blurred. If

Paula was standing there looking at her with concern in her eyes, who the hell was in the bedroom?

Well, shit.

Mortified, Kelly trembled. Her stomach lurched. "Look out." She pushed past Paula, shot into the bathroom, and made it to the toilet just before the contents of her stomach made a reappearance; beer, a shot of tequila, chips and dip. *Yuck.*

"You okay?" Paula asked, rubbing Kelly's lower back.

Groaning, Kelly heaved again. Her throat burned. Her stomach ached as though it'd been turned inside out. "I think I drank too much," she lied, suddenly feeling very sober.

"Oh, darling. I shouldn't have left you on your own for so long. Come on." She tugged on Kelly's arm. "Come and lie down, I'll get you a bucket."

Alarm shot through Kelly. "No!"

Holy crap, what a mess. She didn't want to go back into Paula's room. What if the other woman was still in there?

Fuck, fuck, fuck.

"I just wanna go home." Kelly staggered to her feet, keeping up the façade of being drunk. "I'll get a cab."

"Nonsense," Paula replied. "Colette can drive you."

As much as Kelly would rather not spend time alone with Paula's personal assistant, Colette, she was in no state to argue. "Sure, thanks."

Sticking her head out the door, Paula spoke in a hushed tone to someone who was obviously waiting to use the bathroom. "Murray, do you know where Colette is?"

"Nope, sorry. I haven't seen her for a while. Last we spoke, she said she had a headache and needed to lie down."

No, no, no. Oh please, no, not her.

Kelly's stomach clenched. She clutched the cool hand basin with both hands, hung her head, and focused on taking slow, deep breaths.

"Give us a minute." Paula closed the door and turned back to Kelly.

The care and concern radiating in her eyes made Kelly feel like crap. Her stomach ached, her head ached, her heart ached. A part of her wanted to come clean, but what was Kelly supposed to say?

Hey, Paula, I just cheated on you. Thing is, I'm not sure who with.

Paula picked up a washcloth and wiped the black streaks of mascara from under Kelly's eyes. "Don't worry, your secret's safe with me."

A fresh wave of nausea washed over Kelly. She swallowed hard. "Secret?"

"Not everyone needs to know you can't hold your liquor. I do remember what it was like to be twenty-five." She patted Kelly's arm. "One day you'll learn how to pace yourself, dear."

And here we go again.

Caring one minute, condescending the next.

"Oh, wait a minute." Paula tapped her lip looking thoughtful. "Let me check if Grace is home. She could be in her room. I'm sure if she hasn't been drinking she'll be happy to give you a lift."

"No, please. Go back to your guests. A cab won't cost much."

"You sure? Most people have left now anyway."

"Positive." Kelly hung her head as she exited the

bathroom.

Her gaze landed on Murray's sandal covered feet. She didn't dare look up again until she'd dialled a cab and slipped out of the house.

The loud clunk of the garage door as it banged closed behind her made her jump as surely as if she'd been kicked up the backside.

Fifteen minutes later, Kelly turned the key in the door to her flat, never happier to be home. Her glee was short-lived when she flicked on the living room light and came face to face with a sight she never wanted to see, her long-time friend's backside.

Steve spun around. "Hey, what are you doing home?"

"Bloody hell." Kelly splayed her fingers across her eyes. "Dude, put some clothes on."

As if suddenly realising he was stark naked, Steve glanced down. "You like?"

Kelly scoffed. "You're such a pig."

He waggled his hips. "I prefer donkey."

"Yeah, you're right, you're an ass."

Despite knowing Steve loved to play the clown,

Kelly was in no mood for jokes. She cut a diagonal path across the living room to her bedroom.

The carpet beneath her feet served as a harsh reminder she'd left her shoes on Paula's bedroom floor.

"Goodnight, Steve."

Chapter 2

The following morning, Kelly awoke to her best friend bouncing up and down on the side of her bed.

"Hey, what time is it?" Kelly pried her eyes open.

"It's after ten; time to spill." The bed shook as Nicole got comfortable, leaning against the headboard. "What are you doing home? Please tell me you at least got laid before you gapped it."

Too embarrassed to look her friend in the eye, yet needing to confide in the only person she could, Kelly dragged a pillow over her head. "Yes, I had sex."

The pillow was unceremoniously ripped out of Kelly's hands. She was met by Nicole's inquisitive gaze.

"Why so glum?"

"I don't know *who* with." The confession made Kelly feel worse instead of better. So much for the saying a problem shared is a problem halved.

Confusion knitted Nicole's brows. "Come again?"

Normally, the double entendre would've made Kelly laugh. Instead, she exhaled a heavy breath and the words that had bounced around inside her skull all night came tumbling out.

"Long story short. I had sex with a stranger." She paused, then added, "Without her consent."

Bewilderment flashed across Nicole's face. "Whoa." She held up a hand. "Back up the bus. What the hell happened?"

Shame flooded every cell of Kelly's being as she recalled the sordid events from the previous night. Nicole listened without judgement. The look of empathy in her eyes was more than Kelly felt she deserved.

"Okay," Nicole said as soon as Kelly fell silent. "I'm sure it's not as bad as you think."

Of course it wasn't bad, it was a bloody nightmare. Kelly opened her mouth to say as much but Nicole held up a hand.

"At any time, did *she*," Nicole finger quoted the word, "say no or ask you to stop?"

Heat flared in Kelly's cheeks and she hung her head in shame. "She couldn't."

"Huh? Why not?"

"I stuffed her panties in her mouth."

A smile danced across Nicole's lips. A second later she burst out laughing. "Wow, go you, you horn dog." She punched Kelly in the arm.

"It's not funny," Kelly replied, and she meant it despite the smile she couldn't suppress.

Nicole fiddled with her robe, unwittingly drawing Kelly's attention to the belt.

Only able to endure so much humiliation in one day, no way was Kelly going to tell Nicole she'd also tied the woman's hands to the headboard. Not that she'd done a very good job of it. Apparently, the mystery woman had slipped her wrists free. Yet, she hadn't pushed Kelly away. Why not?

The shrill beep-beep-beep of the fire alarm broke into Kelly's troubled thoughts. The acrid smell of smoke wafted into the room.

"Shit, something's burning." Pain stabbed at Kelly's temples as she threw back the bedcovers and scrambled out of bed. Before she made it to the door, Nicole grabbed her by the wrist and pulled her back.

"Steve's making toast." She rolled her eyes as if that explained everything. "I'll go rescue brunch and make some coffee. Once we've eaten, we'll continue this conversation. Because, honey, before you go beating yourself up, we need to figure out who you bonked and what you're going to do about it."

What Nicole said made sense. Perhaps the unfortunate woman wasn't confused and upset thanks to Kelly.

Yeah right, keep telling yourself that, Kel, and you might actually believe it.

While Nicole sorted out Steve and brunch, Kelly grabbed her jeans and a clean T-shirt and headed for the bathroom. She desperately needed pain killers and her toothbrush. Her head throbbed, and her mouth tasted like she'd licked the toilet bowl rather than just puked in it.

She squinted against the bright light and glanced in the mirror. The image looking back at her made her cringe. Her normally vibrant blue eyes peered back at her, bloodshot and lifeless. Her mousey brown hair stuck out in all directions like twigs on a barren tree.

After locating some pain killers, Kelly chugged back two tablets before stepping into the shower. The warm water pounding on her back felt heavenly. Kelly let out a contented sigh and tried to clear her mind. Her reprieve was short-lived.

The second she closed her eyes images of someone, somewhere, trying to scrub Kelly's scent off their body crashed into her mind. Disgusted with herself, she shut off the water and climbed out.

How had she not known it wasn't Paula? Sure, it had been dark, but didn't women taste different, smell different, sound different? Her eyes went wide recalling the words, *"Wow, am I dreaming?"* No wonder she'd barely recognized the voice.

It hadn't been Paula's, but it wasn't completely foreign either.

***

Back in the living room, Kelly snacked on a bowl of fruit salad and sipped a glass of orange juice. In hindsight, she probably should've downed a large glass of water when she'd arrived home last night, it might've helped stave off her headache. But thanks to a certain person, she'd avoided the kitchen.

As if reading Kelly's mind, Steve winked at her. She rolled her eyes and threw a grape at him, delighted when it hit him in the chest.

He looked at Nicole with puppy dog eyes. "Tell your friend to stop picking on me."

Quick as a flash, Nicole plucked the grape off the floor and dropped it in Steve's coffee.

"Hey, I was drinking that." He scowled.

"Children," Kelly interrupted. "I have a headache."

Steve leaned back on the big blue sofa and placed his left ankle across his right knee. "Sorry, Mum."

When Kelly didn't smile, concern flashed across his face. He dropped his foot to the floor and placed his elbows on his knees, all traces of humour gone. His intense gaze bore into Kelly making her feel like he could see into her very soul.

She'd known Steve longer than Nicole, had introduced them in fact. He was like the brother Kelly never had. Most people assumed she was jealous when her two best friends had hooked up. But they were sorely mistaken, she couldn't have been happier. She was certain one day they'd marry.

"Wanna tell me what's going on? Or is it chick stuff?" Steve directed the question at Kelly, his unwavering gaze drilling into her.

Nicole's silence spoke volumes. It was Kelly's call whether she wanted to share her story with Steve, and if she didn't Nicole wouldn't utter a word of it to him, and Steve wouldn't press her for information.

Bracing herself, Kelly took a deep breath. "Last night I had sex…with the wrong person."

A heavy silence hung in the room. Steve turned to Nicole as if she might elaborate. When she lifted a shoulder, he turned back to Kelly.

"How does that happen?"

How indeed.

Needing to gather her thoughts, Kelly peered out the window. The sun was high in the sky, perfect weather for a ride on her motorcycle. The mere thought of jumping on her Triumph Tiger took the edge off

Kelly's frazzled nerves.

She met Steve's gaze. "The room was dark. I thought it was Paula."

Deep in thought, Steve plucked at the skin on his chin. "But it wasn't?"

"Correct," Kelly confirmed. "After making out with God knows who, I got up to use the bathroom and ran straight into her."

The memory of seeing Paula in the hallway sent a violent shudder through Kelly.

"Well, if it wasn't Paula, who was it?" His confused expression mirrored Kelly's inner turmoil.

"That's just it, I have no bloody idea. Some woman is probably in a state of shock right now, all thanks to me."

Feeling like a disgrace, even though her actions were far from calculated, Kelly buried her face in the crook of her arm. The floodgates opened, and tears streamed down her face.

Before Kelly knew it, Nicole was sitting on the armrest of the chair, stroking her hair and offering words of comfort. Steve crouched next to her on the other side.

He pulled Kelly's arm away from her face.

"Hey, I'm sure it's not as bad as you think." He gave her a reassuring smile. "If I woke up and some girl I didn't know was riding my boner, I can't imagine being upset."

The look on his face was so sincere, Kelly couldn't find it in herself to be offended, unlike Nicole.

"Steve!" Nicole glared at him. "Don't be such a pig."

He poked Kelly in the ribs. "I prefer donkey."

Kelly chuckled and swiped away her tears. "You're an ass."

Pinning his gaze on Nicole, he spread his hands in a placating gesture. "Hey, what can I say? I'm a guy."

In the time that it took for him to turn his attention from Nicole back to Kelly, he went from smug to serious.

He took Kelly's hand in his big meaty paw. "I'm not trying to downplay what happened, but I won't lie, I don't understand what the big deal is."

Nicole's mouth fell open, but before she could berate

him, Steve cut her off.

"Before you get your knickers in a twist, I'm going to get out of here so you two can hash it out until the cows come home, because that's what chicks do, right? Talk about it, talk about it, then talk about it some more.

"In a nutshell, yes," Kelly said.

Nicole jumped to her feet and gave Steve a peck on the lips. "Glad you know when you're not needed."

Witnessing the exchange, Kelly couldn't have wished for two better friends. She wouldn't have told Steve to leave, but he was right. Most men couldn't possibly comprehend what she was feeling any more than she'd ever understand what made men tick.

"And for the record," Nicole smiled sweetly. "You'll be a eunuch if I ever find out you've let someone else ride your mighty pole."

Rather than find humour in the comment, an overwhelming sense of guilt crashed into Kelly. No matter how unintentional her actions were, bottom line was she'd cheated.

As much as Kelly needed Nicole as a sounding

board, she needed to sort through the jumbled thoughts in her head before she shared the heavy load weighing her down.

Kelly uncurled her legs and stood. "Don't rush off, Steve. I'm going for a ride. I need to put my head on straight."

In her bedroom, the sight of her black dress brought her up short. So much for seducing Paula. Actually, it was odd she hadn't heard from Paula given it was almost midday.

Suddenly, Kelly remembered switching her cell phone to silent when she'd climbed into the cab. She'd been too busy beating herself up since to bother turning it back on. Kelly grabbed her phone off the bedside table. Sure enough, she had four unread messages, all from Paula.

Sighing, she slumped onto her unmade bed and swiped the screen.

Hey, babe. I hope you got home okay?

Kelly's heart fluttered. It was nice to know Paula was worried about her.

Hopefully the $20 I slipped into your purse covered

the cab fare.

For some reason Paula often seemed to think money was the way to Kelly's heart. To be fair, Kelly never said no, but she certainly didn't ask for Paula's generosity.

When you finally wake up and drag your lazy backside out of bed, call me. Not everyone can afford to sleep the day away.

What the hell was that supposed to mean?

With her emotions all over the place, Kelly typed out a quick message. "Sorry, slept in. Going for a ride to the beach to clear my head. Will text when I get back."

She jammed her feet into her boots and stormed through the living room. Nicole and Steve stepped aside, giving her the space she needed.

Chapter 3

Kicking her bike to life felt good and brought Kelly a sense of peace. She'd ridden since she was old enough to get her license. As a little girl, her father would sit her on his Triumph Bonneville telling her he'd teach her to ride once she was old enough. That was until he was knocked off his motorcycle by a careless driver and her mum declared she was too young to be a widow.

A week later, the Triumph was never seen again. However, Kelly's desire to ride didn't disappear along with her father's beloved bike.

Memories of her dad always filled Kelly with immense joy, or sadness, today it was the latter. Her mother had no way of knowing fate had other ideas for him. Sadly, selling the bike hadn't been enough to save him from an early grave.

Before Kelly could depress herself any further, she

did up her helmet, kicked the bike into gear, revved the throttle, and gunned it for Highway 56.

The stretches of road between Palmerston North and Himatangi Beach were so familiar, Kelly travelled them with ease, always mindful to keep an eye out for motorists who paid little attention to motorcyclists.

It was a beautiful summer day and plenty of Sunday drivers were heading in the same direction as her.

Half an hour after leaving home, Kelly coasted into the parking area at the beach. After shutting off the engine, she flicked down the kickstand, hung her helmet on the handle bars, and turned sideways on the leather seat.

A light breeze drifted in from the ocean bringing with it the familiar scent of seawater.

Kelly inhaled deeply, tension leaving her body. She shrugged out of her leather jacket and draped it over the seat, then placed her elbows on her knees and admired the scenery.

Sand dunes stretched for as far as the eye could see, cars were parked along the beach, teens collected driftwood, kids built sandcastles, and a woman on her horse galloped along the shoreline, its hooves kicking up water.

Eventually, Kelly's gaze settled on a family sitting on a large blanket, eating fish and chips directly off the paper they came wrapped in. No plates required.

Warmth spread through Kelly as her mind flicked back to many Sundays spent doing the same with her parents and little sister, Joanne. Jo who was now all grown up and attending Victoria University in Wellington.

Watching the father talking to the kids, and pointing to the massive field of sand dunes, Kelly's mind drifted to her childhood. Her father's voice came to her as clear as if he was standing behind her.

"That there sand dune field spreads for over twenty kilometres, said to be the largest in New Zealand."

At the time, Kelly hadn't paid much attention, but with age she'd learned to appreciate the bits and pieces of information her father had shared about their beautiful country.

When the heat of the sun became too much for Kelly, burning through her black jeans and turning her arms pink, she tossed her jacket on, buckled up her helmet, and headed for home.

After a few hours of inner reflection, Kelly felt optimistic and ready to sit down with her best friend to formulate a plan. Either try to forget about what happened, chalk it up to experience, or attempt to find the unsuspecting recipient and apologise.

Annoyance shot through her when Kelly spotted a familiar shiny red car parked out the front of their flat. Damn Paula for turning up out of the blue.

It was out of character for Miss Organised, always announce your arrival so you don't walk in on any nasty surprises, to turn up uninvited.

Without conscious thought, Kelly shot up her elderly neighbour's driveway, parked around the back and slipped off her helmet. Adrenaline pumped through her veins as she crept toward the back door, trying to stay below the fence line and out of sight.

Mrs Thompson appeared in the doorway shortly after Kelly tapped on the glass panel. "Hello, dear, what brings you here?"

"I thought I'd come by and see if you needed a hand

with anything?" Kelly offered up her brightest smile, pleased Mrs Thompson wasn't aware of the emotional turmoil bubbling just below the surface.

After changing two light bulbs for Mrs Thompson, and sharing a glass of iced tea, Kelly deemed it safe enough to return home.

***

As soon as Kelly stepped foot inside, Nicole bounded toward her.

"Give me that." She grabbed Kelly's helmet. "Oh my God, talk about good timing. You dodged a battle-axe." She smirked. "I mean a bullet."

Taking the opportunity to have some fun before things turned serious, Kelly played dumb. "Battle-axe's, bullets, what are you talking about?"

Wide eyed, Nicole tapped her wristwatch. "Paula! She left like two minutes ago. You just missed her." Her voice was shrill.

"Oh, really?" A smile tugged at the corner of Kelly's mouth. She'd never been able to keep anything from Nicole for long. "Good thing I hung out with Mrs T.

until she left."

A low growl rumbled in Nicole's chest. She narrowed her eyes. "Excuse me? You hid next door and left me to deal with your woman?"

The tone of her voice was jovial. She was no more pissed off with Kelly than Kelly would be if the tables were turned. God knew, Kelly had covered for Nicole, more than once, over the years before she'd hooked up with Steve.

"She dropped off your jacket and shoes, grumbled something about you needing to start acting like a responsible adult, sell your bike, and get a real job. I told her she needed to take the stick out from up her arse and accept you for you, warts and all."

The spiel was so out of character, Kelly couldn't believe what she was hearing. Her mouth fell open. "You didn't?"

"Nah, I didn't tell her about your warts. They're safe with me."

Even though Nicole meant well, her comment wiped the smile off Kelly's face. What if Kelly had caught an STD? The woman she went down on could've been a player. It would explain why she hadn't resisted Kelly's advances.

"That's not funny, girlfriend. What if I caught something nasty?"

"You mean like the flu?"

"No, I mean Chlamydia, genital warts, or worse."

Compassion flashed in Nicole's eyes. "Oh, honey. I'm so sorry." She squeezed Kelly's hand, her touch warm and comforting. "Come on, let's figure this out."

After changing out of her jeans and into a lilac minidress, Kelly met Nicole in the living room.

The small fan in the corner did little to lower the temperature. Not that it mattered. Kelly loved the warmer months, and even if she didn't, right then, the heat was the least of her worries.

Kelly lit a lavender scented incense stick and inhaled deeply before dropping into the chair with her name on it. Not literally, of course, but the one she took from her childhood home, with her mother's blessing.

With the click of a button the room fell silent. Nicole tossed the stereo remote on the coffee table and levelled her gaze on Kelly. "Okay, let's start with who we can cross off the list."

Without thought, Kelly replied, "Murray, he was outside the bathroom."

Amusement danced in Nicole's eyes. "Right, and unless you've changed teams, I think we can safely rule out all men who attended the party. Agreed?"

"Agreed." Kelly returned Nicole's smirk. "The only penis I saw last night belonged to your boyfriend."

Nicole's eyes went wide, then she shook her head and laughed. "I told him to put some pants on." She pointed to her eyes. "Focus. Next person."

"Grace, one of Paula's boarders. She was out photographing a wedding."

"How late are photographers supposed to stay at a wedding reception?" Nicole asked. "Isn't it possible she arrived home and you didn't see her? Perhaps she slipped inside and went straight to bed."

"It's possible," Kelly replied, unsure why she hadn't thought of that.

"You'd been drinking, right?' Nicole asked.

"Correct."

"Is there any chance you snuck into the wrong

room?"

Needing a minute to think, Kelly took a swig of her juice. The cool liquid sat in the pit of her stomach like a block of ice. A slither of doubt crept up her spine.

Glancing at the ceiling as if a movie was playing across it, she pictured the three doors opposite the bathroom. Paula's in the middle, Grace's closest to the living room, Lucy's on the other side.

What if she'd been so anxious to get to Paula's room she'd stopped short and gone into Grace's room? Grace could've been fast asleep, until Kelly stumbled upon her.

That couldn't be it. She shook her head trying to dispel the thought. Kelly remembered racing head first into the bathroom, or perhaps it felt that way because seeing Paula when she'd least expected had fuddled her mind.

"I don't know, I suppose it could have been Grace, but I'm ninety percent certain I went into the right room."

"Okay," Nicole replied. "For arguments sake, we'll rule out Grace for the time being. Is there anyone you can think of? Someone who might've passed out in Paula's bed, perhaps they drank too much and needed to lie down."

And just like that, things got worse. "Colette."

Sitting up tall, Nicole looked down her nose and spoke in a posh voice. "As in Paula's mightier than thou stuck up P.A. you can barely tolerate?"

"The very one."

"Well shit." Nicole slumped back against the sofa. "No wonder you look like someone pissed in your Wheaties."

The comment made Kelly chuckle. She loved her best friend and appreciated her attempt to make Kelly laugh. The jibe also took her back to her childhood, when her mother had insisted Kelly and her sister eat Weetbix for breakfast as it was the breakfast of champions.

"What makes you say Colette?" Nicole's question put an end to Kelly's brief trip down memory lane. "From what you've told me, I can't imagine Miss Proper drinking to excess."

It was a fair assessment, but Kelly couldn't get the

hushed conversation outside the bathroom door out of her mind. "When Paula was looking for Colette, Murray informed her Colette had a headache and needed to lie down."

For a moment, neither of them spoke, both lost in their own thoughts.

Nicole tapped a purple fingernail against her lip. "That's not to say it was her. I can't imagine such an uptight woman taking a nap in her boss's bed."

Wanting to believe that was the case, Kelly grabbed hold of Nicole's logic and held tight. "You're right, I think we can cross her off the list of maybes."

"But imagine if it was!" Wide-eyed, Nicole looked excited by the prospect.

Not wanting to imagine anything of the sort, Kelly groaned. "Please, let's not."

Unperturbed, Nicole bounced on the balls of her feet, the sofa jiggling in time to her excitement. "I just had an epiphany. This is a perfect example of the power of the mind. The person you were with could've been someone heinous, yet, you were totally into it because in your mind's eye the woman was hot." She slapped her hands on her thighs. "This is living proof; the brain is the biggest sex organ."

If Nicole thought her epiphany was supposed to make Kelly feel better, she was wrong. In fact, she was so far off track she might as well have been on a train to Auckland.

"Not helping." Kelly mirrored Nicole's actions from earlier and pointed to her eyes. "Focus."

"Oops, sorry, I got carried away. What other babes were there?" Nicole asked.

One name sprung to mind. "Lucy, Paula's other boarder. She made a comment about sneaking off to bed, but I think she was only joking. She likes to tease me."

"Ooohh." Nicole's ears perked up and Kelly could've sworn she saw them twitch.

"Is this the flatmate you think is sexy? Black hair, purple streaks?"

A frustrated sigh escaped Kelly. "Sure, she's gorgeous, but that doesn't mean I want to bang her any more than you want to bang every dude you find attractive."

Nicole quirked an eyebrow.

Chuckling, Kelly shook her head. "I should start calling you piglet. You and Steve truly are perfect for each other."

A dreamy look twinkled in Nicole's eyes. "Yes, we are, and we have you to thank for that. But, honey, this is about you, not us."

Sobering, they continued to hash out names.

Murray was out for obvious reasons. Colette, possible, but unlikely. Lucy and Grace, also possible but highly unlikely.

"Who else do you remember being there before you…you know?" Nicole put her glass on the coffee table.

"A few people I don't recall meeting before. Paula's best friend, Ashleigh." At least she assumed she was still there, but it had been hard to make out the faces of the remaining guests who had been huddled around the brazier.

"Oh, and another woman from Paula's work. I'm pretty sure her name's Kate."

Kelly had only met her briefly but according to

Paula, Kate changed partners as often as she changed her underwear, and she didn't discriminate between men and women. She was somewhat a plain Jane, so she obviously had qualities that attracted both genders to her bed.

Hopefully, that quality was more than being an easy lay because then that would be just plain sad. She'd heard of people with low self-esteem sleeping around as a way of boosting their feelings of self-worth, yet it often had the opposite effect.

Come to think of it, Kate appeared to have been on her own. At least Kelly didn't see anyone who might've been her date. Perhaps she was turning over a new leaf, not that it was any of Kelly's concern.

Frustrated, Kelly sat forward and ran her finger through a ring of condensation on the wooden coffee table.

"We're no closer to discovering who the person is than when we started this conversation."

"You're right." Nicole gave Kelly a sad smile. "We're running around in circles. I'm here for you though. And honey, it might be best if you chalk it up to experience and let it go."

"I can't just let it go. What if I have a disease?" Kelly buried her head in her hands, not caring that her fingers were covered in the watery remnants from her glass of juice.

Nicole walked over to the armchair, crouched down in front of Kelly, and held her hands. "I'm sure you'll be fine, but we need to find out if you have anything nasty. Make an appointment with the doc and I'll come with you."

The compassion in Nicole's voice almost undid Kelly. She stifled a sob. "I can't go to my doctor, he's like a father to me." She'd had the same doctor since she was a little girl. To have to explain what had happened would be embarrassing beyond belief.

"The V.D. clinic at the hospital is walk-in." Nicole stood and picked up her cell phone. "I'll message my boss and ask for tomorrow off."

"Isn't that short notice?" Kelly asked, pleased for the first time ever that she worked Saturdays and therefore had Mondays off.

"I'll tell her it's a family emergency." Nicole

shrugged. "It's not far from the truth; you're like a sister to me, Kel."

As Nicole tapped out a message, Kelly noticed her cell phone vibrating on the chair side table. By the time she picked it up, it'd stopped ringing.

A missed call from Paula.

Resigned to her fate and prepared to face the consequences of her actions, Kelly glanced at Nicole. "I have to tell Paula."

A sudden gust of wind blew through the front door. Kelly shuddered as though someone had walked over her grave.

For some inexplicable reason, she had the uncanny feeling her father's ghost had entered the room, either to offer support or give her a lecture.

Nicole frowned. "That was weird." She levelled her gaze on Kelly. "What do you hope to gain by telling Paula?"

Confused, Kelly exhaled a frustrated sigh. "What do you mean? I could have an STD. Don't you think she deserves to know?"

"Yes. No. Damn, I don't know." Nicole paced the

small living room, her high ponytail bouncing with each step. "I just don't want to see you hurting any more than you already are. And, as far as I see it, telling her right now will only make matters worse."

She came to an abrupt stop and pierced Kelly with a stare so intense Kelly almost recoiled. "Do you love her?"

When a yes or no answer didn't immediately come to mind, Kelly took a minute to ponder the question. She cared deeply for Paula and enjoyed spending time with her. She missed her on the nights they spent apart, but couldn't say she was in love with her. Not yet, anyway.

"I could, love her I mean, given time," Kelly said, her voice barely above a whisper.

On a heavy exhale, Nicole's shoulders sagged as though she was carrying Kelly's heavy load. "Well, if you break this news to her, your time might be up. Why don't you sleep on it, wait till you have your test results, and you've had more than twenty-four hours to digest everything that has happened? Then, if you still feel you owe it to Paula to tell her, knowing it's going to hurt your relationship before it helps it, tell her. If you need me to be with you when you do so, I'll be right by your side."

Love for her friend flooded Kelly's heart. Fighting back tears, she jumped to her feet and pulled Nicole into a bone crushing embrace. "Thank you."

Needing her friends more than ever, Kelly took a step back and put a hand on Nicole's shoulders. "Call Steve, tell him to pick up some beers and come over. We can blob out and order pizza for dinner."

Kelly held her phone up. "I'll text Paula and make up some cock and bull story about why I can't see her for the next few days."

Even though Kelly made light of the situation, she dreaded the stream of text messages that were sure to follow. She could already hear them in her head.

What were you doing out on your motorcycle if you're unwell? Why didn't you text me sooner, or better yet, call? How long does it take someone your age to get over a hangover?

Little did Paula know, Kelly was far from hungover and if a hangover could change the events of last night, she'd gladly take one in exchange.

Kelly sank onto her crumpled sheets and tapped out a message. "Hey there. Sorry, I'm still feeling sick, think it might be something I ate, going to have an early night. Sleep tight. Xx"

The second Kelly hit send, she groaned at her poor word choice. What she'd feasted on last night had been too intoxicating to make her sick. It was the not knowing who she'd devoured that was making her ill.

When her phone vibrated Kelly jumped as though she'd been caught in the act. Taking a deep breath, she swiped the screen and read Paula's reply.

"Fine. Ashleigh needs me right now. We're going out for dinner."

Well that went better than expected. However, Kelly didn't know whether she should feel relieved, affronted, or worried that Paula had blown her off so easily.

Chapter 4

Monday morning arrived all too soon. The sterile environment of the clinic made Kelly shudder. A nurse ushered her into a room and, without preamble, started firing off questions.

"How many partners have you had? Have you had anal sex? Do you need a prescription for condoms? Dental dams?"

Kelly's replies were barely above a whisper. She hung her head in shame, certain the nurse thought she was nothing more than a wanton whore, yet she was nothing of the sort.

Throughout the interrogation, at least that's what it felt like to Kelly, Nicole remained in the room, her silent presence offering comfort. When the nurse picked up a needle, Nicole lowered her gaze, staring at the floor until the last vial had been filled with Kelly's blood.

As soon as the nurse left the room, urine sample, vials of blood, and oral swabs in hand, Nicole shot to her feet. She paced the small room, steam practically pouring from her ears.

"Can you believe that woman?" Nicole held her hand up and looked at her palm as though reading from a script. "Have you had anal sex, Ms Bennett? Do you need condoms, Ms Bennett? Fuck, what part of you're a lesbian did she not understand?"

The tirade was so adorable, Kelly didn't want to burst Nicole's righteous bubble by informing her lesbians could have anal sex, and condoms were often use for covering toys. The diatribe also gave testament to the fact Nicole didn't snoop in Kelly's bedroom or handbag.

The door clicked open and Nicole bolted back to the chair in the corner of the stark white room, the picture of innocence.

The nurse paid her no attention. She addressed Kelly. "We've got everything we need so you're free to go." She patted Kelly's hand. "I applaud you for coming in. We don't get many lesbians through these doors, and I believe that is largely due to the misconception that they are immune to sexually transmitted diseases. While your risk is certainly lower, you're not immune." The nurse smiled, and it softened her entire demeanour. "You really should consider using dental dams if you're not in a committed relationship. They'll greatly reduce your risk of contracting diseases such as Chlamydia and Trichomoniasis."

Even though Kelly wanted to ask what the hell Trichomoniasis was, she bit her tongue to save herself from more embarrassment. She would Google the word in the privacy of her own home.

"How long will it take to get the results?" Kelly asked, certain the next few days would be the longest of her life.

"Most test results will be back within two or three days. The lab results for Trichomoniasis can take up to seven days. However, you'll only hear from us if you need treatment."

The nurse walked to the door, turned the handle, and stepped aside, effectively dismissing them.

Kelly paused in the doorway. "No offense, but I hope we never meet again."

A warm smile crinkled the corner of the nurse's eyes. "None taken, now get out of here and don't come back."

Chapter 5

The following week was rather uneventful for Kelly, as far as work was concerned. Tuesday night, she went over the same scenarios with Nicole as they had on Sunday and Monday, and drew the same blank.

Wednesday evening, Steve came over and all three tossed around a few more theories. The only conclusion they came to was it could've been anyone, except for the two people Kelly saw after leaving the bedroom, Paula and Murray.

Paula texted every day, mostly to say her best friend was having some problems and needed her. Kelly couldn't begrudge Paula of that, and frankly Ashleigh's misfortune worked in Kelly's favour.

By Thursday evening, Kelly managed to watch her favourite TV show, Family Feud, without dwelling on the weekend. The fact she hadn't heard from the clinic was also a good sign, she hoped.

While cracking up laughing over a ridiculous answer one of the game show contestants gave, Kelly's phone vibrated. She swiped the screen and read a text from Paula. The message surprised and delighted her in equal measure.

Smiling, she sent a text to Nicole. "Whatcha doing Friday night?"

A second after hearing Nicole's phone chirp, Kelly's phone was whacked out of her hand by a flying pillow. She glanced in the direction of the missile launcher.

Propped up on her elbow, spread out along the length of the sofa, Nicole pulled a face; half smile, half glare. "Hello, I'm right here."

Determined to one up Nicole, Kelly picked up her phone and held it in the air. "This is proof people in the same room have been known to text each other. Can you believe it?"

Nicole scoffed. "Is that supposed to be news? You suck."

Realizing her joke fell well short of Nicole's earlier epiphany, but not wanting to admit it, Kelly pouted. "You're no fun." She tossed the sofa cushion back across the room.

Nicole plucked it out of the air. "Thanks. As for Friday night, some of the guys from Steve's hockey team are getting together for a barbecue. He said I'm welcome to join him, but he'll understand if I don't want to go. Sometimes, all of that testosterone gets to be a bit much." She screwed up her face. "What is it with guys and booze that turns them into twelve-year-old boys? Frankly, some of the shit they do is damn right idiotic."

Delighted to have the perfect opportunity to talk Nicole out of going, Kelly didn't hold back. "I hear those type of social gatherings can be dangerous." She plastered on a smile. "And as a responsible adult I must advise against you attending."

Once again, the pillow flew across the room, smacking Kelly in the chest.

"You are such a dork." Nicole grinned. "And, according to Madam, it's you who needs to grow up."

Although said in jest, the words knocked the wind out of Kelly's sails. "You're right. Look at us acting like a couple of little kids playing pillow frisbee instead of twenty-five-year-old women."

An angry scowl creased Nicole's forehead. "Oh, no you don't! Don't you dare go there." She stabbed the air with her finger. "You're perfect just the way you are. Don't let anyone tell you otherwise."

Feeling chastised and a little defensive, Kelly asked the question she should've asked months ago. "Is that why you don't like Paula?

The few seconds it took for Nicole to reply felt like forever. Kelly wanted an honest answer, but dreaded it at the same time.

"Oh, Kel. I don't know her well enough to say I don't like her, but she comes across as someone who thinks she's better than everyone else. And that pisses me off."

Amused, Kelly quirked a brow. "Why don't you tell me how you really feel?"

And just like that they were back to playing pillow Frisbee, giggling like school girls. It felt good.

Kelly's mind flashed back to a day at the beach not long after she'd turned twelve. Her dad had picked her mum up and tossed her into the surf after she'd complained one too many times the water was too cold. She had surfaced wiping water out of her eyes and looking like a drowned rat.

After a beat, her mum had climbed to her feet, fists clenched at her sides. Rather than go ape-shit at their father, like Kelly and her sister had expected, their mum had sidled up to their dad and deposited a handful of sand down the back of his shorts.

The girls had burst into fits of laughter, watching their dad waddle toward the water as if he had a giant turd in his pants. Score to Mum!

The event had been retold at many family gatherings, including her father's funeral, and was always met with raucous laughter.

On the drive home from the beach, Kelly's mum had looked at their father with love in her eyes, and turned to her daughters safely buckled in the backseat. "Life's too short to stop having fun, girls. No matter how old you get, never forget that."

Her mum would've been around Paula's age at the time, thirty-five. It was a sobering thought, considering how serious Paula acted most of the time. It also brought Kelly back to the present and her reason for texting Nicole.

"Paula might come across as snotty, but it's all a front. I have the perfect chance for you to get to know her better. If you're happy to blow Steve off…"

The twinkle in Nicole's eyes made Kelly want to groan at her unintentional innuendo. Clearing her throat, she tried again. "Paula's having a potluck dinner Friday night, she said you're welcome to come too."

The suspicious look that crossed Nicole's face shouldn't have surprised Kelly, but it did, and, once again, she found herself making excuses for Paula.

"Her best friend will be there. Perhaps Ashleigh being in town has given Paula a new appreciation for how important best friends are." Kelly blew Nicole an air kiss to sweeten the deal.

"I'll come on one condition." Nicole smiled sweetly.

It was a look that Kelly knew well, one that lured people into a false sense of security. She dreaded the reply to her next question before the words even left her mouth.

"Sure, what condition?"

"If Madam needs shutting up you'll let me watch you stuff her panties into her mouth."

Two or three years ago the comment would've embarrassed the hell out of Kelly. But since dipping her toes into BDSM she didn't feel the need to defend her sexual desires. Different strokes for different folks and all that.

Besides, Nicole was fishing, her smile fading the longer she waited for Kelly to take the bait.

Plastering on a smile, Kelly returned the quip. "Of course you can watch, if that's what floats your boat these days."

Nicole snorted. "Touché. It's a date." Her voice rose in pitch. "And, if the actual recipient of your panty stuffing is there, I'm going to sniff her out."

"Do you realize how bad that sounded coming from a straight woman?"

They burst into a fit of laughter and, for a minute, Kelly let herself believe all was right in her world.

Chapter 6

After a busy day at the café, Kelly slung her backpack over her shoulders, fired her bike to life and headed for home.

Exhaust fumes replaced the aroma of coffee that normally stuck to her nostrils eight hours a day, five days a week.

It had been a good day, devoid of abusive customers. Something about a sunny day seemed to improve people's moods and being Friday, most customers were too busy looking forward to the weekend to be grumpy.

At four-fifteen, Kelly coasted up the drive. She parked her motorcycle next to Nicole's Mitsubishi Mirage in the carport assigned to their flat. Friday was the only day Nicole made it home from work before Kelly.

She had a little over an hour to make a potato salad—with diced bacon and boiled eggs—shower, change, and book a cab so they'd arrive at Paula's by six.

"Hey, honey, I'm home," Kelly called out when she didn't spot Nicole.

The sound of water running alerted her to where Nicole was. Kelly banged on the bathroom door. "Save some hot water for me."

"I can't hear you," Nicole retorted.

Chuckling, Kelly dumped her backpack in her room, tied her hair back, and headed for the kitchen.

At quarter to six, a taxi pulled into the driveway. The driver sat on the horn, even though he could see Kelly and Nicole rushing toward the door.

"Impatient twat," Kelly grumbled under her breath.

If it was customary to tip in New Zealand this guy would need an attitude adjustment. Kelly didn't receive tips but she sure as shit treated her customers with respect. She believed in treating others how she wished to be treated and that wasn't like an inconvenience.

Balancing the potato salad in her lap, Kelly nudged Nicole with her elbow. "Everything okay? You're awfully quiet."

After shooting a quick glance at the cab driver, who was paying them no attention, Nicole replied, "Even though I shouldn't care what your missus or her friends think of me, I guess I'm a little nervous. I want to make a good impression, for your sake."

The declaration warmed Kelly's heart. She squeezed Nicole's hand. "You'll be fine. As long as you stay out of the bedrooms."

The comment made at Kelly's own expense, earned her a smile.

After paying the cab fare, Kelly took the potato salad from Nicole and led the way up the pathway alongside Paula's house.

Laughter and soft voices grew louder as they rounded the corner. Four women were lounging around on the back deck.

Two sat in padded deckchairs, their backs to the sun. Paula and Ashleigh were leaning against the railing, glasses in hand, legs crossed at the ankles.

The second Paula spotted Kelly and Nicole, she strolled across the deck. Kelly's heart skipped a beat, Paula looked damn good. The yellow sundress she wore was simple yet elegant. It complimented her blonde locks and hugged her curves.

As soon as Kelly's foot hit the top step, Paula greeted her with a chaste kiss. She tasted like wine and summer.

"It's good to see you. I've missed you this week."

"Me too," Kelly replied honestly. "Sorry about last weekend."

Paula held up a hand silencing her. "Let's not ruin the mood." She smiled brightly and turned to Nicole. "Come and meet everyone. I'll introduce you. Kelly can put the food in the fridge and get you a drink."

Not wanting to abandon her friend two seconds after arriving, or be bossed around by Paula, Kelly didn't move until Nicole gave her a quick nod conveying she was okay.

By the time Kelly re-emerged, Nicole had been introduced to Grace and Colette and, presumably, Ashleigh who was moving the sprinkler around the backyard.

Her tight skirt rode up as she bent to pull on the hose giving Kelly a mouth-watering view of tanned thighs and a flash of pink panties.

Not wanting to be caught staring, Kelly quickly diverted her gaze. An irrational sense of guilt stabbed at her conscience as though she'd physically touched the woman when all she'd done was cop an eyeful. Admittedly, a very nice eyeful.

Her fiancé was a lucky man. Or was he? Perhaps he was a miserable man if their relationship was on the rocks. Dragging her mind from where it had no business being, Kelly turned back to the group gathered on the deck.

The first person her gaze landed on was Grace. It made sense she was there, considering it was her home for the time being. The next person she saw was Colette. What in the hell she was doing there, other than sucking up to her boss, was anyone's guess.

It was a shame the one person she'd hoped to see was missing. "Where's Lucy tonight?" Kelly asked no one in particular.

Smirking, Nicole handed Kelly a cold vodka and lime out of the esky bag they'd bought with them. She'd insisted they bring their own booze, so Paula could never accuse either of them of mooching off her.

Paula's abrupt reply wiped the smile off Kelly's face.

"Out, she has a life, why?"

Colette, hogging most of the shade provided by the umbrella, and rubbing copious amounts of sunscreen into her pale skin, scoffed.

It was on the tip of Kelly's tongue to retort, "at least she has a life, unlike your P.A." but Ashleigh's voice coming from behind her, and her warm hand on Kelly's bare shoulder left her speechless.

"Chill out, woman, she only asked."

Unfazed by Ashleigh's reprimand, Paula wiped her forehead with the back of her hand. "I've had enough heat for one day." She picked up her wine glass from the top rail of the deck. "Come on, ladies, let's move inside where it's cooler."

"Good idea," Grace said. "We'll be able to eat without worrying about bugs landing on our food."

Chairs screeched across the deck like a synchronized chorus of agreement.

Certain she was the only one who thrived on the

heat, Kelly reluctantly followed suit.

Halfway across the patio, she looped arms with Nicole. "You okay?"

Slowing her pace, Nicole tugged on Kelly's arm and spoke in a low voice. "I'm impressed, but slightly disappointed."

The cryptic words confused Kelly. "How so?"

"Thanks to Ashleigh putting her friend in her place, Paula narrowly avoided a panty gagging moment."

"Do you have to keep reminding me?" Kelly's voice came out harsher than she intended.

The crestfallen look on Nicole's face made her wish she could take the words back. Since she couldn't she poked Nicole in the side and put the comment back on herself. "So, have you sniffed out who it was yet?"

The smile returned. "Not yet, but the night's only young." Nicole pulled her arm free and tapped her nose. "I have a theory though."

Ten minutes later, all six women stood around the huge oak dining room table.

It was no surprise when Paula sat at the head of the table. She motioned for Kelly to sit to her left and

Ashleigh to her right. Grace fell into place beside Ashleigh and Nicole next to Kelly.

Rather than be offended by having no choice but to sit at the foot of the table, Colette sat facing her boss looking as happy as a pig in shit.

If Kelly was the jealous type, she'd take Colette aside and ask if she had a crush on Paula. The way she mooned over her boss verged on the side of creepy.

As the booze flowed so did the conversation. The atmosphere, for the most part, was light and breezy.

Kelly played her part when it came time to dish up dinner. The fact most dishes could be served cold, chicken wings, ham, and salads, meant it was far from a chore. It also gave her something to do other than drink.

While stacking the dishes into the dishwasher, Kelly kept an ear on the conversation in the dining room. Grace held everyone captive regaling them with various events from weddings she'd photographed.

"Last weekend," Grace's voice had an excited edge to it. "The bride's mother asked me to take some pictures of the bridesmaids' unwrapping the gifts. She escorted me over to the table, tapped one of the pretty bridesmaids on the shoulder, and in her most prim voice said, 'Darling, hold up a gift and smile for the camera.' The young woman blushed, stashed something behind her back and replied, 'Um, maybe later, Mrs Jones'."

"Having none of it, Mrs Jones folded her arms across her ample bosom." Grace put on a posh voice and spoke like she had a plum in her mouth. "Nonsense, we're paying the woman to do a job and we haven't got all night. Now hurry up."

When the room fell silent, Kelly stopped wiping out the sink and craned her neck.

All eyes were on Grace as she took a sip of wine, keeping her audience in suspense.

When she didn't lower her glass fast enough, Nicole spoke, "God woman, you're killing us, finish the story."

Kelly didn't need to be able to see Grace's face to know she was grinning from ear to ear.

The table creaked as she placed her elbows on either side of her glass and leaned forward. "The bridesmaid held up a black box with a clear lid." Grace paused for dramatic effect. "She smiled ever so sweetly and turned the box toward me so I could take a picture of the leather wrist restraints and paddle nestled in red velvet."

Nicole smirked and sat back in her chair.

Collette's hand flew to her mouth. "What happened next?"

The fact Ashleigh had her back to Kelly, she had no idea if Ashleigh looked intrigued or dismayed. Kelly made a mental note to ask Nicole later that night.

After hanging up the tea towel, she crossed the note off her list of things to ask and added it to her list of, "it's none of your business, Kelly."

Grace turned sideways in her chair and answered Colette's question. "Mrs Jones flushed beet red and grumbled something about kids these days it must be someone's idea of a sick joke. She stormed off, then stopped and spun back to face me, stating, 'We won't be needing that picture, thank you very much, Ms Porter'."

Just as Kelly was about to re-join the group, Paula's words stopped her in her tracks. "That's the kind of thing Kelly would do."

Blanching, Nicole met Kelly's eyes over Paula's

shoulder. With her heart in her throat, Kelly put a finger to her lips hoping Nicole wouldn't draw attention to her. As much as she dreaded it, Kelly wanted to hear what Paula had to say. Or more specifically, how much she would say. Would she respect the universal rule—what happens behind closed doors, stays behind closed doors?

"Last weekend," Paula continued.

The hairs on the back of Kelly's neck stood on end. She should've shut Paula down, but morbid curiosity kept her rooted to the spot.

"Kelly hinted at tying me up and getting *her kink* on, but then she went and got sick. If she wants to play big girl games, she should learn how to hold her liquor first."

There was no mistaking the emphasis Paula put on the words 'her kink' implying it was something Kelly wanted to explore as opposed to something they would explore together.

The realization that Paula had only ever humoured her sat like a heavy weight in the pit of Kelly's stomach.

The only person who laughed at Paula's revelation was Colette and it sounded more like a nervous giggle than a funny ha-ha laugh.

As if sensing Kelly's presence, Paula glanced over her shoulder. She had the decency to look embarrassed at being caught gossiping about their sex life.

The short walk from the kitchen to the dining room table felt like the longest walk of shame in history. Kelly didn't know whether to be pissed off with Paula or to thank her for opening her eyes. Either way it was time to re-evaluate her relationship.

Right then, though, her mind was set on being the more mature one of the two, and steering the conversation toward safer waters.

"Have you always wanted to be a photographer, Grace?" Kelly asked as she slid back into her chair.

Everyone breathed out at once, dispelling some of the tension in the room.

"Yep, my grandfather gave me my first camera when I turned eight. For the next ten years I drove my family crazy. Everywhere we went I had the lens to my eye, making my brother and parents pose and smile for the camera."

"What about you?" Colette asked Kelly, disdain written all over her face. "Have you always dreamed of being a dish washer?"

Nicole whipped around so fast, her face was a blur. "What the hell is that supposed to mean?"

Touched that Nicole jumped to her defence, but determined not to let Colette goad her, Kelly plastered on a smile.

"It's okay," she reassured Nicole. "My Dad used to take me in his truck with him and we'd stop at roadside diners along the way. The waitresses were always so nice to me, and I loved the ambience of café's, so yes, I guess I did always want to work as a barista."

As if she was on a personal crusade to get under Kelly's skin, Colette tried again. "Wow, a truck driver, your family sure is ambitious." She snorted. "Seriously, what kind of job's that?"

The bitchy comment severed Kelly's invisible line of tolerance. With no more fucks to give, Kelly nailed Colette with what she hoped was a look of utter contempt. "One that got him dead."

There was no mistaking the warning look Paula shot Kelly, but the fact the look was directed at her and not Colette added to her resolve to continue.

"The funny thing is, my mother made him sell his death-trap, as Paula likes to refer to my Triumph, but it wasn't enough to save his life. Ironically, he died cocooned in a metal cage."

"Jesus, Kelly." Paula exploded. "What's got into you tonight? I've told you I'm sorry your father was killed. It's still no reason to tempt fate."

The way Paula said the word 'killed' felt like a punch to the gut. He died, passed-over, or more specifically, met his death when a massive bolder came down in the Manawatu Gorge and sent the huge double milk tanker plunging into the water below.

Nicole leaned in close, her shoulder brushing against Kelly's. "I'm ready to go when you are."

Certain it would please Colette immensely if they left, Kelly held her ground. "I'm not done yet," she said quietly.

Sitting up straight in the tall back chair, Kelly put her hand over top of Nicole's on the table. "Dad drove trucks for ten years. When I turned thirteen, and wanted to earn some pocket money, I would go to work with dad on the weekend and scrub his milk tanker. It was at the depot that I met this wonderful person."

Kelly squeezed Nicole's hand recalling the sullen teenager she'd seen sitting in her father's truck reading a book while he scrubbed it clean.

Spotting Kelly, Nicole had climbed down from the cab, strolled across the yard, and introduced herself. After a brief chat, Nicole turned to walk away. The second her back was turned, Kelly had squirted her with a hose.

As outraged as Nicole had been at the time, over the next month they met up every Saturday morning, and within six months they were inseparable. Despite living on opposite sides of town and going to different schools not a day went by when they weren't in touch.

"Aw, how sweet." Grace smiled.

Ashleigh nodded in agreement.

Colette scowled.

Paula sipped her wine and Kelly would've given anything to know the thoughts running through her head.

"Every job has its merits," Kelly stated.

"Right," Nicole agreed before completely killing the mood.

The way her leg jiggled up and down, brushing against Kelly's, should've alerted Kelly to the fact that even though Nicole was smiling, Colette's attitude had left her simmering.

Nicole glanced around the room then settled her gaze on Colette. "My mother works at an old folk's home."

"Oh, is she an R.N.?" Colette asked, her smile so fake it might as well have been painted on.

Aware Nicole's mother wasn't a registered nurse, Kelly braced herself for Nicole's response.

"My mother's a caregiver and while she might not have any fancy titles or degrees, the world is a better place because of people like her." She shot daggers at Colette with her eyes. "I have far more respect for someone who is paid shit to clean up shit than for someone who gets to where they are by kissing their boss's arse."

"That's enough," Paula warned, her voice deathly quiet.

The tension in the room was so thick it was palpable. Kelly's mind raced along with her pulse. She couldn't recall ever feeling so uncomfortable.

A chair screeched, and Nicole pushed back from the table. She stood, turned her back to Colette and faced Paula head on. "Thank you for the dinner invitation. Sorry for speaking out of line." She glanced down at Kelly and gave her a sad smile. "Clearly I don't belong here."

"No kidding," Colette mumbled under her breath.

It took a mighty feat of self-restraint for Kelly not to launch herself across the table and wrap her hands around Colette's neck.

"Who wants coffee?" Grace asked, bolting for the kitchen before anyone had a chance to reply.

"I'll help," Ashleigh scrambled out of her chair and followed on Grace's heels.

Then, like a knight in shining armour saving the day, or a Dame saving the night, Lucy breezed through the door. "Hey, kids. What'd I miss?"

With her gaze locked on the floor, Nicole mumbled a reply. "We were just discussing what our parents do for a living."

"Oh, how exciting." Lucy rubbed her hands together. "My dad's an undertaker."

"Really?" Kelly asked, taken aback and smiling at the amused look on Lucy's face.

"Nah, but right about now I'm wondering if we need one. Who died?"

Smiling, Paula shook her head. "Come on ladies, let's call a truce. If I wanted to watch a pissing match, I'd hang out with men."

It was a ridiculous comment but when Lucy jumped off the stool and held her hands in front of her jeans, swinging her hips as if she was peeing all over the floor, Kelly couldn't help but chuckle.

Retrieving their cooler bag, Nicole pulled her cell phone out of the side pocket. "I'm going to call a cab, you coming or staying?"

"Coming."

Neither of them smiled at the word that normally evoked all kinds of innuendos, and Paula didn't attempt to stop either of them as they exited the house.

Chapter 7

After a good night's sleep, sprawled out diagonally in the comfort of her own bed, Kelly was finally able to smile when she thought about everything that had transpired at Paula's potluck dinner. While the various dishes people had contributed hadn't revealed any surprises, the conversation certainly had. The look on Colette's face when Nicole put her in her place had been priceless.

Dressed in pink shorty pyjama's, Nicole stumbled into the kitchen, looking more like a child who'd just stumbled out of bed than an adult.

"Morning." She shielded her eyes from the mid-morning sun streaming in through the window.

"Speak of the devil." Kelly handed Nicole a steaming cup of coffee.

Nicole glanced around as if someone else was in the room. "Who?"

"You, you clown. I was just thinking about last night; the look on Colette's face, then Paula's."

"Oh, don't remind me. Sorry if I embarrassed you."

"You didn't. If anything, you did me a favour." Kelly took a sip of coffee; murmuring in delight as the rich flavour washed over her taste buds.

"How so?" Nicole asked around a yawn.

Eager to make the most of the warm day, Kelly cracked open the back door. "Come on, let's sit in the sun and talk."

Once they were seated on the top step, cushions under their backsides and the scent of warm grass tickling their nostrils, Kelly turned to Nicole.

"Last night, I saw Paula through your eyes and I didn't like what I saw. I'm going to break it off with her." Before falling asleep, Kelly had thought long and hard about her relationship and when her heart didn't ache she knew she'd made the right decision.

Care and concern radiated in Nicole's eyes.

Taking a guess as to why, Kelly added, "The only part you played in our breakup was sitting back and letting me make my own mistakes, so don't for a minute think any of this was your fault."

Nicole placed a hand on Kelly's forearm. "It's been a rough week for you, Kel, and as much as I don't think Paula's going to take the news lying down, I can't say I'm sorry to hear it."

She puffed out her chest. "If she goes all Rambo on you, I've got your back." She deflated. "Not really, I'm a lover not a fighter."

The words were so lame they both burst out laughing.

"Thanks, girlfriend." Kelly bumped shoulders with Nicole. "So, tell me, my little sleuth, in amongst all the chaos, did your panty sniffing radar go off?"

With a clunk, Nicole set her coffee mug down on the concrete step. Her eyes lit up. "I wondered when you'd ask."

In awe of her friend, Kelly swallowed a slice of humble pie. Nicole was practically bursting at the seams, yet she hadn't said a word until she was sure Kelly was ready to hear it.

As much as she was dying to know what Nicole had to say, Kelly took the time to ask Nicole if she was okay. "How are you doing? You know you can tell me if you're upset about the way Colette or Paula spoke to you."

An airplane flew overhead. They both glanced up, watching it soar through the clear blue sky until it was little more than a white spot in the distance.

Nicole turned to Kelly. "Hell no, I'm not upset. When she made fun of what our parents do for a living, I wanted to stab her eyes out, with my fork."

Nicole softened her voice and pointed back and forth between them. "You and me, we didn't come from money or brains."

"Hey speak for yourself." Kelly grinned. "I've got plenty of brains, I just didn't want to wear them out at university."

Truth was, Kelly had never dreamed of being a lawyer, or an accountant or anything else that required a degree. She earned half as much money as people in power, but suspected she was twice as happy. She'd never been surrounded by riches, but she'd always been surrounded by love.

"You know what I meant." Nicole nudged her in the

side.

"I did." Kelly planted a wet kiss on Nicole's cheek. "And that's why we're friends. We appreciate the simple things in life."

"Hey, watch who you're calling simple," Nicole shot back.

The easy camaraderie between them was something Kelly cherished. Out of nowhere, a pang of sadness hit her. Why couldn't she meet and fall in love with someone like her best friends, Steve and Nicole?

Kelly shook off the thought. Envy had no place in her heart, it wouldn't change a thing and she never wanted to become bitter or jealous.

"Do you want the good news or the bad news?" Nicole asked, unaware of the thoughts tumbling through Kelly's head.

"Give me the bad news first, and don't tell me you think it was Colette."

"'fraid so." Nicole sighed. "Think about it, it's the reason she's so snippy with you. She's covering her backside."

"Oh my God, do you think so?"

"Nope, just pulling your chain." Nicole giggled. "The good news is I can't imagine it was Colette. The bad news is you're not going to be able to pursue the person I'm ninety-nine percent sure it is, without causing a lot of grief. And now that you've decided to break things off with Paula, I don't think you should go making any confessions."

Having no idea who Nicole was hinting at, Kelly couldn't agree or disagree. "Spit it out. Who do you think it was?

"Ashleigh," Nicole said softly.

Kelly snorted coffee out of her nose. That wasn't the name she expected to hear.

"You okay?" Nicole thumped her on the back. "I tried to break it to you gently."

"Thanks." Feeling like she'd stepped into another nightmare, Kelly wiped her mouth and cleared her throat. "How did you come to that conclusion?"

"Remember when Paula not so subtly divulged to everyone you're into bondage?"

It wasn't something Kelly was likely to forget in a hurry. "Yeah, why?"

"I know you heard every word she said, but you couldn't see every face." Nicole pointed to the narrow concrete path running along the back of their flat. "Ever seen someone turn that colour?"

Unsure if she was following along, Kelly narrowed her eyes. "You mean grey?"

"Yes! That's the colour Ashleigh turned when Paula mentioned you were meant to get your kink on then you got sick."

"Maybe the part about me being into kink embarrassed her."

"I wondered the same at first, but if that was the case she would've blushed not paled." Nicole's voice rose in pitch. "She looked panic struck, Kel, like she was freaking out someone would see right through her. Lower your head."

Humouring Nicole, Kelly did as she was told. She bent her neck and fixed her gaze on her bare feet. Her long hair fell around Kelly's shoulders and framed her face.

"Now, without lifting your head, look at me."

The innocent act of peering through the long, brown

strands made Kelly feel like she had something to hide.

"That's what Ashleigh did," Nicole exclaimed. "She didn't make eye contact with me for the rest of the night. It was almost as if she *knew* I knew."

Unconvinced, Kelly asked the more puzzling question. "What was she doing in Paula's room?"

"Who the hell knows, it could've been for any number of reasons. Remember at our house warming, Tina drank too much and had to lie down for a while? Maybe that's what happened with Ashleigh, or she could've been tired, or staying the night but couldn't crash on the sofa until all the guests had gone home."

Not knowing the answers, Kelly rubbed her friends shoulder. "I'm not disagreeing with you, Nicole. But we're still relying on a lot of guesswork."

The strap of Nicole's pyjama top slid down her arm. "You're right. The only way you'll know for sure is by asking everyone you suspect. And that would be rather silly."

After climbing to her feet, Nicole held out a hand. Kelly let her pull her up then shook out her legs. Nerves pinged as the circulation returned to her backside.

"Ashleigh's a sexy woman for sure. She's also engaged. To a man."

"She's also your soon to be ex's dear friend."

The word dear made Kelly cringe, it was a term of endearment she wouldn't miss.

Nicole, who must've mistaken Kelly's grimace as dread over the impending break-up, patted Kelly on the knee. "I know it won't be easy. Breaking up never is."

Resisting the urge to ask Nicole if she was going to break out in a song, Kelly returned her warm smile. "You're right, even when you're doing the dumping."

It wasn't something Kelly looked forward to and she hoped Paula didn't turn on the tears. But if she did, Kelly would just have to remind herself that their differences no longer attracted her to Paula. And, if Paula's shallow minded attitude and the ugly shadow who followed Paula everywhere, Colette, wasn't enough to make Kelly stick to her guns, looking at her through her friend's eyes certainly would.

A lawnmower fired to life putting an end to their peaceful chat. In unison, they bent and picked up their empty coffee mugs before stepping back inside and closing the door behind them.

Kelly rinsed her cup then held her hand out for Nicole's. The more Kelly thought about it, the more of what Nicole said made sense. Ashleigh certainly had withdrawn, but then again that could be put down to the tension in the room.

Where had Craig been that night anyway? What effect had the tryst had on their relationship? If Ashleigh was plagued by guilt it wouldn't be doing them any favours.

"If you're right, and it was Ashleigh, I feel I owe her an apology."

Just as she was about to bite into a banana, Nicole lowered her hand and narrowed her gaze. "I've said it before and I'm going to say it again. I don't see what possible good can come of approaching her. You need to chalk it up to experience and put it behind you."

It was an experience Kelly didn't intend to ever repeat. Scarred for life, she doubted she'd ever slip into a dark room again with the intentions of having sex.

Chapter 8

Determined to get the inevitable over with, Kelly picked up her phone. A frustrated sigh escaped her lips when her call went to voicemail.

Hello, this is Paula. I can't come to the phone right now. However, your call is important to me so please leave a message and I'll get back to you as soon as I can.

The formal tone of Paula's message, something that used to turn Kelly on, grated on her nerves. More proof it was time to end things.

Beep.

"Hi, it's me. I'm hoping we can catch up later today. Clear the air." Surely, she didn't need to elaborate as to why. "So yeah, call me when you're free."

Kelly disconnected the call, feeling more nervous than before. She didn't want to stew in her own juices and go over and over what she'd say to Paula. Chances were, no matter how much she rehearsed her speech, the words would abandon her once they were face to face.

It wouldn't be the first time she'd lost her train of thought once Paula put her two cents worth in. Kelly picked up her phone, tapped her finger on her leg then put it down again. Deciding fuck it, she picked it back up and tapped out a text message.

Last night you became very ugly in my eyes. I can't possibly date someone who doesn't respect my best friend, or worse, me! You should've told Colette to shut her mouth and swallow her brown tongue instead of berating me. You suck, have a happy life.

Feeling somewhat better, and a tad amused, Kelly held her finger on the delete key.

When her phone rang, Kelly almost dropped it as if she'd been burnt. That would teach her for entertaining the idea of sending such a juvenile text.

She scrambled to right herself, took a deep breath, and answered, "Hi, Paula."

"Good old caller ID sucks the life out of surprising anyone doesn't it?" The playful tone of Paula's voice surprised and worried Kelly.

For some reason, she didn't seem to be pissed off. Rather than put Kelly's mind at ease it worried her. It would've been easier to break things off if Paula was angry and being a bitch. Not this cheerful creature on the other end of the phone.

"I didn't think you liked surprises?"

"Of course I do, as long as they're nice ones." Paula chuckled, then lowered her voice and spoke in a sexy drawl. "Why don't you come over and surprise me? I have the house to myself for at least an hour."

Stress, rather than excitement made Kelly's pulse race. Boy, did she have a surprise for Paula, just not the kind she was expecting. "I'll have a quick shower then be right over."

Twenty minutes later, Kelly hung her helmet on her bike and stared up at Paula's grand three-bedroom home. For the first time ever, the entrance looked foreboding rather than welcoming. With her heart thudding in her chest, Kelly rapped on the solid wooden door.

"It's open," Paula called out, her voice barely

audible through the thick wood. "Lock it behind you."

Kelly did as she was told, then inched her way further inside.

The living room was empty.

"In here," Paula's voice came from somewhere down the hallway.

Trepidation surged through Kelly, the closer she got to the bedroom. She prayed her assumption was wrong. Her prayers went unanswered.

Propped up on her elbow, looking sinfully sexy in a royal blue baby doll negligee and matching briefs, Paula gave Kelly a come-hither look.

"I hope you wore something sexy under those jeans?"

With no other option but to get straight to the point, Kelly pulled the terry robe off the back of the bedroom door and tossed it to Paula; a futile attempt to save some of Paula's dignity.

"I didn't come over here to have sex with you, Paula."

Ignoring the robe, Paula sat upright, swung her legs over the side of the bed, and patted the spot next to her.

The bed dipped as Kelly sat at the bottom end. Which was a stupid move because when she faced Paula the headboard filled her vision.

Thoughts of that fateful night, two weeks ago, punched her in the gut, and steeled her resolve to end things. She didn't belong in Paula's home, or her life.

Paula sidled up next to her. "We haven't had sex for at least two weeks. Don't you find me attractive anymore?"

It was the first time Kelly had seen Paula look so vulnerable.

Why now, damn it?

"You're a gorgeous woman, Paula. It's not that." Kelly didn't add insult to injury by spelling out beauty went deeper than appearances.

"Oh, I get it," Paula said. "Is this to do with you wanting to do that kinky shit? Here." She held her wrists together. "Tie me up if that'll help get you off."

And as predicted, all the speeches Kelly had rehearsed failed her. Unbidden, words tumbled out of her mouth.

"That's the problem, Paula! You don't get it. Kink

isn't about you giving up control just to please another. Letting your P.A. piss all over your friends isn't acceptable either. You go about your day like you're a high and mighty boss, with everything under control, and you don't give a damn what anyone thinks of you. But behind the mask you wear, you're just as insecure as the next person."

An angry scowl creased Paula's forehead. "Who do you think you are, little girl?" Her voice dripped with venom. "How dare you speak to me like that."

Kelly hung her head, the last thing she'd intended to do was offend Paula. "Look. I didn't come here to fight, or as you eloquently put it last night, have a pissing match. You're a lovely woman, you've been great to me. But I don't think we're right for each other."

Paula plucked up the robe and covered her half-naked body. "Are you breaking up with me?"

"Yeah, I guess I am." Her own heart aching, Kelly gave Paula a sad smile.

A flicker of anguish flashed in Paula's eyes before her expression hardened. She held her chin high. "Fine. It won't take me long to find somebody else who's happy to play kitchen bitch and do my bidding."

It was a low blow, one that Kelly let her have. The unshed tears brimming in Paula's eyes said more. Pride and hurt had made her lash out.

Unable to get out of there fast enough, Kelly stood. "I'll see myself out."

"Do that." Paula sniffled and the sound almost broke Kelly's heart.

Being dumped hurt like a bitch. Putting somebody else through the same was no less painful.

Chapter 9

Happy her Saturday shift was almost over, Kelly wiped down the stainless-steel bench, her mind on the next few days off. Sunday, she planned on spending some quality time with her mum and little sister, Jo.

With March only a few weeks away, the summer break would be over before they knew it and Jo would be heading back to Wellington for her second year of study.

The doors between the café and the kitchen swung open and banged against the wall. Kelly turned to see her work colleague, Jacinta, beaming at her, presumably also looking forward to a day off.

Kelly glanced at the clock on the industrial sized oven. "Ten minutes and we can knock off."

Jacinta grabbed the cloth out of Kelly's hand. "I can finish up here."

The huge smile on her face piqued Kelly's interest.

"What are you looking so happy about?"

If it was even possible, the smile grew wider. "It's not every day a sexy woman comes into the cafe."

That wasn't true, they had plenty of good looking regular clientele. However, Jacinta normally swooned after the men.

"Your point?" Kelly quirked an eyebrow.

"She's asking for you."

More than a little intrigued, Kelly stood on her tippy-toes so she could see over the door swinging in Jacinta's wake. When her gaze landed on the sexy woman in concern, Kelly's stomach lurched. "Shit. What does she want?"

"You," Jacinta replied. "Go get her, tiger." She shoved Kelly in the back.

Caught off guard, with no time to brace herself, Kelly stumbled through the doors making a not so grand entrance into the café.

"Hi, what brings you here?" Kelly asked, pleased her voice didn't shake and giveaway the butterflies churning in her belly.

"Can we talk?"

The words were spoken so softly, for a minute Kelly wasn't sure she'd heard Ashleigh right, or perhaps that was wishful thinking.

Had Ashleigh finally decided to confront her about the night Kelly had tried for the last few weeks to put behind her? She wanted to bolt but also owed it to Ashleigh to hear her out.

Maybe it had nothing to do with that night, Kelly tried to convince herself, but in the pit of her stomach she knew better.

"Sure, let me go get my things. The shop's about to close."

"I know." Ashleigh interrupted. "I didn't want to have this conversation at your work, but I had no idea how else to find you." She blushed and damned if she didn't look adorable.

"I couldn't really ask Paula, and I'd appreciate it if you keep this conversation between us, okay?"

That was more than fine by Kelly. "Sure. Nicole's at her boyfriend's tonight, you're welcome to come over to the flat."

The minute the words left her mouth Kelly

wondered if she needed her head read. But it was the one place she was certain Paula wouldn't show her face.

"I'd like that. Lead the way."

On the ride home, Kelly's mind raced along with her motorcycle. Every time she turned a corner, her mind took off in another direction. Should she start the conversation, or wait Ashleigh out? Should she tell Ashleigh she was clean?

No that probably wasn't a good idea. Not only would it be humiliating but Ashleigh could also take it as a slur on her character.

***

Once at home, seated in the living room and unable to stand the silence for a second longer, Kelly took the liberty to speak first.

"I'm glad you're here. I've wanted to apologize ever since that night. I can only guess what you think of me." She wiped her sweaty palms on her jeans.

"You don't have to apologize," Ashleigh said. "Shit happens, and I'm fairly sure you didn't plan it?"

Her warm smile astounded Kelly. How could Ashleigh be so flippant about what happened? It suddenly struck Kelly that perhaps Ashleigh was bisexual and in an open relationship. The thought was so ludicrous Kelly almost laughed at herself.

Rather than continue to let her mind run amuck, Kelly asked the question. "Did you tell your fiancé, Craig?"

A sparkle twinkled in Ashleigh's eyes. "Of course. He thinks it's great and would like to meet you."

What the ever-loving fuck?

"He thinks it's great that I ravished your body? Oh, God, please don't tell me you've come here to invite me to join you two. I don't do threesomes… or men."

The colour drained out of Ashleigh's face. Scowling, she folded her arms across her chest. "What the hell are you talking about?"

Confused beyond belief, Kelly tossed the question back at her. "What are *you* talking about?"

"Paula's potluck dinner. I thought you were excusing yourself for the way you spoke to Colette. But like I said shit happens and I'm sure you didn't plan on being rude to her."

Stunned, Kelly's mouth fell open as she realized she'd made a huge faux pas.

Relaxing her posture, ever so slightly, Ashleigh continued. "Craig has never liked Colette, only tolerated her for the sake of my friendship with Paula. When I told him about you and the way you handled Colette, he looked at me in awe and said, 'Damn I need to meet this woman'."

"Oh," Kelly replied sounding pathetic, and wishing she could take back her comment.

"Craig and I are exclusive. He's the only one who's had access to this body since we got together." A cute blush spread up Ashleigh's cheeks. "I'm not sure why you were under the impression, you and I…you know?" She smiled shyly. "Care to explain? I'm a good listener."

Instinct told Kelly she could trust Ashleigh, not to mention Ashleigh deserved an explanation. "To repeat your words, I'd prefer it if this conversation doesn't go any further."

Swallowing around the lump in her throat, and

needing a minute to gather her thoughts, Kelly stood.

"Can I get you something to drink? Tea, coffee, juice, water? I haven't been to the bottle store yet, so I can't offer you anything stronger." Nerves made her ramble.

"Relax, Kelly. I don't drink and drive, so a glass of water will be fine."

"Ice?"

"Please."

Due to the flat being shut up for the better part of the day the air was thick and humid.

Kelly plucked at her jeans clinging to her legs. "Make yourself at home." She turned on the small fan on route to her room. "I'm just going to change into something more comfortable."

The amused twinkle in Ashleigh's eyes made Kelly chuckle.

Damn she liked this woman.

How on earth Ashleigh and Paula were so close was beyond Kelly, and not something she cared to dissect.

When Kelly returned to the living room, feeling much cooler wearing a pale blue mini-dress, she found

Ashleigh staring at a portrait that held centre stage in the lounge and Kelly's heart.

She handed an iced water to Ashleigh. "Here."

Barely taking her eyes off the picture, Ashleigh took the proffered drink. "I recognize the faces. You and Nicole, right?"

"Yep."

Although the picture had been taken years ago, there was no mistaking the teenage girls grinning from ear to ear.

"And the men?"

"Our fathers."

Kelly stared at the image of her and Nicole, their dad standing behind them hands on their daughter's shoulders, two gleaming milk tankers shining in the background.

"Not only did my dad work with Nicole's father, they were great mates too. As you know, it's how Nicole and I met."

Remorse radiated in Ashleigh's eyes. "I'm sorry I didn't interject when Colette…"

"Stop." Kelly held up a hand. "It wasn't your battle.

Colette was out of line and, if anything, Paula should've been offended that her P.A. was putting down her girlfriend. But, no, she just sat back as though it was totally acceptable."

"You do realize Paula's very insecure? She craves acceptance like a child craves the love of a parent. She'll go to lengths to be the centre of attention."

"I didn't to begin with, but after a while it became more obvious."

The day she'd strolled into the café and asked Kelly on a date she'd seemed like the most confident woman in the world. But over the last month or so, the cracks in her armour had become more apparent, and unappealing. Kelly wasn't the most secure person in the world, but she was a loyal friend and would never let anyone speak down to someone she cared about.

She had to give credit to Ashleigh for being there for Paula. "I'm glad she has a friend who can see the good in her."

It was on the tip of Kelly's tongue to ask Ashleigh if she was one of those people who took in stray friends like stray animals. Not only would it be inappropriate and offensive, but Kelly figured Ashleigh and Paula's friendship went way deeper than she'd ever know, or understand.

Smiling, Ashleigh pointed at the picture. "Tell me about this day. Your father looks extremely proud."

Love for her father blossomed in Kelly's chest as her mind flicked back to the day in question.

"The dairy company had a strict policy on cleanliness, trucks included. As you can imagine, the roads, or should I say dirt tracks to milking sheds are rather…"

"Shitty?" Ashleigh supplied.

"Exactly." Kelly chuckled, wrinkling her nose.

The size of some of the cow patties she'd seen over the years flabbergasted her.

Needing to take a load off her tired legs, Kelly slumped into the nearby armchair.

Following suit, Ashleigh returned to her seat on the sofa.

"On that day, over a decade ago, Nicole and I scrubbed those trucks until they shined like polished silver. The manager of the dairy company stopped by, snapped our photo, and presented us with vouchers to a fancy restaurant. The way our fathers puffed out their chests, beaming with pride, was worth more to me and Nicole than the lavish meal our families feasted on that night."

Kelly didn't know if she believed in the afterlife, but liked to think he still watched over her. More than once she'd felt his presence before telling herself she was being silly.

"This was my dad's chair." She pushed her foot on the floor, lulled by the gentle rocking. "When he died, mum put it in the garage. I guess the pain of seeing it empty was too much for her to bear. I never forgot it was there and when Nicole and I moved into this flat, I asked Mum if I could take it."

Ashleigh's gaze, full of empathy, never wavered from Kelly. The fact she seemed genuinely interested kept Kelly talking.

"Mum burst into tears, wrapped me in her arms, and said, I've dusted that chair off more times than I can remember. At times, when you girls were fast asleep, I'd go out to the garage and sit in your father's chair.

Sometimes I'd smile, other times I'd get angry at him for leaving us."

A tear slid down Kelly's cheek. "I know she didn't mean that in a nasty way, it wasn't like Dad had a choice about dying."

Suddenly feeling self-conscious, Kelly sniffled. "Anyway, mum was delighted and here I sit spilling my guts to you as if I've known you forever."

Ashleigh set her empty glass on the coffee table. "That's the thing, Kelly. I feel it too, it's as if we've known each other for a lifetime."

A phone chirped and they both glanced down.

"It's mine," Ashleigh declared, swiping the screen.

Fascinated, Kelly watched Ashleigh's expression go from neutral, to smiling, to bashful. She glanced up and saw Kelly watching.

"It's Craig." She cleared her throat but didn't elaborate.

Seeing her opportunity to dodge a bullet, Kelly took it. "Well then, you better get going, don't keep the man waiting."

A sardonic smile slid onto Ashleigh's face.

Just when Kelly thought she was off the hook, Ashleigh reeled her back in.

"Oh, no you don't." Ashleigh waggled a finger. "I might be ten years your senior, but I don't suffer from CRAFT yet."

Say what?

Kelly took the bait. "What's craft?"

"Can't Remember A Fk'n Thing."

It took a moment for what Ashleigh said to sink in. Once it did, Kelly burst out laughing, both amused by the acronym and the fact Ashleigh wouldn't say the F word.

"That's a good one. I'll have to tease mum next time she can't find her car keys."

Although, at the tender age of forty-nine, Kelly's mother was still sharp as a pin. Not much got past her, especially when it came to her daughters.

All traces of humour gone, Ashleigh turned serious. "I'm all ears," she said softly. "And rest assured, I won't repeat a word of what you tell me."

The mere thought of that fateful night made Kelly break out in a cold sweat.

She took a deep breath and relayed her story, how she was supposed to meet Paula in the bedroom, seeing Paula in the hallway, not knowing who she'd slept with, and how her and Nicole had concluded it was more than likely Ashleigh, and why.

"I wasn't entirely convinced, and with no way of knowing for certain, I tried to put the night behind me."

When Kelly didn't receive any righteous comments, she finally met Ashleigh's gaze. Her eyes were full of a tenderness that made Kelly want to jump into her arms.

For a hug.

As a friend.

Nothing more.

Yeah, right.

"When you turned up at the café talking in hushed tones and stating we needed to talk, I put two and two together."

"And came up with six?" Ashleigh smirked.

"You got it."

"If it's any consolation, I think you did the right thing not telling Paula. Not that I'll ever admit to saying that."

Once again, Kelly wondered how deep Ashleigh and Paula's friendship went. From where she was sitting, it appeared they kept a lot from each other.

Then again, Kelly didn't tell Nicole everything so perhaps she shouldn't be judging.

As if reading her mind, Ashleigh reiterated her thoughts.

"I have two close friends, but some things even best friends shouldn't share with each other. Know what I mean?"

"Yep," Kelly replied.

"For all you know your flatmate, Nicole isn't it?"

Intrigued and slightly amused by where Ashleigh might be going with this, Kelly nodded.

"Nicole might own a strap-on."

Without thought, Kelly replied, "She's straight."

A slow smile crept across Ashleigh's face. "I know."

When the implications of what Ashleigh was implying hit home, Kelly paled. "Now there's an image I don't need." She chuckled. "Steve would be horrified if he knew we were even discussing the idea of him on all fours and Nicole banging him from… Never mind."

Kelly shook her head before the full picture could take hold.

"Ugh, let's just say I agree with you. Some things should be kept private."

"Right, and I don't need Paula to know I want Craig to spank my bottom." A blush spread up Ashleigh's neck and reached the tip of her ears. "I mean how embarrassing. I'm almost thirty-five not five, and even if I was five, who enjoys being spanked?"

Even though it was a rhetorical question, Kelly couldn't help but reflect on her own experience.

Her first lover had been a switch. Therefore, Kelly had experienced what it was like to take both the dominant and submissive role.

While she could see why giving up control might appeal to others, it did nothing for Kelly. She also discovered when taking the dominant role, she really came alive. Kelly craved the control, the power to give or deny an orgasm.

Ashleigh's voice drew Kelly back to the present.

"I doubt Paula, or anyone other than you, would understand. Anyway, Craig and I both wanted to thank you."

"For what?"

"We've been having problems in the bedroom." Ashleigh's cheeks turned crimson, but she held Kelly's gaze. "He's always taken the lead. Hell, I suppose most men do. But it's never been enough for me. I wanted him to take charge, to restrain me, to spank me, to order me to…" She trailed off. "You get the picture."

Ashleigh truly was adorable. And straight. And engaged.

Kelly bit back a smile, the last thing she wanted was for Ashleigh to think she was laughing at her.

"After that night at Paula's," Ashleigh continued. "Although I was truly embarrassed for you, and the way Paula outed you, I finally realized I wasn't alone in loving kink. When I got home that night, I decided to hell with it and laid my heart on the line to Craig, or more specifically my desires. Hell, if you can't be honest with the person you want to spend the rest of your life with, who can you be honest with?"

Kelly couldn't argue with that, but her mind was still stuck on something Ashleigh said earlier.

"Care to enlighten me why you think it's best Paula doesn't know? Honestly, I thought you'd think I was a coward for not telling her."

"Like I said, Paula's insecure. As much as it kills me to say it, she tends to surround herself with people she deems below her. She's always had straight women as roommates. My guess is so she won't feel threatened by them or worry they might attract the attention of a lover. By not telling her what happened you're protecting the other person as much as yourself."

Worry creased Ashleigh's forehead. "Honestly, Kelly, I believe if she finds out, it won't only be about you. Paula will go on a personal crusade to find out who the other person was, and God help them if she figures it out."

Would this nightmare never end? Ashleigh's words brought the reality of the situation crashing home. Not only would Paula never know what happened, but perhaps Kelly would never know the identity of the other woman either.

Unlike Paula, Kelly didn't have the bliss of ignorance on her side.

Ashleigh's phone chimed. She fidgeted with it in her lap but kept her gaze on Kelly as though it would be rude to look at her phone during such a monumental moment. But Kelly was done talking. She was hungry, and a dull ache had started in her temples.

"Get that." Kelly stood. "I've gotta get a move along anyway."

Ashleigh's hand flew to her mouth. "Oh, gosh. I'm sorry. I didn't realize I was holding you up."

Mentally exhausted, Kelly didn't bother informing Ashleigh the only place she was going was around the corner to the local fish and chip shop.

After pushing herself to her feet, Kelly escorted Ashleigh to the door. "Tell Craig I said hi and I'm glad I could help."

"I will, and thank you again."

Surprising the hell out of Kelly, Ashleigh pecked her on the cheek. "You're a good person, Kelly. I hope you find the one."

With a heavy heart, Kelly whispered, "Me too," as Ashleigh disappeared down the driveway.

Chapter 10

The following morning, Kelly slung her backpack over her shoulders, about to head to her mother's when Nicole and Steve breezed through the door.

"Hey, how was your night?" Nicole asked.

Taking the opportunity to have some fun with her friends, Kelly dropped her bag at her feet and waggled her eyebrows. "Great. You'll never guess who came over."

Steve kicked off his jandals and placed them by the door. "Your sister?"

Nicole elbowed Steve. "She wouldn't be looking as though she got laid if she'd spent the night with Jo."

She turned her attention back to Kelly. "Spill."

Biting her lip to stifle a giggle, Kelly replied, "Ashleigh."

The shocked expression on Nicole's face, eyes wide, mouth open, was entertaining to say the least.

"Are you fucking nuts? If Paula finds out, she'll go mental. And what kind of friend is Ashleigh to be running around behind her best friend's back?"

Spittle flew out of Nicole's mouth. "I told you no good would come out of pursuing her."

"Wow, calm down." Steve put a hand on Nicole's shoulder. "I know you're worried about our friend, but Kelly's not stupid. At least hear her out."

The fight went out of Nicole. She slumped onto the sofa.

Feeling like a jerk for alarming Nicole, Kelly sat beside her and took her hand. "We were wrong."

"Huh?" Steve asked.

"Not you. Me and Nicole."

Certain Steve didn't want to sit around listening to girl talk, Kelly put him to work. "Make yourself useful. Coffee please."

"Aye, aye, madam." Steve saluted as he marched toward the kitchen.

Luckily, Kelly hadn't given her mother a specific time she'd be arriving, so spending half an hour with her friends wouldn't make her mother worry.

"Ashleigh came into the café and asked if we could talk."

Nicole's eyes went wide. "I bet that set off alarm bells. Oh my God. What'd you do?"

A chuckle escaped Kelly's lips. "I spilled my guts, for no good reason. It wasn't her, Nic. Ashleigh's fiancé picked her up shortly before Paula came inside looking for me."

"Hang on a minute. If it wasn't Ashleigh, why'd did she pale at Paula's party? What was that about?"

"I'm not going to tell you the entire story because Ashleigh spoke to me in confidence."

"Okay." Nicole nodded, and left it at that.

It was a trait Kelly admired in her friend. Nicole didn't get upset if she didn't know every sordid detail. She was a fiercely loyal friend and wouldn't expect Kelly to break a confidence any more than she herself would.

"Let's just say, Ashleigh and I like some of the same things. The night of Paula's potluck dinner she thought you could see right through her, then shame overtook her for not standing up to Paula and telling her friend to rein in her P.A."

Understanding flashed in Nicole's eyes. "That's the reason Ashleigh wouldn't look at me?"

"You got it."

Understanding turned to concern. "Now what, Kelly?" Nicole asked.

"I'm going to take your advice and put it behind me."

Which was exactly what Kelly had been trying to do before Ashleigh waltzed into her life and squashed their theory. Anymore guesswork could only lead to further humiliation.

Chapter 11

Over the next few weeks, Kelly kept in touch with Ashleigh. The previous week, Ashleigh had visited the café with her fiancé in tow. Kelly had been about to take a break, so she spent fifteen minutes with them.

Craig was a good-looking man, and it was clear he only had eyes for Ashleigh.

If Kelly could take anything positive from that fateful night, it was that such a wonderful couple had benefited from her blunder.

While sex wasn't the be all and end all of a relationship, in Kelly's mind, it separated friends from lovers.

If there was no intimacy between her and her lover, they might as well just be friends. Perhaps her attitude would change with age. Or if she met someone who wooed her so much with her intelligence, and good company, that sex didn't matter.

The only action Kelly had seen in the past two months was with her own hand. Her vibrator provided her with a swift release but would never replace what she missed the most about being in a relationship; physical intimacy.

A toy could never replicate an emotional connection or the heavenly feel of skin on skin.

Even when she got off with her vibrator, an overwhelming sense of wanting to snuggle up to a lover, and bask in the afterglow, often left Kelly feeling bereft.

Kelly gave herself a mental kick up the backside. If she didn't stop moping around the flat, she'd never meet a potential lover. Although she'd met Paula at the café, when Paula used to frequent the place to impress business associates, chances of meeting another customer Kelly might consider dating were slim to none.

"Don't jump." The warning came from behind.

Startled, Kelly did just that. The cup she'd been holding fell from her grip and shattered on the floor. Thankfully, it was empty.

With her heart pounding against her ribcage, Kelly spun around.

Her boss, Jennifer, quirked an eyebrow and glanced at the mess on the otherwise pristine linoleum floor.

"Shit, you scared the crap out of me."

"Language," Jennifer chided, handing Kelly a dustpan.

Normally more professional at work, Kelly apologized. "Sorry, you took me by surprise. I was miles away."

The signature scent of Jennifer's perfume tickled Kelly's nostrils. "I noticed."

Her boss leaned a hip against the counter, her expression all business. "I have an important assignment and need someone I can rely on. You're top of the list. The pride you take in your work, going the extra mile to ensure a customer is happy, hasn't escaped my notice."

The observation shocked and delighted Kelly. Jennifer wasn't one to sing praises. She was of the mind her employees were paid to do a job and to adhere to high standards.

"The Inland Revenue Department has selected the café to be audited. They are expected to arrive on Tuesday and, all going well, will be done by Friday."

"What does that mean?" Kelly asked. "I mean what does it entail?" she added, not wanting to sound totally clueless.

"Not only will they make sure every dollar has been accounted for, they'll also check all taxes have been paid. Which, by the way, they have."

Kelly didn't doubt that for a minute, her boss was so squeaky clean, Kelly was surprised Jennifer's legs didn't screech when she walked. An image of subtle thighs rubbing together sprung to mind. Trying to rid herself of the inappropriate image, Kelly swept up the shards of glass at their feet.

"Whoever the tax department sends in will also be auditing all personnel files." Her boss's voice trailed off.

When Kelly stood, they were no longer alone.

"Hey, boss. Kel." Jacinta breezed by, retrieved a litre of milk from the fridge and disappeared as quickly as she'd materialize.

"I can't be here all day every day." Jennifer didn't elaborate; she didn't need to.

While it wasn't talked about openly at work, most employees were aware Jennifer's mother was receiving chemotherapy treatment at Palmerston North Hospital, and Jennifer always accompanied her mum to the appointments.

"I want you to assist the auditor. Make sure the files are accessible when needed, and kept under lock and key at all other times."

For some inexplicable reason, the serious look in Jennifer's eyes worried Kelly. Her pulse raced as she awaited her bosses next words.

"I'm putting you in a huge position of trust, Kelly. One that might ruffle the feathers of those who think you're receiving special treatment." Her expression softened.

"That doesn't bother me," Kelly replied honestly.

It wasn't like she hadn't been judged before. And, unlike some of her co-workers who were often late and liked to gossip about customers, Kelly had earned Jennifer's trust.

More than once, a regular client had shared a confidence with Kelly. It was almost as if they thought she was a safe sounding board, especially when they vented about a spouse or family.

God knew, Kelly had shared half her life story with her hairdresser. She hoped it went no further and therefore afforded her customers the same courtesy.

A slither of sunlight glimmered off the key Jennifer dangled between them.

"I won't let you down, boss." Kelly held out her hand.

"I'm counting on it."

The small gold key landed in Kelly's palm. She closed her fist around it, accepting it like a sacred gift.

Jennifer pushed her glasses up her nose, drawing Kelly's gaze to the sadness lingering there.

In that moment, Kelly's heart went out to her boss. She didn't know what would be worse, having her father ripped from her life, or having months to prepare for the fact that a loved one might not survive cancer.

Taking a huge risk of overstepping boundaries, Kelly placed a hand on Jennifer's forearm and gave it a gentle squeeze. "I can lock up tonight, go be with your mum."

Jennifer narrowed her eyes. "Are you after a pay rise?"

Playing along, Kelly replied, "Always."

Without a backward glance, her boss exited the building and Kelly returned to work.

Chapter 12

Tuesday rolled around in record time. Despite having two days off, Kelly arrived at work feeling more tired than rested. Her arms ached from lifting furniture and settling her sister into her new flat in Wellington.

While Jo didn't have a lot of stuff to move—bed, study desk, drawers, book shelves—all of which fitted into their mum's SUV, lugging the furniture up three terraces and two flights of stairs had been a mammoth feat.

The view overlooking the wharf and the city was spectacular, but no way would you find Kelly living in a house perched on a hill in Wellington. Earthquake city.

It didn't seem to bother Jo, and Kelly reminded herself there were no guarantees in life. Between her sister's accommodation and Kelly's love of motorcycles, it was any wonder they hadn't given their mother a heart attack.

Shortly after eight, the door to the café chimed. Kelly glanced up and her heart skipped a beat. There was no mistaking the dark-haired beauty heading her way, hips swaying, high-heels clacking on the tiled floor.

She was as stunning as the day Kelly had met her. Jet black hair framed a gorgeous face, high cheekbones, perfectly straight nose, and luscious full lips.

The white blouse and black pencil skirt she wore hugged her curves perfectly. She was neither fat nor thin, in Kelly's eyes, she was perfection.

The briefcase swinging at her side gave the air of a woman who meant business.

As her gaze settled on Kelly, recognition dawned, and a beaming smile lit up Lucy's face.

"Kelly? Wow, it's great to see you. How have you been?"

Charmed by Lucy's enthusiastic greeting, Kelly tried not to grin like a loon.

"I've been doing okay," she replied honestly. And all the better for seeing you, she didn't add.

Instead, she kept her professional mask in place and picked up a mug. "What can I get you? Latte? Long Black? Espresso?"

Lucy chuckled. "Nothing right now. I've just had coffee."

Trying to figure out why Lucy would be standing before her, Kelly scrunched up her face. After a minute of contemplation, it dawned on her. Food.

She pointed to a silver serving tray with a clear plastic lid. "Blueberry muffin with white chocolate? Fresh out of the oven."

"Mm, now you're talking. Put my name on one." Lucy glanced at her wristwatch.

The white leather strap blended perfectly with her blouse. A very fitting blouse that afforded Kelly a glimpse of tantalizing cleavage. At a guess, Lucy's breasts were more than a handful. But Kelly had two hands, and a mouth, so who cared?

What the fuck? Talk about inappropriate thoughts.

Lucy didn't even bat for the same team as Kelly. Her words from Paula's party—I haven't met the right guy yet—bounced around inside Kelly's skull.

"I'll come back for a muffin when I take a break," Lucy's voice snapped Kelly out of her musings. "If your boss lets me stop for one."

Beyond confused, Kelly folded her arms across her chest. "Come again?"

Ugh, way to go, Kel.

Not picking up on the possible innuendo, or perhaps choosing to ignore it, Lucy handed an embossed card to Kelly.

"I'm here on business. Running into you is an unexpected bonus."

The alluring smile Lucy flashed Kelly ignited her blood. Trying not to blush furiously, she glanced down at the card in her hand. Lucy Tanner, auditor.

Dread over the impending audit turned to elation. As much as Kelly looked forward to spending the next few days assisting Lucy, she needed to get her libido under control if she was going to survive without a lawsuit.

The last thing she needed was a sexual harassment case.

"Come this way, we have to go through the kitchen to get to the office upstairs."

Just as they reached the end of the counter, the door chimed.

Lucy glanced over her shoulder and Kelly followed her line of sight.

The woman cutting a fast track to the counter looked vaguely familiar. Kelly racked her brain trying to place her. Unlike Lucy who apparently knew the woman.

"Hey, Kate." Lucy extended a hand and the woman practically glowed.

Kate, Kate, Kate; average height, average build, average looks.

That's it! Plain Jane, the woman from Paula's ill-fated party.

Could this day get any more bizarre?

Kelly's head spun, it wasn't even nine-thirty and two women from that night were standing before her.

"Nice to see you," Kate said, holding Lucy's hand far longer than necessary in Kelly's opinion.

"Do you come here often?" Kate's gaze roamed over Lucy's body.

Resisting the urge to groan at the lame pick-up line, Kelly cleared her throat, a not so subtle reminder they weren't alone.

Kate released Lucy's hand and turned her attention to Kelly. "Flat white, thanks." Her voice was as flat as her order.

Before Kelly could feel affronted, Kate's eyebrows shot up. She waggled her fingers. "We've met, haven't we?" Her hand stilled, finger pointed to the ceiling. "No, don't tell me."

Her animated gestures and the change of her tone from flat to vibrant, amused Kelly and she found herself grinning. For the first time, she understood why this woman had no shortage of bed partners. Like Lucy, Kate had charisma.

In the back of her mind, Kelly hoped that was where their similarities ended. Even though Kelly had no claim over Lucy, for some reason, the thought of Lucy bed hopping was unsettling.

On second thoughts, she wouldn't mind if Kate and Lucy had one other thing in common. What if, like Kate, Lucy was bisexual?

Kelly squashed that line of thought, not only was she setting herself up for disappointment, but the prospect of dating someone who slept with both men and women had never crossed her mind. She couldn't even begin to imagine the insecurities that might go hand in hand with doing so.

"Kelly." Kate snapped her fingers, startling Kelly out of her reverie.

The conviction in her voice, and gleeful look on her face, reminded Kelly of someone who'd just declared the winning answer on a game show.

"That's me," Kelly said over the hiss of the coffee machine.

"Have here or take away?" Kelly kept her gaze to her customer, Kate, but she could feel Lucy's eyes on her like a physical touch.

"Take away, I have to dash. I normally get my coffee in the plaza. No offense, Kelly. I'm sure yours is to die for."

Kate winked and Kelly blushed unsure if she was supposed to pick up on an underlying innuendo, or if the comment had been innocent.

"I'm meeting one of my clients on his own turf this morning. I'm trying to get him to join the twenty-first century and start using a cloud based accounting system. And, if my mouth doesn't stop getting away on me, I'm going to be late."

Lucy chuckled.

Kelly smiled, handing Kate her coffee to-go.

Kate leaned in and like an invisible force drawing them all together, Lucy and Kelly huddled closer.

"The cost of this." Kate tapped the side of her Styrofoam cup and spoke in a conspiratorial whisper, "Will be buried amongst his bill for my services."

Is that legal?

"You do know Lucy's an auditor?" Kelly said, not sure if she was trying to help Kate or dump her in it.

Unfazed, Kate replied, "I didn't, but I do now." She looked at her watch. "Shit, I've gotta fly. How about we catch up for a drink after work?"

Given the question appeared to be directed at Lucy, Kelly held her tongue, and her breath.

"I'd like that," Lucy replied, her voice soft, her smile sinfully sexy.

A foreign, unwelcome emotion bubbled up inside Kelly, jealousy.

"What about you, Kelly?" Lucy asked.

She's just being polite, the green eyed-monster mumbled in Kelly's head.

Before Kelly could torment herself any further, Jacinta came barrelling through the doors separating the kitchen from the café.

"Oh my God, sorry I'm late. The car wouldn't start." She glanced around nervously while tying her apron strings. "Is the boss here yet?"

Ignoring Jacinta's meltdown, Kate headed for the door hollering over her shoulder, "See you tonight, Aquaba at seven." And with that, she was gone.

"What was that all about," Jacinta asked before her gaze landed on Lucy.

She straightened her spine, and put on her most welcoming smile. "Sorry, Miss. I didn't see you there. Can I get you something or has Kelly already taken your order?"

"She's here on business," Kelly replied, beating Lucy to the punch.

A pang of remorse rippled through Kelly when Lucy snapped her mouth shut. She hadn't meant to speak on

Lucy's behalf, but she didn't know if the staff were fully aware of why Lucy was there.

Keen to get a move along, Kelly made introductions. "Lucy, Jacinta." She turned to Jacinta. "Jacinta, Lucy."

Lucy waved at Jacinta. "Nice to meet you." She glanced at Kelly. "And yes, your co-worker has already taken my order. Shall we?" She picked up her briefcase.

Wide-eyed, Jacinta cupped her hands around her jaw and mouthed, "Go for it. She's hot."

Biting back a grin, Kelly put a finger under Jacinta's chin, pushed her mouth shut, and whispered into her ear, "Don't go there." As an afterthought she added, "Remember, the lady's here on business."

On their way upstairs, Lucy turned to Kelly. "To repeat Jacinta's words, what was that about?"

"Oh, I was just telling her not to forget to fill the pie warmer, and to come and get me if she needs any help."

"Right, and I'm here to check the plumbing."

Unable to help herself, Kelly waggled her eyebrows. "Really? Last time I checked my plumbing worked just fine, but I'm happy to take a second opinion."

When Lucy faltered mid-step, alarm shot through

Kelly. Had she gone too far? What the hell was she thinking? God, they hadn't even made it to the office and she was flirting like a shameless hussy.

As Kelly's foot hit the next step, relief swept over her when Lucy's laughter rang out. She released the breath she'd been holding and exhaled a nervous giggle.

"You're incorrigible," Lucy said, still chuckling as they reached the landing.

Vowing to herself to act more professional, and prove to her boss she was worthy of being assigned the task at hand, Kelly unlocked the office and ushered Lucy in ahead of her.

The room was small but functional. A large desk dominated the left-hand side, and two filing cabinets took up the right. Kelly wrinkled her nose, it also smelled musty.

"Speaking of your plumbing, are you going to join me and Kate for a drink tonight?"

As much as Kelly was tempted to jump at the opportunity to spend more time with Lucy, she refused to play third wheel.

"She invited you, not me," Kelly stated as she strode across the office to let in some much-needed fresh air.

She pushed open the window and inhaled the crisp spring air, along with lingering fumes of early morning traffic.

"Don't play coy, Kelly. It's not very becoming."

The reprimand was like a slap in the face. She wasn't playing coy, she wasn't playing anything. Kelly didn't play mind games. Prepared to defend herself, Kelly pivoted.

The warm smile that greeted her made her forget what she'd been about to say. Instead, she blurted out what had been on her mind since Kate waltzed into the café and sized up Lucy.

"She's hot for you."

That goddamn alluring smile, the one that set Kelly's insides on fire, slid onto Lucy's face.

Without a word, she clicked open her briefcase, got what she needed and sat behind the desk, looking every bit like she belonged there.

Kelly leaned back against the filing cabinet, the cool metal a stark contrast to the heat simmering low in her belly.

The hard drive whirred as Lucy hit the power button. "Password?"

"Huh?" Kelly asked, sounding like an imbecile and hating herself for it.

When the fog lifted, Lucy's request hit home. Kelly gave her the temporary password Jennifer had assigned for the auditor.

"I figured I might as well boot up the computer so I can start gathering the data I need while we talk."

"Sorry, I shouldn't keep you."

"It's okay, I've been known to multi-task. Apparently, it's a woman thing."

Kelly chuckled. "So I've heard."

Doing her own bit of multi-tasking, if talking and working could be considered as such, Kelly pulled out the small gold key Jennifer had entrusted her with and turned to the personnel files.

"I've known Kate for some time now." Lucy's voice drifted over Kelly's shoulder. "While Paula pretends to be understanding of Kate's lifestyle, in going so far as to invite her to the occasional party, it's painfully obvious that Paula's extremely uncomfortable around Kate. However, I get her."

Kelly's stomach went into free fall. How much did Lucy get Kate, and on what level? She fumbled with the lock on the filing cabinet, unsure if she wanted to look Lucy in the eye when she said whatever was coming next.

"What I love about Kate is she's unapologetic about her desires," Lucy said, her tone matter of fact. "She doesn't string anyone along. She loves men and women in all shapes and forms. If she's not hurting anyone, I say all power to her."

The green-eyed monster reared its ugly head again. Was Lucy one of Kate's conquests?

As if reading Kelly's thoughts, Lucy put her mind at ease.

"Kate flirts with me, it's in her nature. But her playful manner is harmless. She hasn't overstepped any boundaries since I turned her down."

Did Kate have no shame? Surely most people checked their gaydar, or bi-dar, if that was even a word, before coming onto someone.

Annoyed on behalf of Lucy, Kelly yanked the key out of the filing cabinet and spun around.

"She hit on you?"

Lucy mock pouted and looked down at her body. "Is that so hard to believe?"

Kelly tried hard not to stare at the cleavage Lucy had unwittingly drawn her gaze too.

"No, that's not what I meant. Weren't you offended?"

"I was flattered, actually."

Trying to understand, Kelly pursed her lips. "Do you like it when women come onto you?"

"You know what, Kelly?" A look Kelly couldn't decipher glistened in Lucy's eyes.

It was a cross between sassy and sultry, and it held Kelly captive. She couldn't look away even if she wanted to.

"The last time you dangled that hook, the night of Paula's party, I had the most bizarre dream." She paused then added, "And you were in it. Crazy, huh?"

Lucy cocked her head to the side as if daring Kelly to say something.

With her heart lodged firmly in her throat, Kelly shrugged, feigning a calmness she didn't feel. "Dreams, they're weird."

Elbows on the desk, chin on her hands, Lucy stared at Kelly, her gaze so intense Kelly broke out in a cold sweat.

"Ever had a dream so vivid you could've sworn it was real?" Lucy leaned back in the chair.

What the ever-loving fuck?

Heat flared in Kelly's cheeks and guilt gnawed at her conscience. She had no way of knowing if Lucy was making general conversation or digging for more.

Kelly had to get out of there, and fast. The last thing she needed was to draw another incorrect conclusion and embarrass herself.

"Can't say I have." Kelly shrugged off the question. "I better go check on Jacinta. Holler if you need anything."

"I will." Lucy picked up a pen and Kelly strode toward the door.

"Oh, and Kelly."

Hand poised on the doorknob, Kelly froze, cold

dread chilling her to the bone.

"Don't forget my coffee and muffin. See you at ten."

***

The next hour and a half went by painfully slow yet way too fast. Kelly hadn't watched the clock at work for longer than she could remember. She loved her job and was never in a hurry to leave.

As much as she wanted to dismiss Lucy's comments as general chit-chat, every time Kelly thought about what Lucy had said, the hairs on the back of her neck stood on end. No matter how often Kelly told herself she was projecting, she couldn't shake the feeling.

When the clock struck ten, butterflies took flight in her belly. For a minute, Kelly considered asking Jacinta, or the kitchen hand, Benjamin, to deliver Lucy's order. But not only would that be cowardice, it would also be letting her boss down.

Slipping back into the persona of barista, Kelly put a napkin and muffin on a plate then picked up a large mug.

Shit, how did Lucy have her coffee? Kelly racked

her brain and came up blank. Had they even discussed that?

Reminding herself Lucy was there on business, and Kelly had a job to do, she bounded up the stairs. The door was ajar, so Kelly didn't bother knocking.

The sight that greeted her was incredibly inappropriate yet oh so right.

A delicious throb pulsed between Kelly's legs as she savoured the sight filling her vision.

Lucy was on all fours, head under the desk, backside in the air, mumbling under her breath.

Urges Kelly had tried to suppress bubbled to the surface. Images of grabbing the ruler off the desk and cracking it across Lucy's backside flooded her mind, closely followed by Kelly dropping to her knees and caressing the tender globes.

"Gotcha," Lucy declared triumphantly.

Not wanting to be caught ogling, Kelly backed up, straight into the doorjamb. The sharp edge bit into her shoulder and the door let out an almighty creak.

Busted.

"Damn," Kelly cursed under her breath.

Still on all fours, Lucy glanced over her shoulder. When her gaze landed on Kelly she smiled, backed up, and slowly climbed to her feet.

"Pen." She held it between them as if to explain why she'd been crawling around on the floor.

Relieved Lucy hadn't called her out for staring at her backside, Kelly pointed to the desk. "There are spares in the drawer, you know?"

A wry smile spread across Lucy's face. "I figured there might be. But, Kelly, I try not to make a habit of putting my hand into someone's drawers without their permission."

Fuck, fuck, fuckitty, fuck.

Another comment that could have an underlying message, or be totally innocent.

The twinkle in Lucy's sparkling green eyes suggested the former. If they kept up this dance, Kelly would be a nervous wreck long before her shift was over.

Taking a huge gamble, Kelly put Lucy on the spot.

"If there's something on your mind, Lucy, just come out with it."

"Okay." Lucy straightened some papers, banging them on the desk. "I have what I need from the employee files so you can lock those."

Just like that, they were back to business. Kelly didn't know whether to laugh or scowl. She did neither. If that was how Lucy wanted to play it, Kelly would do the same. She locked the filing cabinet then turned back to Lucy.

"How do you have your coffee?"

"Two and moo, thanks."

The woman was irresistible. A single comment and Kelly went from brooding to laughing.

"Milk and sugar, or soy and sweetener?"

"I like the real deal." Lucy gave Kelly a pointed look.

"Me too," Kelly replied, trying not to read more into the words than intended.

The rest of the day went by like clockwork. Jennifer came in for a few hours in the afternoon, which meant Kelly had no good reason to return upstairs.

When four o'clock rolled around, Kelly slipped out the backdoor, relieved and disappointed at the same time that she didn't see Lucy as she exited.

Chapter 13

Home alone, Kelly almost drove herself insane with thoughts of Lucy. She had it bad for someone she had no right to be crushing on.

Lucy lived with Kelly's ex-girlfriend, Paula, for goodness sake, and Kelly still didn't know if Lucy was even into women. The two times she'd hinted for information, Lucy had turned the question back on Kelly.

And if that wasn't enough, there was the bigger issue Kelly couldn't ignore. Was Lucy the mysterious woman who'd haunted Kelly's dreams since the night of Paula's party, and, if so, what the hell was she supposed to do about it?

The second Nicole stepped foot inside at seven, Kelly leapt to her feet and gave her a quick hug. "Thank goodness you're home. Where have you been?"

Giggling, Nicole kissed her on the cheek. "Love you

too."

A hint of alcohol lingered on Nicole's breath.

"I've been at Fitzherbert Park. You know Steve plays hockey on Tuesday nights." Nicole narrowed her eyes. "Why, what's going on?"

Caught up in her own misery, that detail had totally slipped Kelly's mind. Come to think of it, Nicole often stayed at Steve's on a Tuesday night, so she was damn lucky Nicole was standing before her, eyeing Kelly curiously.

Taking a minute to let her flatmate dump her handbag and kick off her shoes, Kelly headed for the kitchen. "What are you doing home? Have you had dinner?"

After hanging up her car keys, Nicole followed Kelly to the fridge and nudged her aside. "Yep, I had some pizza." She yanked open the door and pulled out a bottle of wine.

"We all went back to Gary's after the game. I got stuck with his airhead girlfriend. She talks like, you know, like one hundred miles an hour, like, oh my God, like, did you see the shot Gary took? Like, I nearly peed my pants. Like, it was way cool…"

Nicole stuck a finger in her mouth and gagged.

Her own dramas temporarily on-hold, Kelly chuckled. "Are you serious?"

"Deadly." Nicole held up the bottle and Kelly nodded. "I downed half a glass of wine, then used the excuse I had to drive to get the hell out of there."

Kelly took the glass Nicole handed her and they walked side by side back into the living room.

"What about Steve?" Kelly asked.

Nicole took her place on the couch and Kelly slumped into her chair.

"He'll find his own way home, or here. He's a big boy. As you know." Nicole smirked.

"Ugh, don't remind me. I didn't look, honest." Even if she had, Kelly had no way of knowing if he measured up to other guys his age.

Just the thought of getting up close and personal with a dude made Kelly shudder.

She'd never questioned if she was gay or not. She'd known it from a very young age. It was as much a part of her makeup as her brown hair and blue eyes.

As astute as ever, Nicole pierced Kelly with a no-nonsense glare. "Spill, girlfriend, and I don't mean your wine."

Like someone flipping a switch, Kelly went from relaxed to anxious. She took a sip of wine then placed her glass on the chairside table.

"The café is being audited at the mo."

Nicole gave her a single nod.

"Turns out, the auditor is Lucy." The events of the day crashed into Kelly with an intensity so fierce, she could barely think straight. "I don't know what to do, Nic. I think she's the one."

"Naw, I'm happy for you. She's sexy and has a great sense of humour."

Irritation prickled under Kelly's skin. Not with Nicole, but for not being able to articulate herself better.

Taking a deep breath, Kelly tried again. "No silly, not the one one. But the *one*."

A deep frown creased Nicole's forehead. "In English, please."

Embarrassment washed over Kelly as fresh as the

morning after that fateful night. Not trusting her voice, Kelly cleared her throat. "The mystery woman."

A large O formed on Nicole's lips just before the word tumbled out. "Oh, the one from Paula's party. The woman you stuffed her…"

"Yes." Kelly cut Nicole off as if not hearing the words would reduce the severity of what she'd done.

Which was as stupid as burying her head in the sand. Sooner or later she'd have to come up for air and face facts.

The sip of wine soured in Kelly's stomach.

Compassion shone in Nicole's eyes. "Back up the bus." She held up a hand.

The words transported Kelly back to the morning after, and a cold shiver tingled up her spine.

"Tell me more. What makes you suspect it was Lucy?"

Thinking back over the bizarre day, Kelly gave Nicole a quick summary of her interactions with Lucy.

"She made this random comment about dreams being so vivid they seem real."

"What's random about that? Holy shit." Nicole's

voice rose in pitch. "The other night I dreamed I banged my boss. He's hot and all but I'd never want to do the dirty with him."

Kelly snickered.

"I woke up in a panic, my heart was racing and everything. It took me a minute to orientate myself and realize I'd been dreaming." Nicole's cheeks turned pink. "The next day, I couldn't look my boss in the eye." Her hand flew to her mouth. "Shit, don't tell Steve."

Right on cue, there was a single knock on the door and the man himself skulked into the flat.

"Don't tell me what?" Steve asked, a huge grin on his handsome face.

Coming to her friends rescue, Kelly replied, "That she thinks Gary's girlfriends a tool."

Wine snorted out of Nicole's nose. "I didn't call her a tool, but I like your analogy. Mm, what kind of tool? A rake or a shovel?"

Crisis diverted, Steve chuckled. "More like a handbrake. If I'd known she was going to send everyone home by eight, I would've caught a ride with you."

"Oh, poor baby." Nicole jutted out her bottom lip.

Ignoring her sass, Steve turned to Kelly. "Mind if I have a quick shower?"

Appreciating that he asked first, considering he didn't pay the rent, Kelly gave him a warm smile. "That's fine."

Once they were alone again, Nicole picked up where they'd left off.

"The dream reference could've been random."

The knot in Kelly's stomach loosened. What Nicole said made sense, and thinking back, Kelly couldn't deny she'd had more than her share of vivid dreams. Especially when her dad first died. Although, those dreams were more like nightmares when she awoke and the painful reality that he was really gone set in.

Shaking off her melancholy, Kelly concurred with Nicole's assessment. "Agreed."

"Okay, what else makes you think it was Lucy?"

Time for the killer. "She made a comment that I think had an underlying message."

Lucy's face swam in Kelly's vision, the cheeky,

daring glint in her eyes.

"She said she doesn't make a habit of going into anyone's drawers without their permission."

Apparently thinking nothing of the comment, or perhaps trying to decipher a deeper meaning, Nicole looked at the ceiling, chewed her lip, then shook her head.

"I'm not seeing the issue. I know she's there on business, but wouldn't it be rather unethical for her to go sticking her nose into places it doesn't belong? To me, it'd be like rifling through a woman's handbag. It's just not done."

"I get that. It's not so much the drawers, but the way she said it. Drawers—knickers. Get it? Don't go into people's knickers without permission."

"Oh, hun." Nicole chuckled. "I don't mean to laugh but I think your imagination's getting away on you."

Feeling stupid, Kelly lowered her head. Perhaps it was all in her mind. She stopped short of telling Nicole about walking in on Lucy on her hands and knees.

The way Lucy had looked at Kelly over her shoulder, a mischievous glint in her eye, was as if she knew exactly who was standing behind her. The fact Lucy had been expecting Kelly at ten, fuelled Kelly's suspicions. Of course, there was the small chance it had all been pure coincidence.

The bathroom door opened. Steve strolled out, a stream of steam trailing in his wake.

Fresh as a daisy, he perched on the arm of Kelly's chair. "You look troubled. What's up?"

Not wanting to rehash their conversation, Kelly downplayed her worries. "I was just telling Nicole Paula's flatmate is currently doing an audit at work."

"And Kelly's hot for her." Nicole threw her two cents worth in. "Lucy's the woman I told you about after we went to Paula's potluck dinner."

Steve chuckled, making the armchair rock. "The one who said her dad was an undertaker?"

The memory of Lucy's gallant attempt to diffuse a volatile situation made Kelly feel all warm and fuzzy. Picturing her gorgeous face, jet black hair, and piercing green eyes, had something to do with that as well.

Steve poked Kelly in the ribs. "You're just about purring."

Feeling like a smitten teenager, Kelly broke out in a jaw-busting grin. "She's pretty awesome." Reality crept in and the knot in her tummy tightened. "But I'm terrified she's the one from Paula's party."

Unable to look Steve in the eye, Kelly dropped her hands in her lap and fiddled with the hem of her cut-off shorts.

"The one I had sex with. Lucy's been dropping little hints that make me think it was her, she knows it was me, and she wants me to know she knows."

Until Kelly could prove beyond the shadow of a doubt that was what Lucy was hinting at, she wasn't going to admit to anything. In an essence, she was caught between a rock and a hard place.

"Hey." Steve put a finger under her chin. "Don't look so glum, mate. She's talking to you, right?"

"Yep."

"Being nasty?"

"God, no." Kelly jumped to her defence. "She's been nothing but friendly." A little too friendly if anything, but Kelly kept that information to herself. "She actually asked me to join her and a friend for a drink tonight.

As if joined at the hip, Nicole and Steve gasped in unison.

"What the hell are you doing home?" Nicole asked.

"It's a long story." Kelly shot her friend a sad smile.

"I have a proposal."

If Steve's expression hadn't been so serious, Kelly would've joked he was proposing to the wrong woman.

Nicole watched intently from the sofa, leaning against the armrest, sipping her wine.

"Rather than focus on what we don't know, and perhaps never will, Kel," He gave her shoulder a squeeze. "Let's focus on what we do know. You like her, she hasn't accused you of anything or run away screaming."

An image of Lucy running for the hills made Kelly chuckle. When Steve wasn't goofing around he was the rational one of all three.

"Forget about what happened. You can't change the past, but you do have a say in your future. Get to know her, see where it goes."

Without conscious thought, Kelly straightened in the chair and flung her arms around Steve. He put a hand on the wall, narrowly avoiding being knocked off the armrest. His clean scent wrapped around Kelly like a comfort blanket. At the same time, Nicole joined them for a group hug.

In that moment, Kelly knew, beyond the shadow of a doubt, no matter what happened, these two would always have her back.

Chapter 14

After the conversation with Steve and Nicole, Kelly arrived at work feeling optimistic and looking forward to seeing Lucy. She'd do the honourable thing and ask how her night out with Kate went, and not read more into it.

When eight-thirty, and then nine a.m. rolled around, and Kelly still hadn't seen Lucy, her heart sunk. Perhaps due to the business being so small, Lucy managed to gather the information she needed, within a day, and Kelly had lost her window of opportunity.

After delivering an order of sausages, eggs, and toast, to a gentleman at a table by the front window, Jacinta slid back behind the counter and sidled up next to Kelly. "Must be serious."

Glancing at the few customers sipping coffee and looking relaxed, Kelly had no idea what Jacinta was on about. "What?"

"That woman, the one hanging around here yesterday, looking like a government official."

"Lucy," Kelly corrected, hating the way Jacinta referred to Lucy as that woman.

"Yeah, her, the hottie. She was here when I got in at eight. The boss arrived shortly after and they've been holed up in the office ever since. What do you suppose that's about?" Jacinta licked her lips as if she could taste gossip.

Unfortunately for her, Kelly wasn't buying into it. Jennifer trusted Kelly for a very good reason. "She could be a silent partner, for all we know."

Covering her mouth, Jacinta coughed the word "bullshit" into her hand.

The door chimed and Kelly was literally saved by the bell. The next few hours flew by in a flurry of activity as they handled the mid-morning and lunchtime rush.

At twelve forty-five, during a lull in customers, Kelly finally managed to take a quick break.

After grabbing a chicken sandwich, she pushed open the backdoor and stepped outside.

The sun was high in the sky. Kelly revelled in the warmth on her skin. A cool breeze blew through the alleyway bringing with it the faint odour of food scraps from the nearby skip bin.

Leaning against the brick wall, Kelly slid down until her backside connected with warm concrete. A hunger pang gripped her stomach as Kelly placed her sandwich in her lap and picked up one half.

Just as she was about to sink her teeth in, the backdoor to the café swung open and banged closed.

A shapely figure cast a shadow over Kelly's outstretched legs. When she glanced up, her breath caught in her throat.

From Kelly's seated position, Lucy's legs seemed to go on forever. She wanted to climb them like a tree, wrap her legs around Lucy's torso, and cling to her like a possum.

The mouth-watering view was replaced by Lucy's gorgeous face when she crouched next to Kelly. A flash of mauve caught Kelly's eye and she resisted the urge to look up Lucy's skirt.

The corner of Lucy's mouth twitched. "Do you hang

out in back alleys often?"

"Only when I'm hungry," Kelly retorted.

When Lucy didn't so much as crack a smile, Kelly felt like an awkward teenager trying to pick up a girl and failing miserably.

Suddenly all business, Lucy shot a nervous glance toward the door. "I don't want your boss to see me talking to you. She might think I'm sharing confidential information."

"You wouldn't do that," Kelly stated as though she was judge, jury, and executioner, even though she knew next to nothing about Lucy.

Worry lines gave way to a smile. "Thanks for your vote of confidence. Look, we need to talk, Kelly. Are you free tonight? Perhaps we could meet for a drink. Just the two of us?"

A cocktail of emotions ricocheted through Kelly's body. Joy over being asked out, even if it wasn't on an official date. Uncertainty. The troubled look in Lucy's eyes worried her. And hope. Kelly lost herself in the daydream that, at the very least, they would become good friends.

When Kelly didn't reply fast enough, Lucy stood, her knee letting out a crack.

"Never mind, I shouldn't have asked. Sorry for making you feel uncomfortable."

Adrenaline surged through Kelly as she shot to her feet. Her sandwich flew out of her lap and landed in the gutter. Kelly didn't give a damn that her lunch had been ruined. No way was she going to pass up the opportunity.

"It's a date. I mean I'd love to. Name a time and place and I'll be there." Fit to burst with happiness, Kelly added, "With bells and whistles."

The charming smile on Lucy's face spurred her on, and Kelly went all out. "Or boots and leathers." Kelly waggled her eyebrows, leaving Lucy to decide whether she was referring to her motorcycle attire or something far sexier.

The backdoor opened and they both froze. When Jacinta's face appeared, not Jennifer's, Kelly breathed out a sigh of relief.

"Oh, sorry, I didn't mean to interrupt you." Jacinta smiled at Lucy then turned to Kelly. "It's almost one, we'll be flooded with customers again soon."

Jennifer hated it if all hands weren't on deck during peak times, so Kelly was genuinely thankful for the warning.

"Thanks for the heads up. I'll be in in a sec."

After shooting Kelly a saucy wink, Jacinta's face disappeared behind the door.

A piece of paper, seemingly out of nowhere, appeared in Lucy's hand. "Here, this is my private number."

Cursing herself for not bringing her phone outside with her, Kelly took the folded piece of paper and tucked it safely in her bra.

Lucy cracked a smile. "Don't forget to take that out before you shower."

"I won't. I'll add you to my contacts and send you a text as soon as I get inside."

A flicker of uncertainty flashed in Lucy's eyes. "As long as it's not to cancel."

In the blink of an eye, Lucy snapped back to the confident business woman who had marched into the café, two days ago, and turned Kelly's world upside down.

Kelly wondered if Lucy was as nervous as she was about getting together, or if it was nothing more than business to Lucy.

A pang of sadness hit Kelly when she concluded it was probably the latter.

Chapter 15

Finally deciding to wear her black dress, Kelly sized herself up in the mirror. The snug fit showed off her curves without overtly flaunting her body. Not that she had much to flaunt in the chest department.

She turned sideways, and had to admit, what she lacked up top she made up for in the rear. Kelly had a great arse, if she did say so herself.

Firm and round, perfect for spanking. Shame that wasn't her thing. Well it was, if she was doing the spanking.

Her blood pounded when an image of Lucy on her hands and knees sprung to mind.

In the next heartbeat, Kelly reminded herself tonight was about two women getting together for a drink. Of course, in the back of her mind, Kelly hoped it would lead to more.

Nicole had been spending more and more time at

Steve's, and if Kelly made a new friend she'd be happy.

Focusing on the night ahead, Kelly pulled her long brown hair back and tied it in a loose ponytail, leaving a few strands curling around her face.

For the first time in weeks, she didn't cringe when she gazed into her own eyes. The blue irises reflected how she felt. Vibrant.

In the reflection of her mirror, Kelly's gaze landed on Nicole leaning against the doorframe.

"Damn, girl, if I swung your way, I wouldn't let you out of my sight." Nicole looked thoughtful. "Perhaps I should tag along and play chaperone."

Grateful for the confidence boost, Kelly played along. "That won't be necessary, Mum. But I'll take any advice you have to give."

The protective fire in Nicole's eyes made Kelly's throat thick with emotion. She sent up a prayer to her dad. If not for him she quite possibly never would have met this wonderful woman.

"Be yourself." Nicole wandered into the room. "Don't change for anyone. Text me if things turn to shit. I'll come to your rescue."

Not wanting to ruin the only makeup she'd put on, mascara, Kelly blinked back tears and launched herself at Nicole.

"Thank you." Kelly held her friend close, breathing in her familiar scent; vanilla body wash.

Nicole stepped back, her eyes full of love and support. "Come on, I'll drop you off on my way to Steve's. Heed his words, Kel. Live in the moment, don't dwell on the past."

***

Shortly before six-thirty, Kelly climbed out of Nicole's car and bid her farewell. The down side of owning a motorcycle was having to find alternative transport when she didn't want to wear jeans.

Glancing at the sign above the door, Rose and Crown, she smoothed down her dress and took a fortifying breath.

She'd arranged to meet Lucy out front so neither of them would have to sit inside, alone, and endure curious glances from other patrons, or worse, unwanted advances.

If Kelly had asked Lucy to pick her up, she probably would've, happily. But Kelly didn't feel right about it, not yet.

And, if Kelly was to be totally honest, until she knew what was going on, she didn't think it was a good idea for Lucy to know where she lived.

The negative thought vanished on a puff of exhaust fumes. Kelly's heart pounded when a white four-wheel drive pulled into an angle park.

She recognized the car instantly as Lucy's, she'd seen it often enough parked at Paula's.

Shit, Paula.

Kelly crossed her fingers they wouldn't walk into the pub and come face to face with her ex. Although, that was doubtful. The establishment wasn't ritzy enough for Paula.

The autumn night was mild enough that they could sit outside, but Kelly loved the ambience of the fireplace that glowed year-round in the corner of the pub.

Nerves, excitement, and a pinch of arousal, okay, a healthy dose of arousal pulsed through Kelly's veins as

Lucy strolled toward her.

While Lucy had an eye out for traffic, Kelly took the opportunity to give her the once over.

The beige top Lucy wore showcased ample breasts and contrasted deliciously with her dark, tanned skin. White jeans caressed her curves with each step she took. Kelly envied those jeans.

"Hey." Lucy extended a hand and pulled Kelly into a one-armed hug.

She smelled like cocoa butter and Kelly wanted to lick her. Perhaps she already had. That thought extinguished her libido as fast as having a bucket of cold water thrown in her face.

Had Lucy asked her out to confront her?

Get out of your head, Kelly.

"Do you come here often?" Lucy quirked an eyebrow and they both chuckled.

"Only when a sexy lady asks me out." The words flew out of Kelly's mouth before she could stop them. "Ugh, sorry."

"Don't be." Lucy smiled. "Come on, let's get a drink and find a table."

Drinks in hand, seated in a corner booth, Kelly waited Lucy out. She was the one that said they needed to talk and Kelly was happy to listen.

"How was the rest of your day?" Lucy took a sip of her wine and soda.

Just imagining the tart taste trickling down Lucy's throat made Kelly grimace, but she respected the fact Lucy was taking it easy since she had to drive.

As for Kelly's day, once Lucy left and she returned inside, Jennifer had stormed around the café with an angry scowl on her face, opening and closing doors with a bang.

"That bad, huh?" Lucy asked, apparently taking Kelly's grimace as a reflection of her day.

"Not quite. It was rough though. The boss is really upset. Her mum's unwell so I guess the stress of that has flowed over to work."

What Kelly didn't add was that Jennifer had called her into her office and stated whatever the auditor thought she'd uncovered had been an innocent mistake and would be rectified.

Taken by surprise, Kelly startled when Lucy reached

across the table and gripped her hand.

"Kelly, you have to know it was me."

Even though it sounded like a statement, Kelly replied, "I know."

Surprise flashed in Lucy's eyes. She released Kelly's hand as if she'd been burned. "You knew. Yet, you didn't say a word?"

"You were only doing your job," Kelly stated, hating the defensive tone of Lucy's voice.

With her eyes locked on Kelly, Lucy took a long, slow, sip of her drink then sat back and crossed her arms. "What are you talking about, Kelly?"

A nauseating sense of Déjà vu washed over Kelly. Only, this time, she didn't think she was wrong. Fight or flight instinct kicked in. Kelly wanted to bolt, she didn't want to fight. Opting to do neither, she sat tight.

Mirroring Lucy's actions, Kelly took a swig of her beer, but rather than lean back she braced her elbows on the table, and dared to throw the question back at Lucy.

"What are you talking about?" Even though the words were barely above a whisper, there was no mistaking the nervous tremor in Kelly's voice.

After shooting a glance around the pub, Lucy leaned forward, so close Kelly could smell the wine on her breath.

The few seconds it took for Lucy to speak felt like a lifetime. Anticipating what Lucy might say made Kelly's pulse race. She darted a look around, pleased no one was within earshot.

Being a Thursday night, the pub was far from empty, however, most patrons were standing around the bar.

As if she could see right through her, Lucy's gaze drilled into Kelly. "Paula's party."

Shit. And there it was. No more dancing around each other.

Kelly hung her head as shame washed over her. Somehow, she resisted the urge to pull the tie out of her hair and hide behind the long locks.

Bracing herself to face Lucy's wrath, Kelly forced herself to meet her gaze.

Uncertainty shimmered in Lucy's eyes. "It was you, wasn't it?"

Not wanting to spell it out, Kelly waggled a finger between them. "If you're talking about what I think you are."

Lucy bit her lip, and nodded.

Mortified, Kelly fought the urge to look away. The least she could do was look Lucy in the eye when she apologized.

"I'm so, so sorry."

And totally fucking confused. Why wasn't Lucy ripping her a new one?

"Me too." Lucy's voice was so soft, Kelly wasn't sure she'd heard her right. "It took me a long time to get over that night. In fact, I doubt I ever will."

Ouch, embarrassment made Kelly want to lash out. She leaned over and snatched a steak knife off a nearby table.

"Here, give it another twist. I said I'm sorry."

On a heavy exhale, the fight went out of Kelly. What the hell did she think? That one little word, sorry, would magically make everything alright? She almost laughed like a deranged woman.

Even though on some level Kelly knew she was being dramatic, she couldn't stop. In a move that surprised herself, she spun the knife in her hand and offered the handle to Lucy. "Here, do us both a favour and put me out of my misery. Then, maybe you, too, can move on."

The ghost of a smile flittered across Lucy's lips. She sat back and took a sip of her wine.

The way Lucy dismissed her theatrics rendered Kelly speechless, and a little pissed off. Rather than ask what was so damn funny, she clenched her jaw.

In a lightning fast move, the knife Kelly had been wielding like a sacrificial offering was ripped from her hand.

Adrenaline surged through Kelly. Her pulse raced, her breath caught in her throat.

Surely Lucy wasn't about to take her up on the crazy offer and stab Kelly right there, in the corner of the pub.

Before panic could take hold, Lucy tossed the knife on the table and slid into the seat beside Kelly.

The heat radiating off her body was hotter than the fireplace. It was also a hell of a lot more dangerous. The woman was impossible to resist at a distance, sitting so close, all bets were off.

Needing to put some distance between them, Kelly

tried to scoot sideways. Lucy grabbed her hand, stopping her mid-slide. Her grip was firm, her fingers soft, and strangely soothing.

"Kelly, as crazy as this might sound, I haven't been able to get you out of my mind since that night. I was hoping we could spend more time together." The hint of a blush coloured Lucy's cheeks. "As a couple. I want to get to know you, Kelly. All of you."

As much as Kelly wanted to believe what Lucy said, she didn't plan on being taken for a fool.

"I thought you were straight?"

"I never said that."

Maybe not those exact words but Lucy had definitely implied it.

"You said you haven't met the right guy." Kelly resisted the urge to pull her hand out of Lucy's grasp.

"True, and I meant that. The thing is, when Paula was looking for a roommate, she asked me if I date men or women. If I'd been applying for a job I would've called her out for discrimination. But I was looking for a place to live while I save for a deposit to buy my own home. I wondered if it was a trick question. I didn't want to live with a man-hater, so replied men.

"I expected Paula to show me the door, but she replied, 'The room's yours. The last thing I need in my home is more dyke drama.'"

Although it shouldn't have surprised Kelly, her mouth fell open.

"Paula's words." Lucy quickly reassured her.

A thought suddenly hit Kelly, and she didn't know whether to feel sorry for Lucy or pissed off. "And then you kept up the charade?"

"Yes and no. You see, what I said wasn't a total lie. I have dated men, I've had sex with a man."

Trying very hard not to pass judgment, Kelly held her tongue.

"But that's all it was. Sex. The experience was a disaster for more reasons than I care to explain right now. I've dated women too."

Understanding dawned. "That's why you get Kate?"

"I hate to sound cryptic," Lucy said. "But once again, the answer is yes and no. Kate's bisexual. She loves cock and pussy in equal measure."

Trust Lucy to be so frank just as Kelly took a sip of

her drink. A chuckle burst forth and beer fizzed up the back of Kelly's nose, making her eyes water.

Half laughing, half serious, Lucy handed Kelly a napkin. "Sorry to be so crass. What I'm trying to say is, I'm attracted to the person, the entire package, not just what's between their legs."

What Lucy said computed on one level but was also hard for Kelly to get her head around. Steve was her best friend, he was the nicest guy anyone could hope to meet, but she'd never, ever, considered sleeping with him. Because, duh, he was a guy.

"I can almost see the cogs turning, Kel. Talk to me, tell me what's going on in there." Lucy tapped Kelly's temple.

"Firstly, I'm glad you're not a man-hater, my best friend's a dude. But…"

A mischievous glint shimmered in Lucy's eyes. "But he doesn't have the equipment you like?"

Oh my God. How did Lucy do that? The woman was astute, incredibly sexy, and had a wicked sense of humour.

Biting back a grin, Kelly continued. "Right, and he

burps and farts and smells like man."

Lucy grinned. "And you're innocent of all three?"

Right on cue, wind bubbled up Kelly's windpipe. Damn beer. She put her hand over her mouth and suppressed a burp. "Point taken. And for the record, I don't fart, I whisper in my panties."

"Me too," Lucy replied. "Especially when they're stuffed in my mouth."

Blushing furiously, Kelly steered the conversation back toward safer waters.

"Wind aside, believe me when I say, I'm trying to understand where you're coming from."

"What about your friend, the one I met for all of five minutes at Paula's potluck dinner?"

"Nicole, we've been best friends for more than a decade. She and Steve are an item."

"She's cute," Lucy said.

"She's fucking gorgeous." Kelly narrowed her eyes. "And taken."

Without missing a beat, Lucy drilled her point home. "Would you do her?"

"Hell no, she's like a sister to me. And even though

she's stunning, to tell the truth, I've never been sexually attracted to her."

"But she has the bits you like? So what's the issue?" Lucy cocked her head to the side.

"It's about more than that. Sex is great, but I have to be attracted to the person."

Kelly had never been into casual sex. She had to connect on more than a physical level, even if it turned out to be a one-time thing.

In a show that eclipsed Kelly's theatrics, Lucy gasped and covered her mouth. "Goodness me, Kelly. Surely, you're not suggesting attraction goes deeper than anatomy?"

Kelly chuckled. "Okay, okay." She held up a hand in surrender. "Point taken."

They still had a lot to discuss. First and foremost, what the hell had Lucy been doing in Paula's bed and why wasn't she running for the hills? Something Kelly was determined to find out. The sooner the better.

A couple breezed by and sat at the neighbouring table. Great. So much for talking openly.

Now that she was sure Lucy didn't want to stab her

with a pitchfork, or steak knife, Kelly felt more relaxed about the offer she wanted to make all along.

"I have the flat to myself tonight, how about we finish this conversation there? Then you can have a real wine instead of that half and half stuff you're sipping on."

"And how am I going to get home if I have a few wines at your house?"

That goddamn alluring smile, the one that set Kelly's insides on fire, slid onto Lucy's face. "Are you asking me to sleepover?"

The thought hadn't occurred to Kelly, until that moment. Rather than assume anything she gave an open-ended answer.

"If you drink too much you might have to. I guess that's up to you." Kelly ran her thumb over the back of Lucy's hand, trying not to imagine tying her wrists to the headboard.

When Lucy didn't move, just stared right into Kelly's eyes, guilt gnawed at Kelly's conscience.

"Look, Lucy." Kelly pushed a stray lock of Lucy's raven black hair off her face. "I promise I won't do anything without your consent. If we only end up talking, I'm okay with that. If you want more, I'm absolutely onboard with that."

A jolt of white hot desire pulsed between Kelly's legs when Lucy put her hand on Kelly's bare thigh. The heat of her palm reflected the fire in Lucy's eyes.

"I didn't stop you that night, Kelly. And I don't intend to start now. What we did was wrong, but we can't turn back time."

Kelly hated that Lucy felt responsible for something she had no part in. Well she had a big part in it but not by choice. "What I did," Kelly said, taking responsibility for her actions.

"Don't play coy, Kelly." There was a smile in Lucy's voice.

Suddenly, a thought slammed into Kelly like a runaway cattle truck. Lucy didn't stop her despite slipping her wrists free. Not only that, she'd also made a joke about having her panties stuffed in her mouth.

At long last, the weight Kelly had been carrying lifted off her shoulders.

She reached across the table and snagged the stem of

Lucy's wine glass "Here." She handed the glass to Lucy. "Finish your milk."

Like an obedient child, Lucy drank the last of her wine and soda.

Feeling like a giddy teenager, Kelly drained the dregs of her beer, rubbed her tummy, and burped.

The woman at the next table smirked. Her male companion scowled. The look on his face as good as said, "That wasn't very lady like."

Kelly couldn't help but wonder if he would've given her the thumbs up if she'd been wearing her motorcycle boots, black jeans, and leather jacket.

His eyes almost bugged out of his head when Lucy entwined her fingers with Kelly's and whispered none too quietly, "Let's get out of here. You look better out of that dress than in it."

Light glimmered off the woman's wedding band as she handed her husband a napkin. "Wipe your chin, darling, you're drooling." She winked at Kelly and Lucy. "Have a nice night, ladies."

"Thank you, you too," Kelly said, pleased to know the woman was secure enough in her marriage not to feel threatened by her husband ogling two attractive women, and quite likely harbouring lesbian fantasies.

Anticipation tingled up Kelly's spine as she strode toward the exit, hand in hand with Lucy.

Chapter 16

On the ride home to her flat, Kelly posed the question that had been plaguing her since earlier in the evening. "You've slept with both men and women, right?"

The corner of Lucy's mouth kicked up, but she kept her eyes on the road. "One man, two women. But who's counting?"

Holy shit, only three people. Kelly could triple that, and she was younger than Lucy, which begged another question. "How old are you?"

Another smirk. "You're not shy in coming forward when you don't have to look someone in the eye, are you?"

"Guilty as charged." Kelly smiled, enjoying the friendly banter.

The sign to Knowles Street loomed up ahead. "Take the next right, my flat's halfway down on your left, number twenty-nine."

Lucy flicked on the indicator and waited for a car heading in the opposite direction before turning right. "Twenty-nine, closer to thirty."

"Huh? Oh, never mind." Kelly cursed herself for being slow on the uptake. She'd just asked how old Lucy was for goodness sake. With any luck, the uncanny coincidence was a good omen.

While Kelly had successfully ascertained Lucy was indeed in her late twenties, she'd also successfully sidetracked herself from the point of her first question.

"I guess you identify as bisexual, right?"

"Not exactly." Lucy pulled up outside the row of flats. She'd done a better job of keeping an eye on the road than Kelly, that was for sure.

After shutting off the engine, Lucy turned to Kelly. Her eyes warm, her expression serious. "I identify as me, Lucy Tanner. While I respect some people find peace in being able to shout out hey, I'm gay, I'm queer, I'm pan, or whatever makes them feel accepted, I don't like to be labelled. If someone enjoys bondage, but isn't into pain, does that mean they're any less into

BDSM than a sadist who has an aversion to being restrained?"

Clearly, it was a rhetorical question and a topic Lucy was passionate about. She barely paused long enough to draw her next breath. Kelly didn't care, she was totally enraptured. She could listen to the melodic tone of Lucy's voice until the cows came home.

"What about a woman who enjoys strap-on sex, does that mean she secretly wants to be with a man? I don't think so, but others would beg to differ. If Kate marries a man will that make her straight? Or if she marries a woman will it mean she's gay, not bisexual, end of story?"

Suddenly, Kelly felt like she'd hit a raw nerve. "Sorry, I meant no offense."

A mischievous glint twinkled in Lucy's eyes. It was a sassy look Kelly had come to recognize.

Anticipating Lucy's next words, Kelly flung open the door and bolted out of the car.

"Don't play c…"

The thud of the car door drowned out the last word along with Lucy's raucous laughter. Kelly stood on the sidewalk grinning so broadly her cheeks hurt.

Lucy was an interesting mix of confidence and vulnerability that turned Kelly on.

***

Inside, with the heavy drapes pulled and the only light coming from a lamp in the corner of the small living room, the atmosphere was more subdued. The time for jokes and innuendos over.

After lowering the volume on the iPod dock, Kelly selected shuffle and hit play. When the lyrics *Take It Easy* filled the room, the irony wasn't lost on her.

Watching Kelly from the sofa, right leg crossed over her left, Lucy quirked an eyebrow. "You never cease to amaze me, Kelly. Weren't the Eagles a little before your time?"

Ecstatic Lucy recognized the song, Kelly sauntered across the room.

"That's rich coming from a woman only four years older than me who recognized the old timers immediately." Kelly slumped onto the sofa, close enough that their bodies brushed together. As strong as the temptation was to pull Lucy into her lap, Kelly resisted the urge.

"You got me," Lucy said. "To be honest, I prefer soft rock, especially from the seventies and eighties."

In the dim light, Kelly glanced up at the picture of her father hanging on the wall. "My Dad loved the Eagles. I find their music soothing."

"I'd love to hear all about him one day, but..."

"Now's not the time," Kelly finished for Lucy, sparing her from an uncomfortable moment.

"Agreed." Lucy tucked a lock of her black hair behind her ear.

For the first time that evening, Kelly noticed Lucy wore tiny ruby-red earrings. The studs barely bigger than a pinhead.

After a beat, Kelly decided to dive right in. "Okay, that night."

No longer looking so confident, perhaps because they were on Kelly's turf, Lucy's throat worked as she swallowed.

Taking a fortifying breath, Kelly soldiered on. "I made a huge mistake."

"I don't blame…"

Not wanting to be absolved quite so fast, Kelly held up a hand. "Please, let me finish."

"Okay." Lucy plucked at an invisible thread on her beige top.

"As you found out the hard way, I'm into Kink, or BDSM, call it what you will. However, I'd never force myself on anyone, so, for that, I am truly sorry."

A bead of sweat trickled down the back of Kelly's neck. She hadn't realized how difficult it would be to utter the words.

Without a trace of humour, Lucy asked, "May I speak?"

The way she sought out Kelly's permission sent a jolt of desire coursing through Kelly's body. Shaking off thoughts of Lucy begging for release, Kelly nodded. "Go ahead."

Lucy set her glass on the coffee table and turned to Kelly.

For some reason, Kelly felt like Lucy needed comforting. She held out a hand. Lucy took it and scooted closer.

"Remember when you first started dating Paula."

"Yes." Kelly rubbed her thumb over the back of Lucy's hand.

"What room did she have?"

Casting her mind back six months, Kelly pursed her lips. An image of the bedroom at the end of the hallway sprung to mind. "The last one."

"And a few months ago, she moved to the middle one, right?"

"Correct," Kelly replied unsure if she was following along.

"Did you ever move house as a kid?"

The change in conversation gave Kelly whiplash. She frowned. "No."

"But you moved here."

A snort burst out of Kelly. "Well done, Einstein. Your point?"

"Ever get lost on your way home?"

If Lucy was somehow implying Kelly got lost on her way to Paula's bedroom, she was way off track. Humouring Lucy, Kelly tapped her lip in contemplation. Out of nowhere, a memory slammed into her. Kelly smiled, still able to hear her mother's laughter.

"A few months after I moved into my first flat, I jumped on my motorbike, tore out of the parking lot at work, and gunned it for home. Next thing I knew, I was outside Mum's place. Out of habit I just headed in that direction. I caught myself doing it a few more times after that and had to turn around."

"Exactly, it's called muscle memory. And, like I said, you didn't go into the wrong room."

The look of despair in Lucy's eyes undid Kelly. She leaned the side of their heads together, so Lucy wouldn't have to look her in the eye if she was struggling to go on.

"It's okay," Kelly said softly.

"After having a few drinks, I wasn't thinking straight."

They both chuckled. Nothing about what happened had been straight or thought-out.

"Buzzed and tired, after using the bathroom, my feet took me to the bedroom I originally moved into. At first, when you walked into the room, I thought you knew what you were doing, that perhaps you'd taken my comments in the kitchen as a come on, or a challenge. As awareness took hold, I realized you thought I was Paula." Lucy's voice trailed off.

Needing to hear the rest, Kelly put a finger under Lucy's chin and forced her to meet her gaze.

A blush crept up Lucy's long, elegant neck. "By that time, I was too embarrassed, then too aroused, to put a stop to things. Please don't hate me." The anguished tone of Lucy's voice was gut wrenching.

"I know I should've pushed you away." Lucy turned scarlet. "Or closed my legs."

Hating that Lucy felt responsible, Kelly interjected, "You know what, Lucy? I think we both need to stop the blame game. Neither of us are masochist yet, it would seem, for weeks both of us have done nothing but beat ourselves up."

"I've never done that." Lucy picked up her wine glass. "Not literally anyway. But I've tied myself up. Not very well, but well enough to get off."

The declaration sent a jolt of lust through Kelly.

"That night, I discovered the meaning of sexual

fulfilment. After coming down from the mind-blowing orgasm, the first I've experienced with a partner..."

A sense of pride shot through Kelly only to be replaced by a pang of sadness for Lucy. She couldn't even begin to imagine reaching twenty-five and never having had an orgasm with another, let alone approaching thirty.

"Once my head cleared," Lucy said. "I panicked and pretended I'd been asleep and thought it was a dream. When you said you had to use the bathroom, I saw the perfect opportunity to slip out of Paula's bedroom and back to my own. And like I said, Paula would kill me if I even looked sideways at you. So, rather than pursue you, I took the cowards way out and went out of my way to avoid you."

"That's why you weren't at Paula's potluck dinner?" Kelly mused out loud.

"Correct. When you broke up, I wondered if it had anything to do with what happened that night. Not wanting to cause you, or myself, any more pain, I tried to forget you."

Having no intention of letting Lucy forget about her,

Kelly smiled. "But, lovely lady, apparently fate had other plans for us."

Lucy raised her glass, Kelly picked up hers and they clinked them together.

"Amen to that. I don't normally audit small businesses, but my work colleague, Mark, was away sick so you got stuck with me."

The mention of a man's name had Kelly's mind jumping tracks faster than a train wreck.

"Did you get your kink on with the dude you slept with? I'm not sure if I can compete with a man." Even though Kelly said it as a joke, the serious look on Lucy's face suggested she took it as everything but.

"Don't ever think you have to compete with a man, or anyone else, Kelly. I thought I was broken, until I met you. The one and only guy I dated, I discussed my desires with at length. When we finally acted on them, he slapped my bottom. He was very heavy-handed, and it hurt. A lot. Rather than be this great sexual moment, I wanted to jump up and punch him in the nuts."

Inappropriate or not, Kelly couldn't hold back a chuckle. She cupped her crotch. "If you ever feel the desire to punch me between the legs, please tell me *before* it gets to that stage."

When Lucy tipped her head back and burst out laughing, Kelly's heart sung for joy. Her lecherous gaze zoned in on the jiggle of Lucy's boobs. Damn she had a nice set.

Regaining her composure, Lucy went from jovial to serious. "Where do we go from here?"

My bedroom, Kelly wanted to say, but held off. They still needed to set some boundaries.

"I might not come across as worldly and confident to others, because I'm not," Kelly said. "But behind closed doors, I get off on being in control. It's got nothing to do with my job or needing to feel validated, it's just the way I'm wired."

"I get that, Kelly. Believe me, I do. I have a high stress job but my desire to submit has nothing to do with having to let that go. I didn't have to worry about paying bills or saving to buy a house when I was fifteen, yet, that's the first time I woke up tangled in my sheets. Fighting to get free, I somehow ended up with the blankets bunched between my legs…" A blush crept up Lucy's neck. "And, I experienced my first orgasm. As I got older, I invented more ways to restrain myself and get off. How pathetic is that?"

Sensing an opportunity to lighten the heavy mood, Kelly threw a revised version of Lucy's words back at her. "Keep playing coy, Lucy. It's very becoming."

Smirking, Lucy poked her tongue out.

With the speed of a sleek black panther, Kelly pounced on Lucy. In one fluid motion, she had Lucy on her back, pinned between herself and the sofa cushions.

"For the record, I don't think you're any more pathetic than others have made me feel because of my desires. However, I think you need a lesson in etiquette."

Heat shimmered in Lucy's eyes and Kelly ran with it.

"Do you normally crawl around office floors on your hands and knees? What if the kitchen hand, young Benjamin, had walked in on you with your backside pointed to the door and your skirt practically around your hips?"

The memory of the gorgeous sight lit a fire in

Kelly's belly. The sooner she had Lucy out of her jeans the better.

Lucy's eyes went wide, her expression an adorable mixture of amusement and horror. "Oh, my goodness, I didn't even think of that." Lucy sucked in a breath, her breasts heaving against Kelly's chest.

Heat sizzled between them and Kelly yearned to feel skin on skin. With any luck, Lucy would take the bait Kelly had dangled and she'd be naked before long.

"Shit, that could've been awkward. I heard light footfalls on the stairs and assumed they were yours."

Boom! Gotcha.

A slow smile spread across Kelly's face. "Are you saying you purposely dropped your pen with the intention of teasing me?"

"Oops. Busted." Lucy bit back a smile.

For a minute, Kelly wondered if they needed to back up, but considering their relationship had started out arse about face, almost literally, there wasn't much point in that.

"Do you know what I wanted to do when I walked in on that beautiful sight?"

"No, Miss."

The submissive tone of Lucy's voice, coupled with the coy look in her eyes, ramped up Kelly's excitement.

Before lust overtook her, Kelly needed to know, beyond the shadow of a doubt, that Lucy was on the same page. And more importantly, that Lucy knew she had the power to stop things with a single word.

"I'm not in the habit of using a safe word." Kelly stroked Lucy's cheek.

A flicker of uncertainty flashed across Lucy's face.

Wanting to reassure Lucy with a gentle kiss, Kelly lowered her head. Lucy's pupils dilated and her heavy lids closed seconds before their lips met.

Heat exploded inside Kelly, rocking her to her core. She'd had her mouth all over Lucy's body, but nothing could've prepared her for the intensity of their first kiss.

A soft moan escaped Lucy when she parted her lips, allowing Kelly entrance. Their tongues danced the dance of new lovers; long, slow, exploring, and panty melting hot. Bracing her weight on her elbows, Kelly ran her fingers through Lucy's silky black hair.

The flat of Lucy's palms pressed into Kelly's back,

holding her close. Breast to breast, their hearts beat a rapid tempo. Kelly yearned to be inside Lucy.

Needing to come up for air, Kelly broke the kiss. "Phew." She fanned out the neckline of her dress. "Is it hot in here, or is it me?"

"Both."

"You're pretty hot, too." Kelly returned the compliment. "As I was saying, do you need a safe word?"

"I don't know, do I?" Uncertainty contorted Lucy's features, and Kelly didn't like it one bit.

"No means no to me, Lucy, and stop means stop. But more than that, I'd like to think I know when to push and when to pull back. However, considering we're just starting out, and I don't want a punch in the twat…"

Just as Kelly had hoped, the comment earned her a chuckle.

"I wouldn't do that." Lucy grinned.

"No, but you might think it and I don't want you to ever go along with a scene just to please me."

Eager to wrap up her speech before she totally killed the mood, Kelly pecked Lucy on the lips. "Pick a safe word. I don't think you'll need it, but I'm sure we'll both feel better knowing you have one."

A faraway look glimmered in Lucy's eyes. Seconds later, her focus returned.

"Candyfloss," Lucy said with a decisive nod.

"Fitting word for a sweet lady with lovely pink cheeks."

A frown crinkled the bridge of Lucy's nose. "That's not why I picked it. I hate the stuff, made myself sick on it as a kid." Her expression softened. "If I utter that word, you'll know I'm not happy."

Lucy bent her knee, and whether intentional or not, the heat of her thigh burned through Kelly's underwear, sending a jolt of horny anticipation dancing up her spine.

"Now that we've established a safe word, do I need to sign a contract?" Lucy asked, mischief dancing in her eyes.

Delighted to be back on track, Kelly nipped at Lucy's neck. "Oh, sassy, too."

Giggling, Lucy squirmed like a worm, goose flesh erupting on her skin.

Somewhat reluctantly, Kelly pried herself off Lucy and stood. "Time to show you what I wanted to do when I walked into the office at ten on Tuesday."

Lust surged through Kelly. "Resume the position." She pointed to a spot on the floor.

Without hesitation, Lucy slid off the sofa and presented herself on all fours. Kelly pulled the coffee table out of the way and walked a slow circle around Lucy, drinking in her intoxicating form; the shape of her shoulders, the slope of her back, the flare of her hips—all of which were concealed by too many clothes.

"Nope, that's not how I remember it." She slid her hand under the waistband of Lucy's white jeans, luxuriating in the shiver that ran through Lucy, and the feel of her bare flesh against the back of Kelly's hand.

"Up you get. The jeans need to go, you were wearing a skirt and gave me quite the show."

Just then, a song Kelly's father used to listen to, caught her attention. The lyrics were so apt, she turned up the volume.

When Kelly turned back around, Lucy had already climbed to her feet. She flashed Kelly a seductive smile and deftly popped the top button of her jeans.

Lucy's eyes burned into Kelly. The power of their unspoken words stunned her. This was what Kelly craved, the unmistakable connection of lovers. She didn't know Lucy well, but she knew her well enough to know she wanted more, lots more.

A feeling of euphoria washed over Kelly as she perched on the edge of the coffee table, settling in to enjoy the show.

Lucy toed off her shoes, then lowered her jeans, inch by slow inch, swaying her hips in time to Joe Cocker singing…

Baby, take off your coat,
Real slow,
Take off your shoes,
I'll take off your shoes,
Yes yes yes…

The eroticism of the moment stole Kelly's breath away. She no longer knew who was running the show and right then she didn't care. If Lucy suddenly ordered her to her knees, she'd probably do her bidding. Well maybe not, but if Lucy kept up the erotic dance, Kelly would end up a puddle at her feet all the same.

When Lucy straightened and kicked her jeans aside, Kelly's breath hitched. A triangle of pubic hair, as black as the hair framing Lucy's face, pointed to where Kelly longed to be.

"No panties?" Kelly quirked an eyebrow and reached to turn the volume down.

With the music on low, Lucy reverted to looking shy. "I like the feel of the denim seam against my..." She paused as if searching for the right word. "My lady bits."

Eager to get her hands on the parts Lucy was coy about naming, Kelly sidled up next to her. She leaned in close and whispered in Lucy's ear. "You like the rough seam on your cunt, your pussy, your labia."

Kelly slid her middle and forefinger through the thin triangle of hair, and lower. "Your clit?"

Lucy gasped when Kelly snapped her fingers closed.

"Yes, Miss Kel. Those bits," Lucy said, her voice thick with desire.

Damn, she liked the sound of that.

Kelly nipped Lucy's neck. "I approve of the title."

She cupped Lucy's mound, absorbing her slick heat. "But you're not off the hook for purposely teasing me. Payback's a bitch and I'm going to enjoy every minute I draw out your pleasure."

Kelly brushed Lucy's entrance with the tip of her finger, drawing a whimper out of Lucy.

"Make no mistake, once we cross the threshold to my bedroom, you'll be at my mercy, understood?"

"Yes, Miss Kel. Take me to your dungeon."

Biting back a smile, Kelly pointed her finger of doom at Lucy. "That's the last wisecrack you get to make."

The hint of a smile disappeared so fast, Kelly wondered if she'd imagined it.

Lucy held her arms out, wrists together. "I am yours to do with as you please."

The earnest look in her eyes, such a stark contrast to Paula's pathetic outburst when she'd presented her wrists to Kelly, made Kelly's chest tight.

She swallowed around the lump in her throat, now was not the time to get emotional. Not that Kelly had ever been any good at separating the two—physical and emotional attraction—hence never having had sex with a total stranger.

What Lucy said earlier about wearing labels came back to Kelly. Considering she wasn't a harsh top, and didn't enjoy dishing out extreme pain, many wouldn't consider her a domme, mistress, whatever. But she knew what she liked and what worked for her, and that was all that mattered.

Shaking off the thought, Kelly addressed the woman she was falling for, hard and fast. Hell, who was she kidding? She'd already fallen for Lucy.

As inviting as Lucy's offer was, Kelly had no intention of restraining Lucy until her top was off, her gorgeous breasts fully exposed.

"We'll get to that." Kelly put a hand on Lucy's wrists and pushed her arms down.

Footsteps pounded up the driveway and they both froze. The silhouette of a figure whizzed by and Kelly let out a breath, feeling as relieved as Lucy looked.

"The back flat," Kelly explained.

More often than not, she didn't even notice when her neighbours came and went. Thankfully, they were respectful and kept the noise down.

Even though Nicole generally texted when she was coming home if she'd said she wouldn't be, Kelly decided to play it safe.

She plucked Lucy's jeans up off the floor. "How about we adjourn to my bedroom?"

"Good idea." Naked from the waist down, Lucy trailed behind Kelly.

Chapter 17

In the privacy of Kelly's bedroom, Lucy's eyes sparkled. Her body radiated enthusiasm, making Kelly's toes curl and her throat dry.

The scent of cocoa butter filled Kelly's nostrils as she stepped before Lucy. "Arms up."

Lucy did as she instructed, and Kelly slid her top up, thankful when Lucy bent forward so she didn't have to stand on said curled toes to pull it all the way off.

And there Lucy stood, looking fucking gorgeous, wearing nothing but an alluring smile and a pink bra that matched the colour of her kissable lips.

Kelly didn't bother hiding her approval. "Fuck, you're beautiful."

"Thank you, Miss Kel."

She trailed her finger up Lucy's sternum and across her breasts. Lucy sucked in a breath, her nipples straining against the tight confines of her bra.

"Assume the position you presented me with in the office."

To make the scene more authentic, Kelly could always loan Lucy a skirt, but what fun would that be?

For the second time that night, without hesitation, Lucy dropped to all fours.

Aware it was possibly the first time Lucy had been in such a vulnerable position, Kelly didn't want to give her too long to consider her next move.

This early in the game, rather than build excitement, Lucy could panic, or worse, feel like she was nothing more than an object for Kelly to use and discard at will.

"You okay?" Kelly asked as she lit a lavender scented candle and slipped out of her dress.

"Yes."

"Tell me how you're feeling?"

Lucy's posture was relaxed, back swayed, her face obscured by her hair hanging down like a short black curtain.

"Exposed, aroused, vulnerable, excited…"

"Look at me," Kelly commanded, hoping her attire would increase Lucy's excitement.

When Lucy's gaze locked on Kelly, desire shimmered in her eyes. "Wow, Miss Kel. I knew you'd look great out of that dress. You truly are stunning."

Glowing, Kelly ran a hand down the front of her soft leather corset. "I told you when you asked me out, I'd be there with bells and whistles, or leathers. One out of three aint bad."

"It's two out of three, Miss Kel," Lucy said.

Rather than throw Lucy's words back at her, who's counting, Kelly took the opportunity to reprimand her.

Circling behind Lucy, she raised her hand. Just as she was about to deliver an open-handed slap, Kelly remembered Lucy's unpleasant experience of being spanked and pulled up short. Improvising, she grabbed a worn canvas belt out of her top drawer and lightly slashed it across Lucy's backside.

Lucy flinched, then exhaled a low moan. She glanced over her shoulder and Kelly saw nothing but raw desire shining in her heavy-lidded gaze.

"That was for getting lippy. Don't sass me in my bedroom." Kelly tapped her foot. "Have you had enough?"

"No, Miss. May I have another?"

The words were music to Kelly's ears.

A delicious throb pulsed between her legs as she swished the belt back and forth across Lucy's backside, taking care not to hit her with the buckle.

Lucy swayed her hips, moaning softly with each stroke.

"When I walked into the office and saw you on your hands and knees, I wanted to crack the ruler across your rump."

After one final slash, slightly harder than the first few, Kelly tossed the belt across the room. It landed on her dresser with a thud.

"Then I wanted to do this." Kelly dropped to her knees and caressed the stripes crisscrossing Lucy's backside. Her skin was pink and warm. Her buttocks firm and round, and oh-so smooth.

The scent of Lucy's arousal tickled Kelly's nostrils when she rocked back on her knees as if seeking more contact.

"Greedy girl." Kelly chuckled.

Confident she'd warmed Lucy up enough to enjoy

an open-handed slap, Kelly delivered a whack. When Lucy let out a soft mewl and thanked her, Kelly's heart grew wings and soared.

"Have you learned your lesson?" Kelly trailed a finger down the seam of Lucy's puffy, wet lips.

"Yes, Miss Kel," Lucy said, her voice hoarse. "No more crawling around on my knees, unless you order it."

Damn straight.

"I like a fast learner. Now crawl your sexy arse over to the bed and position yourself in the middle, spread eagle on your back."

Not needing to be told twice, Lucy moved so fast it was more of a scamper than a crawl. She reminded Kelly of an excited puppy being given permission to jump up on the bed.

Except, rather than sniff the blankets, turn in a circle, and plonk down without ceremony, Lucy laid down with grace. Her body an open invitation.

Chapter 18

It'd been a long time since Kelly had had such a willing and trusting partner laid bare before her. And because of that, she didn't have an arsenal of restraints and toys at hand. But she prided herself on being able to make do with what she had.

"I want you to tell me if anything makes you uncomfortable, okay?"

Lucy's gaze locked on Kelly, as though in a trance, she gave her a barely perceptible nod.

Kelly plucked up Lucy's white jeans and tied the bottom of the left leg around Lucy's ankle, then crouched and secured the right pant leg to the leg of her bed. Snatching up her black jeans, she'd forgone wearing earlier that night, Kelly repeated the same process on the other side.

"Beautiful." Kelly stood at the foot of the bed, barely able to believe she was about to climb the legs she thought she'd only ever dreamed about.

"When you towered over me, out the back of the café, I wanted to climb your legs like a tree."

"Are you calling my thighs tree stumps, Miss Kel?"

There was a smile in Lucy's voice and Kelly admired her for not taking life too seriously.

"A native bush with pretty blossoms beckoning…"

Before Kelly finished speaking, Lucy pulled the pillow over her head and groaned.

"Ugh, if you refer to my lady bits as petals, I might have to use my safe word."

Inhaling the heady scent of Lucy's arousal, Kelly slid between her thighs and blew on her wet centre.

"You won't get any flowery words out of me. I'm going to feast on your gorgeous pussy, cunt, labia. No more jokes."

Lucy's groan of protest turned to a moan of pleasure when Kelly flicked her tongue across her glistening lips.

"Oh, Kel. Fuck." Lucy bucked her hips and fisted the sheets.

Anxious to rid Lucy of her bra, Kelly slid higher, the

heat of Lucy's body burning through her corset. "Lift."

With nothing but desire shining in her eyes, Lucy did as she was told, her breasts rising along with the arch of her back.

Just as Kelly was about to slide her arm under, she spotted a shiny clasp between the cups. A front opening bra.

Elation shot through Kelly. Lucy had obeyed her instructions, without mirth or question, when she very easily could've pointed out the obvious.

"You get an extra lick for that." Kelly swept her tongue over Lucy's ribcage.

A shiver ran through Lucy and gooseflesh erupted on her skin.

Pushing herself up, Kelly straddled Lucy's lap and pulled her into a sitting position. Without thought Kelly found her mouth on Lucy's. Their tongues duelled, their passionate embrace more intoxicating than the finest wine.

When Kelly snaked a hand between their torsos, Lucy broke the kiss. She watched with rapt attention as Kelly unclasped and slid Lucy's bra off her shoulders.

For a minute, Kelly considered stuffing it in her mouth, then decided against it. She didn't want to risk injuring Lucy with the underwire, and, she wanted to hear every cry of pleasure she enticed out of Lucy.

After tossing the bra aside, Kelly hungrily pulled one of Lucy's nipples into her mouth. She swirled her tongue around the puckered flesh, then sucked, hard.

Lucy swore quietly. "Fuck." The word was barely above a whisper as though her throat was too thick to force it out.

Head tipped back, weight braced on her hands, Lucy's body was completely open to Kelly. The amount of trust she afforded her made Kelly's heart skip a beat. After releasing her nipple, Kelly lavished the same attention on Lucy's other breast, cupping the heavy weight in her hands. "Fuck, you've got great boobs."

They were full and round. The pinkish brown areolas blended deliciously with her dark complexion.

"Thank you, Miss Kel." A coy smile tilted the corner of Lucy's mouth. "I'm glad *you* approve."

The emphasis on the word *you* told Kelly there was a

story to be told. She filed a mental note to ask Lucy about it later.

Even though Kelly could happily bury her face between Lucy's breasts and feast on them for hours, she had other plans.

Namely, recreating their first time together, but this time with all parties onboard, and the lights on.

Once Lucy was flat on her back, the heavy weight of her breasts dipping to the sides, Kelly shimmied off the bed and collected the belt she'd tossed on her dresser.

Just as she was about to issue her next order, Lucy's hands gravitated toward the headboard as though drawn by a magnetic force.

"Good girl," Kelly said, securing Lucy's wrists together with one end of the belt and looping the other around her headboard.

Lucy's breathing became ragged, leaving no room for doubt that being bound turned her on.

Fuelled by Lucy's arousal, Kelly moved to the foot of the bed and then climbed the legs she'd dreamed about for the last two days.

For the next several minutes, she kissed, licked and

sucked every inch of Lucy's thighs. Licking along the inside of one leg, barely grazing her centre, then descending the other.

Each time Kelly got close to her core, Lucy bucked her hips and half-heartedly pulled at her bonds.

"God woman, you're killing me. I know you said you were going to tease me, but right now I think you're a sadist."

Kelly pinched the delicate flesh of Lucy's inner thigh, and squeezed, hard.

"Ow, ow, ow."

"What'd you call me?"

"Okay, okay, I take it back, Miss Kel. You're not a sadist."

Smiling to herself, Kelly kissed the spot better. Lucy's musky scent wrapped around her and Kelly's mouth watered imagining—remembering—the taste of her.

A gasp tore from Lucy the second Kelly's tongue made contact. She licked the seam of Lucy's labia, then gently parted her folds, tasting and exploring.

Lucy's soft whimpers intensified as she writhed

beneath Kelly. Turned on by the passionate sounds, Kelly licked Lucy's outer lips, then sucked and pulled on her inner labia, toying with the silky flesh.

Lucy rocked her pelvis, thrusting up to meet Kelly. "Oh, fuck, that feels so good."

"Do you want me to fuck you, Lucy-Lou?" The affectionate name took Kelly by surprise. She had no clue where it came from, but Lucy didn't seem to mind.

"Yes, please. Please, fuck me." Lucy sounded delirious.

Happy to oblige, Kelly flicked her thumb over Lucy's clit and inserted a finger. Lucy bore down on her, her inner walls hot and tight. Arousal pooled low in Kelly's belly. She inserted another finger. When it slipped in with ease, she plunged deeper and began a relentless rhythm, pumping in and out.

"Oh, God. I'm not going to last long if you keep that up."

The breathy words made Kelly's own body pulse with need. Riding the orgasmic high with Lucy, she fucked her mercilessly. With her free hand, Kelly ran it over Lucy's sweaty abdomen and palmed her breast.

Lucy's stomach muscles rolled.

Slowing her pace, Kelly thumbed Lucy's clit, rubbing it in slow, torturous circles, just above the hood so the stimulation wasn't so intense it verged on painful, rather than pleasurable.

When Lucy's body tensed, her breathing laboured, Kelly commanded, "Come for me."

The headboard banged against the wall and Lucy breathed out the word fuck as her climax hit, inner walls gripping and releasing Kelly's fingers.

Unable to get enough of the beautiful woman thrashing about on her bed, in orgasmic bliss, Kelly lapped it up, literally and figuratively. Her heart soared that she'd given Lucy the second orgasm of her life with a partner. She looked forward to giving her many more.

Once Lucy's breathing slowed, and her body stilled, Kelly met her gaze over the top of her pubic mound and smacked her lips together. "Damn, you taste good."

Lucy bit her lip. "I hope I didn't make a mess."

Kelly glanced down at the rather large wet spot gracing the centre of her purple duvet, and didn't give a damn, it would all come out in the wash.

"I don't think I've ever been so wet," Lucy said softly.

"Me either." Kelly didn't need to put a hand in her bikini briefs to feel how slick she was. The heavy ache and relentless pulsing between her legs told her as much.

She inched her way up the bed, peppering kisses over Lucy's abdomen and breasts before crashing her lips to Lucy's.

Needing to feel Lucy's hands on her, Kelly reached up and untied the belt. The second her wrists were free, Lucy's arms wrapped around Kelly. She held her tight, kissing Kelly long and deep, as though she couldn't get close enough.

Emotion flooded every cell of Kelly's being. She couldn't recall ever feeling so wanted.

"Wow, that was quite the kiss," Kelly said, resting her forehead against Lucy's.

A coy smile tilted Lucy's lips. "I've never tasted myself on another person. The combination of me on you was pretty hot." Her flushed cheeks turned a darker shade of pink. "I always thought it'd be unpleasant."

"A lot of firsts tonight, huh?"

"The best kind."

Kelly gazed into Lucy's alluring green eyes; the woman who came across as confident, worldly, yet was everything but when it came to sex.

A thought suddenly hit Kelly. "Have you tasted another woman before?"

"Oh yeah," Lucy said, looking slightly amused. "Many, many times."

Needing no further reassurance, Kelly bolted upright, pulled her panties to the side and straddled Lucy's face.

In the back of her mind, Kelly wanted to know what had made Lucy smirk, but right then her need for release, and for this moment to be about the two of them, took precedence.

True to her word, Lucy knew what she was doing. Kelly held still, revelling in the exquisite sensations lighting up her body, as Lucy expertly devoured her.

The satiny soft feel of Lucy's tongue gliding along the length of her slit was like an electrical current sparking every nerve ending to life. Her stomach fluttered, her toes curled, and her clit throbbed.

On the precipice of climax, Kelly thrust her pelvis chasing her own release. Lucy stilled, holding her tongue flat, letting Kelly take her pleasure. That action alone, the giving of herself, tipped Kelly over the edge.

Her inner walls spasmed and Kelly's entire body pulsed with an intensity that left her breathless.

Still gripping the headboard, Kelly glanced down. The sight of Lucy smiling up at her—lips glistening with Kelly's arousal, her gorgeous face framed by Kelly's thighs—was an image she never wanted to forget. Like the flash of a camera blinding her, Kelly blinked, imprinting the image on the back of her eyelids.

Once feeling returned to her limbs, Kelly slid down the bed, released Lucy's legs and flopped down beside her. Side by side, they smiled warmly at each other.

A loud grumble interrupted the comfortable silence. Kelly put a hand on her stomach. "Was that yours or mine?"

Lucy chuckled. "I'm not sure."

Nerves had got the better of Kelly before meeting Lucy so she'd barely touched her dinner.

"Hungry?" Kelly asked.

"A little. You gave me quite the workout."

"Pfft. I took it easy on you, young lady."

"Ohh, I like that. Mm, hmm." Looking smug, Lucy nodded. "Young lady. Yep, that's me."

"You're only as old as the person you're feeling." Kelly joked. "Stick with me and you'll be forever young."

"Hey, isn't that a song?"

"Ugh." Taking a page out of Nicole's book, Kelly pointed to her eyes. "Focus." In less than a minute, they'd ping-ponged between, food, age, and music.

Kelly rolled off the bed and grabbed two nightshirts out of her dresser drawer.

"Here." She tossed a shirt to Lucy, then unlaced her corset and slipped the other nightshirt over her head.

"Come on, let's get a snack."

***

Propped up in bed, a platter of grapes, cheese, and

crackers between them, Kelly felt like she'd died and gone to heaven. She couldn't have wished for a better outcome for the evening.

Looking even more at home in Kelly's home than she had at the café, if that was even possible, Lucy crunched on a cracker. A crumb disappeared between her cleavage and, as she absently plucked it out, Kelly's mind flicked back to what Lucy had said earlier.

"You really have got gorgeous breasts." Kelly glanced down at her own chest, barely visible through her loose-fitting nightshirt. "What did you mean when you said you were glad I approved? I mean to say, what's not to like?"

Lucy took a sip of wine and put her glass on the bedside table. "I had my first bra before I turned twelve. Being heavy chested as a teenager was hell. I can laugh about it now." She cupped her breasts and jiggled her boobs. Kelly smiled.

"I used to wear baggy tops but now I refuse to. The 'girls' still get a lot of attention, most of it I ignore, but yours I appreciated."

Totally able to relate to the angst of being a teenager

with body parts that received unwanted attention, Kelly leaned over and planted a kiss on Lucy's cheek.

"When I was younger, I hated my backside. At school, I hung out with my best mate, Steve. Friends of his, who assumed we were dating, would make immature comments like, Go, dude. I'd totally tap that. And other inane things like more cushion for the pushin'."

Over time, Kelly had learned to ignore the comments and love her body for what it was. Was anyone truly ever happy with how they looked? Kelly doubted it, and, she was eternally grateful that she had all her faculties and limbs. Not everyone was as fortunate.

"This backside." Kelly wiggled her bum on the bed "Has the perfect amount of padding for riding my motorcycle."

"I've never been on a motorbike." Lucy popped a grape into her mouth and passed the nearly barren bunch to Kelly. "Would you take me for a ride one day?"

"It would be my pleasure. In fact, I'd planned to make a trip to Wellington to visit my little sis next weekend. Wanna come?"

A worry line creased Lucy's forehead and Kelly's stomach churned. Had she been too presumptuous? Surely not. Lucy had said she wanted to get to know all of her and her sister was an important part of Kelly's life.

"I think my arse would be flat as a board if I had to sit astride a bike for two hours straight. Perhaps we could start with a shorter trip."

"Oh. yeah." She had a good point, one Kelly hadn't thought of. "Never mind. Perhaps you can meet Jo, my sister, some other time."

"Hey, don't sound so dejected. I'd love to come with you."

"I don't have a car." Kelly picked up the empty platter and set it on her bedside table.

Caught up in her own misery when her bright idea had come crashing down around her ears, Kelly didn't even consider the fact they had other options. Until Lucy spoke.

"Don't play c..."

Biting back a smile, Kelly plucked up a pillow and

wielded it in the air. "Don't say it."

She tossed the pillow aside, pinned Lucy to the bed, and launched into a full-on tickle attack.

Giggling, Lucy thrashed about trying to get free. "I was going to say I have a car."

"Were not."

Kelly kept up the torment until tears streamed down Lucy's cheeks and she was laughing hysterically.

"Stop."

"Never." Kelly nipped Lucy's neck and dug her fingers in deeper. "Take it back. I wasn't playing coy."

"I take it back." Lucy's smirked. "You were sulking."

Kelly moved the tickling from her stomach to her ribs, upping the ante. Lucy screamed and laughed.

"Okay, okay. I take it back."

"Say it like you mean it." Glad she wasn't the one on the bottom, Kelly gave Lucy an evil grin.

Thrashing about wildly, Lucy said, "Candyfloss."

Relenting, Kelly rolled off. "Not fair. That's not what a safe word's for."

With the back of her hand, Lucy wiped tears from

her eyes.

Kelly stroked her cheek. "Naw, don't cry."

They laughed and called a truce.

"Come here." Kelly held her arm out and Lucy snuggled into her side. The bedside clock glowed nine. Kelly hoped her next question didn't ruin a perfect evening. She considered making a joke and telling Lucy she couldn't leave because she'd been drinking. But considering Lucy had only had a glass over the last hour and a half, that would be a cop out. So, she stuck to being honest.

"I'd really like you to stay the night, Lucy." Kelly put a finger under Lucy's chin and kissed her softly. "But don't feel like you have to. I'll understand if you need to get home."

And I'll be crushed and cry like a baby the minute you walk out the door, Kelly refrained from saying.

"I'd like that, too," Lucy replied, her eyes full of warmth.

Over the moon with happiness, Kelly leapt to her feet. She knew it was immature but couldn't help herself. Trying to keep her balance on the mattress dipping as she danced in a circle, Kelly fist pumped the air. "Yes, yes, yes."

Like an acrobat, she jumped off and gave a bow. "Would Ma'am like a shower?" Kelly extended her hand.

Shaking her head in amusement, Lucy took it and slid out of bed. "If you promise to wash my back."

"Deal."

As they walked hand and hand to the bathroom, Kelly briefly considered asking Lucy if she needed to let Paula know she wouldn't be home. Then she recalled Paula's terse words from the night of her potluck dinner when Kelly had asked where Lucy was, "Out, she has a life," and doubted Paula cared.

Not only that, Kelly didn't want to ruin the night by opening that can of worms.

Chapter 19

The following morning, Kelly awoke before her alarm went off at six-thirty. She didn't often get up before seven but Lucy had asked her to set it early so she had time to duck home and change before work.

Rather than let the angry blare of the alarm wake Lucy, Kelly kissed her on the cheek and gave her a gentle shake. "Wakey, wakey, sleepyhead."

Groaning, Lucy stretched and rubbed her eyes. "Do I have to."

"'Fraid so, we can sleep in tomorrow. I mean you can, and I can. Not necessarily together. Here. In my bed."

An eye cracked open, followed by a wide smile. "You're cute."

"I'm rambling." Kelly hated when she did that, let her insecurities bubble forth.

She slid out of bed and handed Lucy her clothes

after untangling the pant leg still wrapped around the foot of her bed. The image brought a smile to her face.

"Do you have time for coffee before you have to go?"

"Always. Especially when the sexiest barista in town offers to make it for me."

Seven o'clock rolled around in record time.

Halfway across the lounge to see Lucy out, Kelly's phone chirped. She swiped the screen and read the message from Nicole.

"Forgot something I need for work. Put your pants on, I'm coming home."

While trying to formulate a witty reply, out of the corner of her eye, Kelly saw Lucy's face drop.

"Hey, what's that look for?"

"Do you often have naked women in your bed?"

Ah, there it was. The barely contained vulnerability that bubbled just below Lucy's confident exterior. A trait Kelly admired.

She took Lucy's hands in her own. "I've owned that bed for over a year, and you, Lucy-Lou, are the first woman to spend the night in it, with me, between those sheets."

Lucy's game face slid back on. "Well, in that case, I'm honoured." She gave Kelly's hand a squeeze. "Thanks for a great night. I'll talk to you later."

***

All day Friday, Kelly bustled around the café feeling like she was walking on air. She couldn't recall ever being so smitten. She'd wanted to ask Lucy to come over that night, but also wanted to give her space if she needed it. Just because they had great chemistry didn't mean they had to be joined at the hip, as much as Kelly wouldn't mind that.

When she received a text from Lucy saying, "Staying home tonight, flatmates having friends over for drinks," Kelly's heart plummeted.

Like a slap upside the head, the reality of their situation hit her hard. For obvious reasons, they couldn't flaunt their relationship for as long as Lucy paid rent to Paula.

A nauseating sense of guilt clawed at Kelly's insides.

That's what you get when you have to keep your relationship a secret.

"I'm not doing anything wrong," Kelly screamed into the wind as she sped home on her motorcycle.

That night, the frequent text messages Kelly received from Lucy put a smile on her face.

"Miss you."

"Miss you more."

"You're hot."

"You're hotter than a hot fudge sundae."

"You're lame."

"You're lamer than a three-legged donkey."

"What? That doesn't even make sense, go have another drink!"

Turning her attention back to the movie she'd totally lost the plot of, Kelly put her phone on the chairside table.

Friday night spent with her besties enjoying a few cold ones, and snacking on pizza, was far from a hardship. And better yet, Jacinta had swapped her Monday shift with Kelly, so Kelly had the weekend off.

"Care to share." Steve shielded his eyes. "You're

practically glowing over there."

"We were just texting about donkeys."

"What?"

"That's what Lucy said."

In a lightning fast move, Steve snatched Kelly's beer and took a swig.

When he tried to hand it back, Kelly held her fingers up in a cross. "Ew, boy germs."

The television went silent, the picture paused. Nicole raised an eyebrow. "Okay, children. Get it all out, then we can watch the movie."

"I want some of what she's drinking." Steve pointed like a petulant little brother. "I think she's on drugs."

"It's called love, babe." Nicole plucked up a piece of pizza and severed a stringy piece of cheese with her finger.

"Why don't you get like that around me? All gooey-eyed and lovey-dovey?"

"Because you're an arse and I want a donkey."

With a theatrical groan, Steve spread his lanky frame across the floor and slapped his forehead. "Shoot me now."

Nicole winked at Kelly and Kelly high-fived her on the way to the kitchen. Grabbing a cold beer out of the fridge, her mind wandered to Lucy. What would she make of Kelly's crazy friends?

***

Saturday morning, Kelly had just finished cleaning her motorcycle when Nicole appeared on the porch hollering, "phone."

Not wanting her cell phone to get wet, Kelly had left it inside. "Thanks, hun." She blew Nicole an air kiss, then plucked the phone out of her hand before it stopped ringing.

"Hello."

"Hey, it's me."

Hearing Lucy's sexy voice made Kelly break out in a huge grin. Her skin tingled and her heart skipped a beat.

Assuming correctly who it was, Nicole mouthed, "Ask if she wants to come with us to mini-golf."

Mini-golf? That was news to Kelly, but she wouldn't miss it for the world. She gave Nicole the thumbs up and turned her attention back to Lucy.

"Did you sleep well?" Kelly absently ran her toes through a puddle of water under her sparkling clean Triumph.

It was warming up to be another hot day and she intended to spend every hour she could outdoors enjoying it. If she could do that with Lucy by her side, all the better.

"I did. I dreamed about a very sweet lady."

"Anyone I know?" Kelly asked, picturing Lucy's alluring smile.

"Yeah, I think you know her well. Better than me," Lucy said. "But I'm looking forward to getting to know more about her."

Even though it felt weird being referred to in the third person, it was kind of cute, so Kelly played along. "I hear she has a mean golf swing. Care to find out?"

"I'm not sure that's such a good idea. My work colleagues are still searching for the golf balls I lost at last year's Christmas function."

An image of Lucy taking a huge swing only to watch the golf ball sail off into the trees, never to be found again, made Kelly chuckle.

"I meant mini-golf. We're heading to The Putt Hutt on Napier road. You and me can team up against Nicole and Steve. What do you say?"

Just as Kelly was about to offer to pick Lucy up, Lucy beat her to the punch.

"Sounds great, I'll be at yours in ten."

A mixture of dread and relief shot through Kelly. She put a hand over her pounding heart.

Damn, that was close.

Kelly wasn't sure how long she could dance around the fact her now girlfriend lived with her ex-girlfriend, and she couldn't just bowl around and pick her up.

It was a tricky situation to say the least. On one hand, she wanted to address the topic with Lucy, but at the same time she was at a loss of what to say. It was far too early to have any say in where Lucy should, or shouldn't, live.

Hopefully, they would have plenty of time to talk during the four-hour round trip to Wellington next Saturday. But before then, Kelly needed to come up with a way to ask Lucy when she anticipated buying her own home, without being as nosy as to ask how much money she had, and how much more she needed.

Banishing any negative thoughts, Kelly headed inside to get changed. For the time being, she'd take what she could get.

***

Seventeen holes of golf later, neck and neck, team Nicole and team Kelly stood around the last hole.

"You go first," Kelly said to Lucy.

"Good call." Steve stepped back, and ushered Lucy forward. "Losers first." He smirked.

Kelly waved her golf club at him. "Hey, watch who you're calling a loser, mate."

"There won't be any losers, just first and second." Nicole gave Lucy a warm smile and Kelly loved her for it.

"Great, I get partnered with someone who couldn't care less whether we win or lose." Despite Steve's gruff reply, there was no mistaking the love in his eyes when he draped an arm across Nicole's shoulders, dwarfing her petite frame.

By the time Kelly turned back around, Lucy was lining her golf club up. She hit the ball and it puttered up the hill, ran out of steam and rolled all the way back to her feet.

"That's one," Steve said.

"We can count." Nicole and Kelly snapped at the same time.

Steve ran his thumb and forefinger across his lips in a zipping motion.

"Take your time," Kelly gave Lucy a reassuring smile.

"Room please." Lucy made a shooing motion.

The light green sundress that clung to her gorgeous curves, fluttered as she lined up her shot, wiggling her hips.

When Lucy pulled the club back, Kelly held her breath and crossed her fingers she'd get a hole in one.

The ball shot up the runway, bounced off the backwall, and flew back toward them. All three girls jumped, but Smug Steve didn't move fast enough. The ball smacked him in the shin.

"What the f…" He gripped his leg and hopped in a

circle, making such a grand show anyone would think it was broken.

Two young boys with worried looks on their faces pointed. One tugged on the bottom of his father's shirt to get his attention.

"Steve, you're scaring the kids." Nicole stuck a thumb over her shoulder.

"Sorry, nothing to see here." He dropped his foot and rubbed his leg. "Damn that hurt."

"I truly am sorry," Lucy said, looking and sounding sincere. "I told Kelly, me and small balls don't get along."

Steve's knees drew together, and Kelly snorted. Lucy had a way of wording things that often made Kelly wonder if they'd been intentional or totally innocent.

Nicole sidled up next to Lucy and bumped shoulders. "I like you."

Smiling broadly, Steve squeezed Lucy's shoulder. "Me too. You passed the test."

Lucy quirked an eyebrow, her gaze locked on Kelly. "I didn't know I was being tested."

Gaping like a fish, Kelly punched Steve in the shoulder. "It's not like that. Tell her."

"I did. She passed the Steve test. You're like a sister to me, now I can rest easy that I won't have to slash your missus's tyres."

"Oh, my goodness." Eyes wide, Lucy's hand flew to her mouth. "Paula had a flat tyre this morning." She narrowed her eyes. "You didn't, did you?"

Kelly's heart jumped into her throat. Her friends were very protective, but she never thought Steve would stoop so low. She folded her arms and levelled her gaze on Steve.

He flinched as though she'd shot daggers at him. "Shit, no." He backed up, arms held out in surrender. "I was kidding, honestly. I wouldn't do something like that."

Lucy cocked a finger gun at Steve and winked. "Bang, gotcha."

Once again, Kelly's mouth fell open. Lucy kissed her on the cheek. "Sorry, I didn't mean to alarm you, but someone has to beat this dude at his own game.

The look on Steve's face spoke volumes. Although

he tried to act like he hadn't been bested, Kelly knew him well enough to know he was impressed with Lucy's fast thinking.

Scratching the stubble on his chin, Steve said, "You'll keep."

The last golf hole seemingly forgotten, Kelly put an arm around Lucy's waist. "You're right, she is a keeper."

When Lucy's face lit up and she leaned into the embrace, Kelly couldn't wait a minute longer to be alone with her.

"You guys win." Kelly handed her golf club to Steve. "Let's get out of here, it's too nice of a day to be indoors."

Chapter 20

An hour later, Kelly was in her element, basking in the warmth of the sun on her face and a soft body moulded to her back.

Lucy had taken to the bike like a pro. Kelly wasn't a fan of carrying nervous pillion passengers, but Lucy's body moved with hers as if they were one, leaning with her into each corner and straightening as they exited.

And there were a lot of winding roads between Palmerston North and Apiti.

If it wasn't for the heat of her body, her arms wrapped tightly around Kelly's waist, and the tantalizing feel of her breasts pressed into Kelly's back, Kelly would've forgotten she was there.

After climbing a steep incline and descending the other side, Kelly coasted over an old bridge, tapped Lucy on the leg and pointed to the river below. It was a spot Kelly loved and had stumbled upon quite by accident.

A few meters past the bridge, she slowed as a gate barely visible from the road came into view. Her headlight flashed across BARTLETS RESERVE as she turned onto a narrow gravel path. Day or night, Kelly rode with her headlight on. It gave her a sense of security that she would be more visible to motorist.

Once the path gave way to grass, she continued to the far end of the clearing and parked alongside a thicket of blackberry bushes.

The air was humid and carried the scent of dry grass. Kelly put the kickstand down and pulled off her helmet. Lucy climbed off the bike, tugged her helmet off, and shook out her legs.

"Wow, that was fantastic." Lucy beamed, her smile brighter than the sun. "Even if I have got a numb bum." She rubbed her backside as if to prove her point.

Like a ghost, Kelly sidled up next to Lucy and pinched her butt, delighted when Lucy squealed and jumped.

"Ow."

"I'd say you've still got plenty of feeling there. If

you're not sure, I've got other ways to test the theory."

"Really?" Lucy draped her arms around Kelly's neck.

Birds chirped, and the gurgle of the river faded into the background as Kelly lost herself in the green depths of Lucy's eyes.

Her temperature spiked, and it had nothing to do with the sun beating down on them. As tempted as Kelly was to relieve Lucy of some clothes, she refrained from doing so. Kelly hadn't shared this place with another soul and she wanted Lucy to experience the beauty as she had.

Breaking their intense gaze, Kelly pulled the backpack off Lucy's shoulders and grabbed her hand. "Follow me, and be careful."

Minutes later, after tramping down wayward blackberry vines, and holding others up while Lucy ducked underneath, they emerged onto a riverbank. A few stray vines had snagged Kelly's forearms but other than one or two surface scratches she was none the worse for wear.

And, she would endure cuts ten times worse to see

the awestruck look lighting up Lucy's face.

She stood with her hands on her hips, taking in the scenic view. "Beautiful."

A bead of sweat trickled down Kelly's back. "And bloody hot."

She pulled a towel out of the backpack and spread it out on a relatively even patch of ground.

"You're not wrong." Lucy shucked out of the jacket Kelly had loaned her. It was too tight to zip all the way up, but no way would Kelly let her on the bike without long pants and long sleeves.

Kelly had only had one spill and the unrelenting surface of the road had torn through her jeans and jersey, leaving her knees and elbows grazed and bruised. The memory of that day made Kelly shudder. It didn't even bear thinking about how much worse her injuries would've been if she'd been wearing shorts and a tee.

Within seconds, they'd discarded their jackets, socks, and shoes. Kelly wiggled her toes imagining the cold water washing over her feet.

The rockface on the opposite side of the valley cast

shadows over the ground. It had to be at least sixty-foot tall. The tip of two power poles and their dangling wires peeked over the top. If they were the only thing that peered over the cliff, Kelly would be happy.

She suspected the cliff bordered the edge of a dairy farm they'd past a few kilometres back.

"Skinny dip?" Sitting on the towel, Kelly rocked her backside and slid her jeans down her legs.

A coy smile tilted the corner of Lucy's mouth. "I'm not skinny enough."

"Are you kidding? You've got curves in all the right places. And who cares, anyway? There's no one within a country mile." Kelly gave Lucy's thigh a reassuring squeeze.

"True, and you've seen it all before anyway."

The saucy wink Lucy shot Kelly made her insides tingle. If Kelly didn't need to cool off, she would've jumped Lucy right then and there.

Sitting beside her, Lucy worked her jeans down her legs, then yanked her shirt over her head and tossed them on the pebbled beach.

And there she sat, looking fucking gorgeous, in a

pink bra and matching briefs.

Kelly fanned her face. "Goddamn you're sexy. I don't know what's wetter, me or the water."

A snort bubbled out of Lucy. "Such eloquence."

When Lucy stood, Kelly's gaze roamed up her legs, coming to a rest on the dark triangle hidden beneath her briefs.

Saliva pooled in Kelly's mouth when a plan Lucy wasn't yet privy to bubbled to the surface.

Oblivious to her sweet backside taunting Kelly with each stride, Lucy hollered over her shoulder, "Last one in's a baked potato."

Chuckling, Kelly pulled her shirt off. Feeling brave, she ditched her bra and glanced up just in time to see Lucy wince when she stood on a sharp stone.

With no intention of doing the same, Kelly slipped her feet into her boots, not giving a damn how ridiculous she looked.

The heavy clomp of her footfalls gave her away as she closed in on Lucy.

Lucy's head whipped around. Her surprised expression gave way to amusement when her gaze dropped to Kelly's feet.

"Laugh all you like." Kelly slapped Lucy on the butt as she sped by. "I like baked potatoes."

"Roast, not baked." A pebble hit Kelly square in the back.

Rather than react, a wicked smile spread across Kelly's face. Lucy would pay for that.

Chapter 21

Refreshed after a quick dip in the river, Kelly piggybacked Lucy from the water's edge back to their makeshift blanket. The feel of her wet body plastered to Kelly's back was exquisite torture. Kelly wasn't strong enough to carry Lucy for long, but she also never wanted to put her down.

The squelch of her feet in her boots made Kelly rethink her wisdom. In her haste to outdo Lucy, she hadn't taken a towel to the riverside.

Once she made it back to their clothes, and towel, Kelly lowered Lucy to her feet.

A frown creased Lucy's forehead. Fairly certain she knew why, Kelly bit back a smile.

"How am I supposed to dry these?" Lucy plucked at her wet bra, and snapped the waistband of her briefs. The worry line morphed into a grin. "Or are we going to live dangerously and ride home commando?"

As much as Lucy would love that, Kelly had other plans. If she didn't, she would've told Lucy to pack her bikini as well when she'd texted Lucy to bring jeans.

"Sorry, I have a hard rule about appropriate clothing for riding. Looks like we'll have to spread them out to dry." Kelly pointed to a fallen log a few feet away. "We shouldn't have to wait for long."

Although it was no longer unbearably hot, the afternoon sun still held plenty of heat.

"And how do you propose we pass the time, Kelly?" Lucy cocked her head, a sexy smile on her face.

"That's Miss Kel, to you." Kelly slipped her proverbial domme hat on. "And, I do believe I owe you a punishment."

A spark of desire flashed in Lucy's eyes. "What for?" She narrowed her gaze.

A jolt of arousal shot through Kelly when her fingers connected with the rope she'd stashed at the bottom of her backpack.

She stood and addressed Lucy. "Did you, or did you not, toss a stone at my back? And don't even think about lying to me, young lady."

Like a perfect submissive, Lucy bit her lip and lowered her gaze. "It was a pebble, Miss Kel."

Okay, perhaps not perfect, but perfection was overrated. Kelly admired Lucy's sass. Rather than chastise Lucy for answering her back, Kelly took the opportunity to throw some of Lucy's words back at her.

"I'd peel these off." Kelly tugged on Lucy's briefs. "But I don't make a habit of going into people's drawers without their permission."

Lucy's lips twitched, confirming her innocent comment had been nothing of the sort.

Thankfully, unlike that day at the café, Kelly could now find humour in the comment rather than have a coronary. Sure, her heart was racing, but that was for entirely different reasons.

The loud snap of elastic on wet skin echoed in Kelly's ears when she released the waistband. Elation shot through her when Lucy didn't so much as flinch, just held Kelly's gaze as if awaiting further instruction.

Kelly put her hands on her hips. "Strip."

A hint of worry skidded across Lucy's face. Her gaze flittered left, then right, over Kelly's shoulder, across the river, to the top of the rockface, then settled back on Kelly.

Apparently, like Kelly, Lucy wasn't an exhibitionist. As much as Kelly liked the element of surprise, she had no intention of exploiting Lucy's worries.

Intent on erasing Lucy's fears, Kelly walked behind her and kissed her shoulder blade. She ran her tongue over a droplet of water that dripped from Lucy's hair. Her skin was hot and slightly pink, another good reason to get out of the sun.

Slowly, Kelly undid the hooks on Lucy's bra. One. Two. Three.

"Don't worry, I'm not going to tie you up for all the world to see." She trailed a finger under the crease of Lucy's left breast.

Lucy shivered, goose flesh erupting on her skin.

"This gorgeous body is for my eyes only."

Hanging on to Kelly's every word, Lucy looked incredibly beautiful and vulnerable, the combination was a heady drug. Lucy trusted her. And that was everything to Kelly.

Lucy sucked in a breath and let it out slowly as Kelly

slid the straps down her arms.

Questions swam in Lucy's eyes, but she didn't voice them, further cementing her trust in Kelly.

Kelly picked up the towel, shook the grit off, and handed it to Lucy.

As if reading Kelly's mind, Lucy wrapped it around her body, knotted it above her breasts, and kicked her underwear off.

After spreading their wet clothes over an old log, Kelly plucked up the length of rope and grabbed Lucy's hand, towing her behind her.

"I have the perfect way to pass the time while these are drying. Did you notice the big tree on our way to the riverbank?"

"I did!" Lucy said, her voice shrill.

Her enthusiastic response revved up Kelly's excitement. It also led Kelly to believe Lucy suspected what Kelly had in store for her, and she didn't intend to disappoint.

Halfway along the narrow path from the reserve to the river, stood a tall birch tree, with a clearing approximately ten-feet in diameter surrounding the base.

The gurgle of water turned to white noise as Kelly's senses honed-in on Lucy and their surroundings.

Slithers of sunlight crisscrossed the ground. A tall tree pierced through the foliage of wild blackberry vines surrounding them like black and red curtains.

In that moment, Kelly felt like a director on a stage, and it was fucking exhilarating.

Kicking at the ground with the toe of her boot, Kelly cleared away some stray vines. Lucy did the same, then toed off her shoes. The promise of what was to come, and not wanting a foot full of blackberry thorns, halted any would-be jokes about their attire.

With a sharp tug on the knot of the towel, it fell to the ground. Kelly backed Lucy up until the tree brought them to an abrupt stop. Their lips met in a bruising kiss. There was nothing gentle about it. Teeth clashed, tongues duelled. Hands roamed.

The rapid increase of Kelly's heart from something as basic as kissing Lucy, never ceased to amaze her. She wanted Lucy with a passion that left her breathless.

"Goddamn, you're one fine woman, Lucy-Lou."

Kelly grazed her teeth over the tendon on Lucy's neck, loving the feel of Lucy's strong pulse.

Exhaling a soft whimper, Lucy gripped Kelly's backside, dug her fingers in, and pulled her close.

"Tut-tut." Kelly stepped out of her reach and waggled a finger. "You don't get to take liberties. You've been a naughty girl."

An adorable pout formed on Lucy's lips.

"Don't give me that look, missy. Turn around and hug the tree."

A frown.

"Don't make me ask twice. Wrap your arms around the tree." Kelly pulled her belt through the loops of her jeans and then kicked them off, glad to be free of them chafing on her centre.

What on earth Lucy enjoyed about going commando was beyond Kelly. The only reason Kelly had slipped her jeans back on, without underwear, was so they'd be nearby if she needed them in a hurry.

Cutting Lucy some slack—for not complying immediately—Kelly basked in the attention as Lucy's gaze wandered over her body. Her scrutiny was so intense, Kelly felt it like a physical caress. Her nipples tightened, and her pulse raced.

"I think I'd rather look at you, Miss Kel." Lucy batted her eyelashes.

As tempting as it was to smile, Kelly refused to reward Lucy's bratty behaviour for a minute longer. If she wanted Kelly to take control, then she needed to learn how to follow instructions.

"Turn around, now. Put your arms around the tree," Kelly gritted the words out, slow and controlled, leaving no room for argument.

It had been the right call. All traces of humour vanished.

Lucy's eyes glazed over. "Yes, Miss Kel. I've been naughty, please punish me."

Fuck, could she say anything hotter?

Once Lucy had her back to Kelly, her arms as far around the tree as they would go, Kelly took a minute to admire her body. The slope of her back, the round globes of her buttocks, her curvy thighs.

Then, Kelly lingered a little longer, letting anticipation build, tormenting herself as much as Lucy.

When a loose bit of bark above Lucy's head caught her eye, Kelly reached for it, pressing her breasts into Lucy's back.

The sudden contact made Lucy jump, but she held her position, arms glued to the tree trunk.

"Good girl," Kelly whispered into her ear. "Don't forget your safe word."

She didn't intend to flog the life out of Lucy, but Lucy might freak for whatever reason.

"I trust you won't hurt me, Miss Kel."

"Much." Kelly chuckled, dragging the strip of bark down the length of Lucy's back.

Kelly slashed the birch across her hand, testing the weight, imagining the sound it would make when it connected with Lucy's bare flesh.

Like a cat stretching, Lucy arched her spine. It was all the encouragement Kelly needed.

"Count for me." Taking care to warm Lucy up, Kelly landed a soft blow.

"One, thank you, Miss."

Like a pro tennis player, Kelly delivered two blows in quick succession; forehand, followed by a backhand.

"Two. Three. Harder please."

A jolt of desire shot from Kelly's nipples to her clit. She appreciated the guidance given she couldn't see Lucy's face to read her expressions.

"Your wish is my command." Kelly wound up and delivered a hard blow. The ensuing red stripe intersected with the crease of Lucy's arse forming a perfect letter t.

A quiver rocked Lucy's body. "Four."

The husky tenor of her voice turned Kelly on. Soothing the burn, Kelly ran her hand over the offending mark.

"Can you take two more?"

"Yes, Miss Kel."

The scent of soil wafted up from the ground as Lucy shuffled her feet, moving them further apart, as if to brace herself.

When the next blow landed, Lucy groaned. "Five."

Her resilience sparked a fire deep inside Kelly. She was tempted to make the last strike really count, but at the same time, Kelly didn't want Lucy to be too tender to lean back against the tree. As it was, the wood would probably scratch her bare flesh.

Eyeing up the crease where thighs met butt-cheeks, Kelly swished the birch strip one final time.

"Six." Lucy's body sagged.

Desperate to get her hands on Lucy, Kelly ate up the small space between them and spun her in a circle.

Lucy's cheeks were flushed, her eyes full of desire. Their lips met, and like always, the passion that flowed between them robbed Kelly of her senses. Lucy's arms wrapped around her and Kelly melted into the embrace.

When the need to devour every inch of Lucy became too much, Kelly broke the kiss. "You took your punishment well."

"Thank you, Miss."

"Now for your reward."

Lucy watched with rapt attention as Kelly picked up the rope and ran it through her fingers. It snaked across Kelly's palm like a rough caress. "What do you think I'm going to do with this?"

For the second time that afternoon, Lucy's eyes darted left, then right. "Tie me up?" she asked, her voice excited, her gaze wary.

Kelly tied a knot in one end of the rope, forming a small loop.

"Correct, I'm going to bind you, but loosely enough that you can slip free if we need to make a quick exit."

Kelly smiled, and any tension that had been between them vanished on a gentle breeze.

In seconds, Lucy's wrists were bound, the front of her gorgeous body completely exposed to Kelly. Arms back, breasts thrust out. It was another image Kelly added to her mental snapshots of Lucy.

"How do you feel?"

Flashes of their first night together ran through Kelly's mind when Lucy replied in kind.

"Exposed, vulnerable, excited."

While Kelly could relate to the last part, she was in awe of Lucy for putting herself in such a vulnerable position.

The mere thought of being restrained, especially out in the open, freaked Kelly out. Thankfully, that would never happen. Kelly couldn't imagine Lucy ever ordering her to do anything, much less Kelly obeying her commands.

With a hand on each breast, Kelly rolled Lucy's nipples between thumb and forefinger.

Lucy's eyelids lowered, then flew open when Kelly squeezed and twisted, hard enough to elicit a yelp. Not intending to cause any lasting pain, she released the taut peaks and sucked one then the other, soothing the ache and drawing little whimpers from Lucy.

"Fuck." Lucy moaned. "I want to touch you so bad. To run my fingers through your hair."

As if they were connected, the mere suggestion of Lucy running her fingers through Kelly's hair made her scalp prickle.

Out of the corner of her eye, Kelly saw Lucy's hand flex. The rope around her wrist prevented her from touching Kelly, and served as a silent reminder she was at Kelly's mercy.

Anxious to feel skin on skin, she released Lucy's nipple with a pop and plastered the front of her body to Lucy's. The heat rippling between them was off the charts.

Time stood still as Kelly luxuriated in the warmth of Lucy's skin, the wonderful scent of her hair, and the stunning green eyes holding her captive.

Kelly fisted Lucy's hair and kissed her hard. Lucy parted her lips, expelling a whimper as she allowed Kelly entrance.

"I love having my hair played with, so hold that thought." Kelly dropped to her knees. "For now, you can simply dream about grabbing my head, while I lick, suck, and fuck you until you're begging for release."

A tiny whimper escaped Lucy's lips, her eyes glassy with lust.

The second Kelly's tongue made contact, a groan tore from Lucy. Like the birds that took flight, Kelly's heart soared. She loved how utterly responsive Lucy was.

"You horny girl." Kelly held up her fingers, glistening with Lucy's arousal. "Is this all for me?"

"Yes." Lucy inhaled sharply. "You do that to me, Miss Kel."

With that, Kelly was on Lucy like waves lapping at a beach. She licked, nipped, and sucked every inch of Lucy's labia, enticing delectable whimpers from her lips.

When Lucy's thighs tensed as if poised on the edge of release, Kelly pulled back and slapped her mound.

"Fuck." Lucy exhaled a tortured groan.

Burning with desire, Kelly continued to smack her clit with one hand while finger-fucking her with the other.

Tiny tremors rocked Lucy's body, a sheen of sweat glistened on her forehead, and her breathing grew shallow.

"Oh, Miss Kel, I'm so close. Permission to come?" It was more of a plea than a request.

The white rope pulled taut around her wrist when Lucy flexed her hands as if trying to reach out and pull Kelly closer.

"Where do you want me?" Kelly teased. "Here?" She swiped her tongue along the length of Lucy's labia, savouring her unique taste and inhaling her musky scent. Both were out of this world. She tasted and smelled fucking amazing.

"Yes, yes, like that."

In the back of her mind, Kelly was conscious they were at a public reserve. A fact that was as distracting as it was exhilarating.

Focusing her attention on the beautiful woman writhing before her, Kelly thumbed Lucy's clit and buried her fingers deep inside her.

"Come for me." Kelly curled her fingers forward and massaged Lucy's G-spot.

A guttural moan tore from Lucy.

Seemingly all at once, her body sagged, she clutched the tree, and cried out.

The heady feel of her pulsing around Kelly's digits, the sound of her raspy breaths, and exhaled curses—fuck, oh my God, fuck—was the hottest, most humbling thing Kelly had ever witnessed.

She'd dreamed of bringing a partner to orgasm with an intensity that blew both their minds. The reality surpassed all of Kelly's expectations. In that moment, she was lost to Lucy, to the dream of them growing old together.

The undeniable truth of the matter—she'd fallen hard and fast for Lucy—rocked Kelly to her core.

As though her legs didn't want to hold her up anymore, Lucy's body went limp. She slid down the tree. Just before her naked backside hit the ground, she braced herself, her butt hovering millimetres above twigs and dirt.

"Shit. Perhaps that's not such a good idea."

Kelly pulled the towel out from under her knees. She slid it forward. "Here."

Lowering herself the last few inches, Lucy gave Kelly a grateful smile. "Thanks, I'm boneless."

Far from done with Lucy, Kelly stood. "Well, lucky for me, it's not a bone I'm after."

Kelly's legs pinged as circulation returned. Despite the towel cushioning her weight, the rough ground had left dents in Kelly's knees.

Hands still bound, and making no attempts to slip free, Lucy licked her lips. Her hungry gaze zeroed in on where Kelly wanted—needed—her most.

Practically able to feel Lucy's mouth on her, Kelly put one foot between Lucy's thighs, hiked her other leg up, and settled her foot on a knot jutting out of the side of the tree.

Like someone savouring the heavenly aroma of their favourite brew, Lucy inhaled deeply.

"You want some of this?" Kelly grabbed a handful of Lucy's short black hair and pulled her head back.

The intensity of desire simmering in Lucy's eyes rocked Kelly's world. Lucy wanted her as much as she wanted Lucy.

"I want all of it, of you, Miss Kel." Lucy licked her lips.

Aching from pent up sexual tension, Kelly thrust her pelvis forward. Before she could draw her next breath, Lucy wrapped her lips around Kelly's swollen clit. Her tongue was warm and wet, and she kept up a steady rhythm that had Kelly hurtling toward orgasm in record time.

Pleasure zinged through Kelly's veins, and it was her turn to expel expletives.

"Fuck."

Head back, sunlight crisscrossing her face, Kelly clutched the knee of her raised leg.

Tiny moans coming from Lucy vibrated through her, intensifying her arousal. Before long, a cacophony of their cries of pleasure filled the small space between them.

Fighting to suck in air, Kelly's muscles tensed as the rising crescendo of pleasure robbed her of her senses. Her toes curled, her legs shook; exquisite sensations bombarded her body.

Out of nowhere, Kelly's orgasm slammed into her like a cattle truck, and hit her with as much force. All the breath left her body. White spots danced in her vision. Struggling to remain upright, she lowered her leg.

Lucy slowed her movements, retreating from where Kelly had become too sensitive.

Sucking in air, Kelly dragged her jeans closer and sat beside Lucy. "You literally steal my breath away."

"Thank you, Miss Kel." Lucy sounded unsure. She leaned her head back against the tree and stared up at the sky.

Having none of it, Kelly gripped Lucy's chin and forced her to meet her gaze. "I meant it, Lucy. The mere sight of you takes my breath away. I don't mean just the sex, which, by the way, is fucking amazing."

Lucy chuckled and Kelly's heart soared. The only thing she loved more than hearing Lucy laugh was being the cause of it.

"It's pretty amazing," Lucy said. "We're amazing, together."

Kelly had the urge to ask a question that had been on her mind since Thursday night. If she was to be honest, she hadn't asked before now because she was terrified of the answer.

But after such an intense moment, she couldn't put it off any longer.

"Do you think we should slowdown? I can, you know. If you want me to." There, she'd said it and survived.

"I've been thinking that very same thing," Lucy said.

A little unsure if she wanted to hear the answer, Kelly held her breath. "You have?"

Lucy chuckled. "Of course I have. I'm a planner by nature. Hell, I'm paid to look for things others don't see." She shrugged. "It's what I do, analyse."

The mysterious reply did nothing to alleviate Kelly's concerns. She would back off if that was what Lucy needed. Although, she suspected that would be as crushing as having to walk everywhere instead of riding her Triumph. It would be difficult, but she'd cope.

"The thing is, Kelly, all my life, I've taken the time to really get to know the person I was dating before being intimate with them. And none of those relationships worked out. As soon as it came to sex, everything went downhill."

Even though Kelly understood what Lucy was saying, she still felt insecure.

"So, what you're saying is we have the chemistry but might not have what it takes to go the distance?"

"You really are cute, Kel. All powerful and dominant one minute and insecure the next."

"Are you making fun of me?" Kelly harrumphed, not at all offended.

"We all have our insecurities, I find yours endearing."

"As are yours," Kelly said.

"Touché." Lucy smirked. "Now stop distracting me. To answer your question, I don't see why we should back up. We have chemistry, trust, and respect. Those are the things that matter most to me, Kelly."

"Me too," Kelly said softly.

"I knew a couple who decided to tie the knot."

Kelly chuckled. The timing of Lucy's words couldn't have been better.

Lucy glanced down at the hand Kelly had just freed. "Not that kind of knot."

"I know." Kelly slid across Lucy's lap and released her other hand. "Go on."

"They married after being together for ten years, divorced a year later. There are no guarantees in love and life, Kel. You just have to trust your instincts and make the most of every God given day."

Never had a truer word been spoken. Kelly of all people knew the truth of it.

She swallowed the lump in her throat, cupped Lucy's cheek, and kissed her on the lips.

Overwhelmed by a sudden rush of emotion, Kelly blinked back tears. "There you go again."

"Huh?" Lucy furrowed her brow.

"You, stealing my breath away."

Whatever Kelly had done to deserve such a wonderful, intelligent, and loving woman, was beyond her. But she would heed Lucy's words and enjoy every minute they spent together.

The distant rumble of a vehicle grew louder.

They both froze.

With her heart hammering in her chest, Kelly met Lucy's wide-eyed gaze and held a finger to her lips.

The crunch of tyres on gravel was unmistakable.

"Shit, that car's heading this way."

Slowly, as if the slightest sound would alert someone to their secret cubby-hole, Kelly uncurled her legs and climbed to her feet. Once she had her jeans on and Lucy had secured the towel around her body, they huddled close and made a beeline for the riverbed, and their clothes.

A heavy silence hung in the air as they quickly dressed. Once they were clad in the clothes they'd arrived in, Lucy exhaled a relieved sigh. Kelly let out a nervous giggle, Lucy snorted, and within minutes they were both laughing.

"I think we've had enough excitement for one day." Kelly slung the backpack over her shoulder. "Let's get out of here."

Lucy stared at the dense foliage. "What if we come

face to face with someone on the other side of the blackberry bushes?"

Kelly shrugged. "So what? We've been for a swim."

After a beat, Lucy relaxed and winked. "Swimming in lust."

Giddy with happiness, Kelly stepped in front of Lucy and parted the blackberry vines. "Follow me."

"Always." Came from over her shoulder.

That one simple word wrapped around Kelly's heart and squeezed tight.

Chapter 22

The following week was bittersweet for Kelly. One minute she was flying high, the next she crashed and burned. However, the highs surpassed the lows and kept her buoyant.

As much as she understood, and respected Lucy's need for discretion, keeping their relationship on the downlow was proving harder than she'd anticipated.

Work kicked Kelly's arse. The best thing about that was Friday arrived in record time. Just as she was about to leave for the day she was summoned to Jennifer's office.

"The boss wants to see you." Jacinta grabbed the dishcloth out of Kelly's hand. "She didn't look happy, perhaps she's going to give you a DCM slip."

Not at all concerned, Kelly dried her hands on a towel and shook her head. "I don't work Mondays, so I hardly think she'll give me a Don't Come Monday—

you're fired—slip."

Jacinta jutted out her bottom lip. "Spoilsport, you're no fun."

Although Kelly put on a brave face, her mind raced as she bounded up the stairs. Perhaps there was some truth in what Jacinta said. Kelly couldn't imagine what. She'd arrived at work on time every day, and hadn't had any customer complaints, at least not that she was aware of.

Jennifer hadn't shown her face all day yesterday, and Kelly had kept the ship afloat. The knot in her stomach tightened. Had something happened to Jennifer's mum? God, Kelly didn't want to deal with that last thing on a Friday, but if Jennifer needed a shoulder she would offer her one.

She knew first-hand the pain of being avoided by people who didn't know what to say during a time of grief. She also knew often a shoulder meant more than any words.

Taking a deep breath, Kelly tapped on the door.

"It's open." The tone of her boss's voice, all business, gave away nothing.

The flowery scent of Jennifer's perfume was the first thing that hit Kelly as she stepped into the small room.

The second thing that hit her was an image of Lucy on her hands and knees. Kelly bit the inside of her cheek to suppress a grin.

Using her pen like a pointer, Jennifer indicated to the chair in front of her desk. "Sit."

The old wooden seat groaned as Kelly sat making her feel like she'd gained ten pounds. She really needed to stop eating takeaways, but Nicole was rarely home these days and cooking for one sucked.

The impulse to tap her fingers when the silence stretched out made Kelly antsy. To avoid doing so, she hitched her thighs up and tucked her hands underneath.

Finally, Jennifer stopped shuffling papers around and locked eyes with Kelly. "You know I drive down your street on my way home some nights, don't you?"

More confused than ever, Kelly frowned. Surely her boss hadn't called her into her office to discuss her driving habits. Many motorists used Knowles Street as a bypass to avoid heavy traffic.

"No, I didn't." Kelly shrugged, unsure what the big

deal was.

"I went that way on Wednesday." Jennifer gave Kelly a pointed look that as good as said, "you know where I'm going with this?"

Having no clue, Kelly flicked her mind back to Wednesday night. The memory made her heart flutter. She'd been home, Lucy had spent the night. Kelly shook her head before a silly grin overtook her face.

When the reality of what Jennifer was implying hit home, Kelly's mouth fell open, hanging slack as if it had come unhinged.

Jennifer slowly nodded. "You had a visitor. I recognized the car, and face."

Certain her personal life and who she chose to spend her free time with had nothing to do with her boss, Kelly's nostrils flared. "And?"

"If I'm not mistaken, it was the woman who audited the business. The woman whom I entrusted you with."

"I've known Lucy for a while." Kelly held her chin high. "I'm seeing her again tonight. Not that it's any of your business. Why don't you cut to the chase and tell me what this is really about?"

Stunned by the words tumbling out of her mouth, unbidden, Kelly broke out in a cold sweat. Had she lost her mind? If her job wasn't on the line before, it surely was now.

"Don't forget who you're talking to, Kelly," Jennifer's voice carried a warning, but her expression remained warm. "Need I remind you, you're still on my dime?"

As quickly as the boxing gloves had come out, all the fight went out of Kelly. Jennifer had always treated her with respect and she deserved the same in return, even if Kelly was confused as all get out. "

"Sorry, that was out of line."

Jennifer accepted her apology with a sharp nod.

"I don't know how much Lucy told you about the audit. More specifically what came to light."

Heat prickled up Kelly's spine. Lucy hadn't disclosed a word of her findings. Rather than react, she clenched her jaw.

"Not much if the scowl on your face is anything to go by."

"Correct," Kelly replied, not trusting herself to utter

more than a single word.

A smile softened Jennifer's features. It also drew Kelly's attention to the wrinkles around her eyes. Jennifer looked tired. On closer inspection, she looked downright rung out.

"How's your mum?" Kelly asked.

"Not good."

Without elaborating, Jennifer got right back to business. "I just want you to know, I'd never intentionally underpay an employee." She cleared her throat. "Minimum wage went up right around the time Mum first got sick."

Feeling awkward, like her boss wanted to be absolved of a cardinal sin, Kelly squirmed in her seat. "You don't have to explain yourself to me."

"Please, I need you to hear me out. Despite my mind being elsewhere these days, it's something I never should've overlooked. It also brought to my attention, I can't do this on my own. For the business to continue to thrive, I need a 2IC.

Unfamiliar with the acronym, Kelly frowned. "Huh?"

"Second in charge." Jennifer glanced up then back to her notepad. "Ben has been given a pay increase and back paid the shortfall. I've come to rely on you, Kelly, to be my eyes and ears, to ensure the place runs smoothly during my absence."

"Thank you." A mixture of pride and embarrassment washed over Kelly. She prided herself on doing a good job, and while it felt good to have her boss recognise that, receiving praise gracefully never came easily to Kelly. It made her feel conceited, a trait she detested in others.

"I want you to start inducting new employees, carry out monthly audits to ensure all files, food handling certificates, tax declarations, and pay rates are current. It's a big responsibility and your pay will increase to reflect that. What do you say? Are you up for the challenge?"

Fighting back the insane desire to jump up, fist pump the air, and do a happy dance, Kelly stayed seated.

Besides she wasn't entirely happy with how the conversation had gone. She scrunched her face up. "I'll have to think about it."

Wondering if she'd gone insane to even be considering the offer, Kelly soldiered on. "You questioned my friend's integrity, whether or not we'd discussed your business, which felt like a slur on my character."

A broad smile split her boss's face in two. "I knew I'd made the right choice in offering you the position. I admire your spunk, Kelly." She underlined something on her notepad then dropped the pen. "I wasn't questioning Lucy's integrity. However, most couples chat about work, and keep confidences, so I wouldn't have been surprised, or angry."

"Whoa, wait a minute." Kelly held up a hand. "Who said anything about being a couple? Like I said, I've known her for a while. We're friends." Technically, it wasn't a lie.

Jennifer clucked her tongue. "I might be getting old, but I'm not stupid. You've been walking around here on cloud nine. I haven't seen you smile so much since you broke up with that other woman."

The way Jennifer referred to Paula as the other

woman made Kelly cringe.

Jennifer's gaze flicked to Kelly's legs and Kelly became acutely aware that she was perched on the edge of the seat, the lip biting into her backside. She had no memory of shuffling forward.

"Look at you. You're champing at the bit to get out of here. I'm not going to push for more, but don't lie to me about your relationship."

"She lives with my ex," Kelly said, a simple explanation of why she couldn't shout out that they were dating.

"Oh." Jennifer nodded her understanding. "That complicates matters."

A humourless snort burst out of Kelly. "You think?"

Jennifer stood and crossed the office. "You're off the clock, go make the most of your weekend." She shut the window and pulled the curtains, blocking out the late afternoon sun.

"What's said in this room stays in here. Your secret's safe with me, Kelly."

"Thanks." Kelly headed for the door, doing an awkward walk-run. She didn't want to seem too anxious to flee. Her boss had just offered her a promotion, for goodness sake.

Crap.

Kelly stopped in the doorway. "By the way, boss."

"Yes." Jennifer closed the lid on her briefcase.

"I accept your offer."

They smiled, a silent acknowledgement of mutual respect passing between them.

With nothing more to be said, Kelly bolted down the stairs, jumped on her bike, and gunned it for home. She grinned the entire way.

The minute she got inside, she sent out a group text to Steve, Nicole, Ashleigh, Jo, and her mum to inform them of her job promotion.

She couldn't wait to share the news with Lucy, in person.

Chapter 23

Sunday morning, Kelly awoke to the sun streaming through a gap in her curtains, the back of a soft body moulded to her front. Relaxed and content, she breathed in Lucy's scent and kissed the back of her head.

Lucy stirred, mumbled something incoherent, and burrowed into her pillow.

Reluctant to move, but also excited about the day ahead, Kelly flipped the covers back. The sight of Lucy's baby doll negligee bunched around her waist made Kelly's breath hitch. The tantalizing image was almost enough to make her reconsider their plans.

"What time is it?" Lucy grumbled, pulling the sheet back up.

"Time to hit the road." Kelly rolled out of bed and yanked the blankets off.

"Oh shoot, yeah." Lucy shot up in bed, rubbing sleep from her eyes. "I almost forgot. You short-circuited my brain last night." She flashed Kelly a wicked grin.

The memory of making love into the wee hours of the morning sparked a flame in Kelly's belly.

Shower, she needed a cool shower.

Stark naked, happy for the first time in a long time that Nicole had abandoned her on a Saturday night, Kelly gathered up some clean clothes and tossed Lucy her overnight bag.

"You can join me in the bathroom or take a few minutes to wake up properly and have second dibs. Come to think of it," Kelly said, "That might be a better idea, or we'll never get out of here."

A knowing smile lit up Lucy's features.

On impulse, Kelly bounded across the room, cupped the back of her head, and planted a chaste kiss on Lucy's lips.

"See you in the kitchen after you've showered. I'll have coffee and toast waiting."

"Aye, aye, captain." Lucy saluted.

As strong as the pull was to pin Lucy to the bed, Kelly walked away. "You'll keep."

***

An hour later, the sign to Himatangi Beach came into view. Lucy pulled to a stop at the T intersection, checked for traffic and turned left.

"I love the beach," Kelly said.

Keeping her eyes on the road, Lucy flicked down her sun-visor. "Oh, really? When was the last time you were there?"

"Shit, did I say that out loud?" Kelly hadn't meant to, she'd rather talk about Lucy than herself, and in all honesty, she didn't want to answer the question.

Hoping to dodge a bullet, Kelly returned fire. "What about you, do you like the sea? New Plymouth has some lovely beaches, right?"

One thing Kelly had discovered about Lucy was that six months ago, she'd relocated from New Plymouth to Palmerston North, for work.

"The beaches are gorgeous. I miss building sandcastles with my nieces and nephews."

How many were there, four or five? "Remind me again how many you have?"

"Five." A warm smile spread across Lucy's face. "My eldest brother has two boys and a girl, and my younger brother, or should I say the middle child, has a boy and a girl. My parents spoil the kids rotten."

"I'll bet." Kelly smiled, happy to hear about Lucy's family, to see her eyes light up when she talked about them.

"Now it's your turn to answer my question, Kelly."

Shit.

So much for deflecting.

A knot formed in Kelly's stomach as she searched for the right words, the right tone, light and breezy or regretful? On one hand she regretted what happened, but on the other, how could she when it led to where she was? Well on her way to falling head over heels in love.

"It was the day after Paula's party." She flipped down the sun visor.

"Which one?" Lucy asked nonchalantly. "I mean, which party."

Kelly wiped her sweaty palms on her dress. She really didn't want to spell it out. Shame washed over her every time she thought about her actions that night.

When Kelly took too long to reply, Lucy glanced in

her direction.

Taking one look at Kelly's unsmiling face, Lucy mouthed, "Oh, that party."

Finding her voice, Kelly replied, "Yeah, that party. I was a wreck, I didn't know what to do. I needed to think. The sea helps clear my mind, so I headed straight for the nearest beach, Himatangi."

"You, Ms cool, calm, and collected, were distraught? Colour me surprised."

Unsure how to respond, Kelly turned the tables. "What did you do the next day?"

"Masturbated." Lucy shrugged like it was a no-brainer.

Unbidden, and totally against her will, a dull ache throbbed between Kelly's legs. Knowing she hadn't left someone scarred for life, quite the opposite according to Lucy's declaration, made Kelly giddy with relief.

"I had nightmares about you, well I didn't know it was you, trying to erase me from your mind, to scrub my scent off you."

"Oh, Kel." Lucy's words were heartfelt. "I'm so sorry. If only I'd had the strength to stop you. But no, I just gave in to the moment…"

No, no, no, no no, no!

Kelly cupped her ears, shocked that Lucy was taking responsibility for Kelly's actions. "It wasn't your fault, Lucy. I went down on you without your consent, and it fuckin' kills me knowing that!"

Gravel kicked up and the car came to an abrupt stop when Lucy skidded to a halt on the side of the road. She pulled Kelly's hands from the dashboard where she'd braced herself.

"Listen to me, what happened wasn't premeditated. Yes, the outcome could've been ugly, but unless you call what we have together ugly, you need to build a bridge, cross it, and spank my arse."

Getting off her pity-pot, Kelly cupped Lucy's cheek and tried a different tact. "Did I ever tell you that night's the best thing that ever happened to me?"

"Better." Lucy shoved the car in gear, checked for traffic, and continued on her merry way, grinning from ear to ear.

Kelly marvelled at their contrasting personalities. When Kelly needed grounding, Lucy was her anchor.

When Lucy needed guidance, Kelly took the lead.

A car whizzed by, overtaking them at some ungodly speed. Kelly's heart jumped into her throat. "What a fucking idiot."

Lucy slowed and moved to the side, letting the guy sneak back into their lane before he had a head-on collision with a truck heading in their direction. The truck driver blasted his horn and shook his fist.

"Someone's in a hurry to arrive dead on time. You okay?" Lucy squeezed Kelly's thigh.

"Yay, I trust your driving. It's the other tossers that worry me."

Ironically, for one of the straightest stretches of road in the lower North Island, the Himatangi-Foxton straight had seen more than its fair share of fatalities.

Shortly after eleven, Kelly texted Jo. "Hey, Sis. We've just driven past the Ferry terminal. See you soon."

Jo's reply was instantaneous. "Cool, we're already here, will meet you in the foyer."

Warmth spread through Kelly's chest. She couldn't wait to see her sister, to meet her boyfriend, Tim, and to introduce them to Lucy.

"Look at you, all smiley blue eyes over there," Lucy said as she indicated left and exited the motorway.

Kelly rubbed her hands together. "I know, I feel like a teenager on her first trip to the big city. Have you been to Te Papa before?"

"Nope, I normally avoid Wellington like the plague. I hate the rat race, and I dodge politics at all costs."

"Hey, just because Parliament's here doesn't mean everyone talks…"

Noticing the huge smirk on Lucy's face, Kelly stopped midsentence. In the next heartbeat, the rest of what Lucy said registered. Lucy had offered to drive to Wellington, despite her dislike of navigating the city.

She reached across the car and trailed a finger down Lucy's cheek. "Thank you."

Pulling to a stop at a red light, Lucy glanced at Kelly. "You're welcome. Being with you is no hardship, Kel. I'd drive through Auckland if I had you by my side."

"I promise never to do that to you. When I take you on a romantic getaway to the Sky Tower, I'll whisk you away in my private jet."

Even though Kelly laughed it off as a joke, an idea took root and blossomed. She didn't have access to a jet, but she had savings and could pay for airfares.

Chapter 24

After finding a park, which was no easy feat due to many parking buildings being condemned after the 2016 earthquakes that rocked Wellington city, Kelly and Lucy strolled hand and hand to Te Papa Museum.

Although it wasn't Kelly's first visit to the centre, the stunning architecture still robbed her of breath: six levels of high ceilings, gleaming glass, bronze walls, suspended skeletons of extinct mammals, and exhibits for as far as the eye could see.

"Wow," Lucy said.

"Beautiful, isn't it?"

"Scary." Lucy stared straight ahead.

Following her line of sight, Kelly took in the imposing 3.6-metre-tall trolls. William, Tom, and Bert. Infamous for greeting guests on the red carpet at the World Premiere of *The Hobbit*.

"They won't hurt you, promise. They're made of

fibreglass."

"Not them, silly." Lucy turned to Kelly, concerned etched across her face. "I wouldn't want to be in here if an earthquake hits."

"Don't worry." Kelly was quick to put Lucy's mind at ease. "I did my homework. Te Papa's built on one hundred and fifty-two isolators to protect it from movement." Kelly tapped Lucy on the nose. "And, I'll have you know, this massive building was constructed with enough steel to stretch from Wellington to Sydney?"

"Is that right, little Miss Encyclopaedia?"

Before Kelly could reply, she was almost knocked off her feet when Jo slammed into her and wrapped her in a bear hug. "About time you got here."

Peering over Jo's shoulder, Kelly locked eyes with a young man sporting an enigmatic smile and hair the colour of oranges.

"Don't say it," Jo whispered in Kelly's ear.

"He's handsome." Kelly squeezed Jo tighter, ecstatic her sister, who liked to joke about carrot-tops, had matured enough to see beyond appearances.

"He treats me like a princess." The smile in Jo's voice was contagious.

It would seem Jo was as smitten with her beau as Kelly was with Lucy.

"Your girlfriend's got sexy eyes."

"Your boyfriend's looking at us funny."

"He probably thinks we're talking about him."

"We are." Jo snorted.

Aware they had an audience, and there were introductions to be made, Kelly stepped back.

"Hi, Tim. I'm the good-looking sister." Kelly winked at Jo who mouthed *dream on*.

"Nice to meet you." Tim took her proffered hand and rather than shake it, brought it to his lips. His kiss was soft and brief, the gesture fucking adorable.

"The pleasure's all mine. Jo's told me so much about you."

"All good, I hope." She glared playfully at Jo.

Ignoring the sisterly banter, and clearly comfortable around new people, Tim extended a hand to Lucy. "And you must be Lucy?"

"Indeed." Lucy waggled her fingers, her expression

saying I expect the same treatment.

With a slow bow, Tim kissed her hand then straightened and draped an arm around Jo's shoulders.

"Is he always this charming?" Kelly asked.

"Always," Jo replied, admiration shining in her eyes.

After dragging her gaze off Tim, Jo smiled at Lucy. "Nice to meet you. Kelly wasn't lying, you're a knockout. I'd do you if I swung that way."

"Jo!" Kelly shot daggers at her sister with her eyes.

"Just yanking your chain, Sis. You're so easy to wind up."

Unfazed, Lucy grinned. "Okay, kids. Now that we've got the niceties out of the way, how about we relax?"

There wasn't an ounce of tension between them, but Kelly appreciated the sentiment.

"Where to first?" Jo asked. "Should we start at the top and work our way down, or at the bottom and slowly work our way up?"

"What are we talking about?" Kelly winked.

Tim smirked.

Jo's mouth fell-opened. "Perv."

"What?" Kelly held her arms out, in a 'what'd I say gesture.'

Lucy pinched her butt. "Behave."

Tim offered a third option. "How about we go directly to the café on level four and go from there. I don't know about you ladies, but I'm starving."

***

Three hours later, after a lot of fun, and exhausted from wandering from exhibit to exhibit and absorbing all the information, the foursome found themselves back on level one.

"Anyone want to take a look in the souvenir shop?" Kelly asked.

Jo stepped aside when two young boys barrelled past, waving black and white New Zealand flags high in the air.

"Isn't that kind of lame, buying souvenirs from your own country?" Jo asked.

"I don't know about that," Lucy said. "I used to collect every kind of cow I could get my hands on. Soft toys, figurines, hats, you name it."

"Now—" Jo smirked. "—You have a heifer with long brown hair, big blue eyes, not much of an udder and a nice beefy rump."

Too happy to be pissed off with Jo for inferring Kelly was a cow, much less her colourful and somewhat fitting rendition, Kelly burst out laughing. "Nice description, Sis."

Lucy squeezed Kelly's hand and without missing a beat, returned Jo's cheek. "You and Kelly could be twins, the similarities are startling, don't you think, Tim?"

Tim rubbed the ginger stubble on his chin, looked heavenward and then replied in the safest way possible for a guy with three women staring him down. "I need to use the bathroom, back soon."

As he walked away, the bottom fell out of Kelly's world. One look at the woman storming their way and her happy mood vanished.

Chapter 25

Like a deranged woman on a mission, Paula barrelled her way into the middle of their circle.

"Oh, now it all makes sense." She looked at Kelly and Lucy's joined hands. "How long has it been going on? Under my bloody roof! You have until noon tomorrow to get out," she practically screamed at Lucy. "If I get home and your stuff is still there, polluting my house, I'll have it removed and donated to the Salvation Army."

Anger radiated off Jo in thick waves. "You can't do that."

Ignoring the curious glances shot their way, Kelly put a reassuring hand on her little sister's shoulder. "Don't worry, Paula's full of hot air."

Paula pressed her lips together in a thin, angry line. "Really? Try me."

"Been there, done that, didn't like it," Kelly

deadpanned, delighted when Paula's mouth fell open.

"How dare you. How dare both of you. I treated you with nothing but kindness, and you…" Paula turned her angry glare on Lucy. "You, Lucy. I gave you a roof over your head and you repay me by lying and stealing my girlfriend?"

"I didn't lie to you," Lucy said softly. "And I didn't steal your girlfriend. We didn't start dating until you broke up."

"Oh, I don't doubt that, but I'm sure you were screwing each other well before then. I figured Kelly was getting it from someone else, but never thought to look under my own roof."

Jo tapped Kelly on the shoulder, a mischievous glint in her eyes. "Is she always this obnoxious, Kel? Sheesh, no wonder you never wanted me to meet her."

Anger contorted Paula's features. "Who asked you, pipsqueak?"

Okay that was pushing it.

Reigning in her fury, Kelly spoke in a low, controlled voice. "If you know what's good for you, Paula, you'll walk away. We received your message, and will do your final bidding."

Unbeknown to Paula, she'd done Kelly a favour. Once they got home they'd no longer have to hide their relationship.

Concern gnawed at Kelly's insides when Lucy wouldn't meet her gaze. But she wasn't about to ask what was troubling her while Paula was within earshot.

When Paula's gaze locked on something, or someone, over Kelly's shoulder, the tension that rolled off her was so thick it was palpable.

"There you are, sweetheart."

There was no mistaking the tenor of Colette's voice. Like fingernails on a chalkboard the high-pitched screech made Kelly cringe. She didn't turn around though, it was more entertaining watching the emotions playing out across Paula's face. None of them happy.

Her cheeks turned crimson, whether from anger or embarrassment, Kelly couldn't be sure. Probably both. The fact Colette was now calling her boss sweetheart was almost laughable.

"I told you, I'd meet you in the tearooms." Paula breathed heavily.

Kelly wouldn't have been surprised to see fire burst forth from her nostrils.

"I know, but you've been gone for so long, I started to worry you got lost. It's a big place, you know?" Colette whined like a petulant child.

In that moment, Kelly didn't know who she pitied more, Colette or Paula. On second thoughts, they deserved each other. The thought made Kelly smile.

After a brief stare down with Paula, Colette finally took stock of the three women before her.

Feeling smug, Kelly smirked and waved. Jo and Lucy stood mute.

Ignoring all three of them, Paula held a finger to Colette's lips. "I'll be right there, now go."

"Fine, just make sure you don't give any money to gold digger over there." Acting like the self-entitled bitch she was, Colette poked her tongue out at Kelly then spun on her heels.

The comment bounced off Kelly like a poorly aimed dart. While she didn't doubt Colette had always thought Kelly only dated Paula for her money, she no longer needed to defend herself.

Somewhat proud she'd resisted the urge to call after Colette, "enjoy my leftovers," Kelly took the opportunity to turn the entire debacle back on the person making a scene.

Folding her arms across her chest, Kelly quirked an eyebrow. "Pot, kettle, black? How long have you two been cosy?"

"It's not like that." Paula looked at the floor, her bravado gone.

The fact Paula's obnoxious P.A. was now calling her sweetheart suggested otherwise.

"Tell it to someone who cares."

Kelly entwined her fingers with Lucy's and linked her other arm with Jo's. "Come on, ladies, there are more entertaining exhibits to see than this...this…" Kelly trailed off leaving Paula to fill in the blank.

***

After nabbing Tim on their way past the bathroom, Kelly put her arm around Lucy's waist and guided them toward the ground floor.

Tim walked with a stoop, his ear close to Jo's mouth as she no doubt gave him a rundown of the drama he'd narrowly avoided.

The good-natured humour they'd all enjoyed had been replaced by a dark gloomy cloud. One minute they'd been exploring the wonders of the world, the next a volcano had erupted and spewed shit on them.

"You okay?" Kelly squeezed Lucy's side, pulling her closer.

"No." Lucy shook her head. "But I will be."

Her sad smile punched Kelly in the gut. Fuck Paula and the high and mighty horse she rode in on.

Back outside, loitering around the front entrance, Tim spoke first. "I have a work van. If you need a hand to move, I can follow you back to Palmerston."

A strong desire to launch herself at Tim rocked Kelly to her core. "You really are sweet, aren't you?"

He shrugged.

Jo burrowed into his side. "He is."

Looking at her little sister, all grown up, Kelly swallowed the lump in her throat. If one good thing came out of today, it was knowing that Jo had met a good man.

Lucy let out a humourless chuckle. "That's a lovely offer, Tim. The thing is, I have no idea where I'm moving to."

The penny finally dropped, and Kelly could've kicked herself. No wonder Lucy had looked so distraught. At the time, Kelly's mind had immediately flicked to the fact Paula had done them a favour. She'd overlooked the bigger picture. Lucy was soon to be homeless.

Actually, no she wasn't, not if Kelly could help it.

"You can stay with me." Kelly beamed, feeling proud of herself, and excited by the prospect.

Jo's eyes lit up. "Great idea."

Lucy's piercing gaze bore into Kelly. "Don't you think we should talk about that first?"

"Oh yeah," Jo said, sounding as flat as Kelly felt.

Even though what Lucy said made sense, Kelly couldn't deny the disappointment that weighed heavily on her shoulders. Her emotions were all over the place.

The next thought made Kelly's stomach lurch. What if Lucy moved back to New Plymouth? Surely she wouldn't.

"How about Mum's place?" Jo asked.

"That could work," Kelly replied. "Mum would love the company."

"I couldn't impose on your mother." Lucy shook her head, her black hair fanning out like a raven about to take flight.

On second thoughts, perhaps it wasn't such a bright idea. Kelly's mum appeared to have come to enjoy her own space, to such an extent that a few weeks ago she'd asked Kelly to text ahead of time if she planned on visiting.

At the time, Kelly hadn't thought much of it. Now though… No, she wouldn't go there, not while there were more pressing matters to take care of.

Zeroing in on something over Kelly's shoulder, Jo's eyes went wide. "Don't look now."

A sense of Déjà vu crawled up Kelly's spine. However, unlike the night Lucy had uttered those same words, Kelly didn't turn around. She didn't need to, she could sense Paula's presence.

Craning her neck, Lucy glanced behind them. "Shit,

here we go again." After what felt like forever but was only a matter of seconds, Lucy exhaled a breath, shoulders relaxing. "It's okay, they've turned left, toward the carpark. At a guess, not only did Paula piss on our parade, but she's ruined her day out as well."

"Damn, and I thought I could turn scarlet," Tim said, looking equal parts appalled and amused. "That woman's angry scowl could give a vampire squid a run for its money."

"Say what?" Lucy scrunched up her face.

"Another time." Tim grabbed Jo's hand. "You two need to talk. How about we take a rain check on the cable car until next time you visit. Because there will be a next time. You'll get through this." He spoke with such conviction, Kelly's spirits lifted.

"Yes, we will."

Jo launched herself at Kelly, wrapping her in a fierce embrace. "Love you, Sis."

"Love you too, Jo-Jo." Kelly stroked Jo's long mousey brown hair. Lucy hadn't been far off the mark when she'd quipped that Jo and Kelly looked alike. They had the same blue eyes as their dad and the same thick mop of hair as their mum.

With a final squeeze, Jo extricated herself from Kelly, turned to Lucy, and held out her arms. Lucy stepped into the embrace like a lifelong friend.

Watching them hug made Kelly tear up. She couldn't recall Jo ever hugging one of her girlfriends, much less be anything more than cordial.

After bidding Tim and Jo farewell, Kelly's smile faded. She took Lucy's hands in both of hers. Her expression matched Kelly's, anxious, but whereas Kelly's hands were dry, Lucy's were hot and clammy.

"Nerves getting the better of you?"

Lucy smiled, but it looked forced, painful even. She pulled her hands free and rubbed her palms together as if the friction would dry them out.

"It's hot." She looked away, and Kelly let it go.

In spite of being pissed off that their day had turned to shit, she was determined to stay positive for Lucy's sake.

"Everything will work out. I'm a firm believer in the saying, 'When one door closes, another opens'."

The twinkle in Lucy's eyes made Kelly feel self-conscious. She wasn't normally one for making sentimental declarations. But then again, her entire perception of what a relationship was all about had changed.

"Nice analogy, Kel."

"Oh." Kelly chuckled, finally understanding why Lucy looked amused. "I meant when a door figuratively closes, not literally."

"I know." Lucy fiddled with her shoulder bag. "I planned on moving out within a month or two anyway. I won't miss all the social hob-knobbing."

"See, you're already finding positives. Now give me a genuine happy smile." Kelly put a finger on each side of Lucy's mouth and pulled her lips up.

"Stop it." Grinning, Lucy smacked Kelly's hand away.

"Better." Kelly's heart inflated, like it always did when Lucy flashed her a smile, one that reached her eyes and lit up her face.

Kelly's phone chirped. For a minute, she considered ignoring it. Then her mind ran rampant. It could be Jo, her mum, Nicole, or worse, Paula.

Lucy started walking toward the carpark. "You gonna get that?"

Kelly fell into step beside her. "I should, it might be Mum."

It was Jo. "You've got a good woman there. Let me know what happens, I'm worried about you. About you both."

A huge smile spread across Kelly's face. On impulse, she grabbed Lucy by the arm and yanked her to an abrupt stop.

"Oops, sorry," Kelly apologized to a scowling couple as they stepped around her.

"Here." She shoved her phone into Lucy's hand. "Read this."

Eyeing Kelly curiously, Lucy shielded the screen from the sun. Her frown morphed into a silly grin. "That's sweet. But I don't want her to worry about me."

Across the road, a green sedan made a hasty exit from the service station leaving a puff of exhaust fumes in its wake.

Lucy wrinkled her nose and coughed. "I hate the smell of petrol."

"I kinda like it," Kelly confessed.

"You like petrol fumes but hate petrol heads. Got it," Lucy said with a decisive nod.

Even under duress she was on form. It was another trait of her personality that Kelly found alluring.

"Let's grab a cold drink for the road. We have a two-hour drive to figure out what to do, okay?"

"Sure." Lucy punched the button by the zebra crossing.

A breeze ruffled the bottom of her slacks and drew Kelly's attention to her strappy sandals. Kelly couldn't say she was a foot person, but Lucy had beautiful feet, long and elegant, like the slope of her neck.

"What are you looking at me like that for?" Lucy narrowed her gaze.

"Like what." Kelly feigned innocence.

Lucy leaned in close and whispered in Kelly's ear, her warm breath sending tingles up Kelly's spine. "Like you want to eat me."

"Oh, that. That's my normal look around you."

The little green man flashed, and the walk sign dinged. They crossed the street, swept along with the crowd like a piece of driftwood floating downstream.

Chapter 26

Half an hour later, they were well on their way home. As the traffic thinned so did the tension radiating off Lucy.

"You really don't like the motorway, do you?" Kelly asked.

"No. I feel like I have to have eyes in the back of my head. Not only that, but with all the one-way streets, if I'd miss a turnoff we would've been screwed."

"And not in a good way," Kelly mumbled.

Well aware time was of the essence, Kelly was impressed that Lucy stuck to the speed limit, a hundred kilometres.

She had no clue how much furniture Lucy owned or how long it would take to move it, but she did know where it could be stored if need be. Certain it was another thing Lucy would argue about, she didn't bring it up right then.

"Speaking of being screwed," Kelly said. "You told me why it didn't work out with the guy you dated. What about the women?"

"Woman," Lucy said, her wary gaze on the Sunday drivers weaving in and out of traffic like they had a death wish.

"Huh?" Kelly asked, sounding like a moron, and wondering what Lucy had meant by the singular word woman.

Her mind flicked back to the conversation she had with Lucy on their drive from the bar back to her flat. Kelly clearly recalled saying, "You've slept with both men and women, right?" And Lucy's reply hit her with just as much clarity. *"One man, two women. But who's counting."*

"Is that steam I see?"

Taken aback, Kelly whipped her head around and looked out the passenger window. Waves crashed against rocks and sprayed high into the air.

"It's mist." Kelly bit back a smile.

Rather than look offended, Lucy reached over and tugged her earlobe. "I meant you, dummy. Smoke's practically pouring out of your ears. Tell me what's burning up that overactive brain of yours?"

"This isn't about me and my inquisitive mind, Lucy. I shouldn't have asked."

"I don't mind answering your questions. The conversation's a pleasant distraction. We can't do much until we arrive back in Palmy. So, hit me with it."

"I'm sure you said you'd been with two women. But you said woman like it'd only been one." Suddenly feeling shy, Kelly's cheeks heated. "Not that it's any of my business."

"Don't play co…"

"La, la, la, la, la." Kelly plugged her ears, delighted when Lucy burst out laughing.

Between them, they were doing a wonderful job of avoiding the bigger issue.

"It was one, it's now two. You're the third person I've had sex with."

Shock and honour warred within Kelly.

Lucy gave her a sheepish look. "This is probably going to sound conceited." She turned back to the road. "I know I'm easy on the eye, some might even say attractive."

"Fucking gorgeous," Kelly interrupted, unable to contain herself.

"Thank you, but at times, that's been a curse. It brings new meaning to pubs being meat markets. It's a rare occasion that I can enjoy a drink with a friend or work colleague without being hit on. Most people assume I've been around the block a time or two."

She let out a self-deprecating laugh. "I'm sick of hearing, oh you're twenty-nine and single, not ready to settle down yet, too busy playing the field?"

Feeling like she'd opened a can of worms, Kelly was tempted to apologize. The thought of Lucy accusing her of being the C word again, stopped her.

"What about the other woman? Did she spank your arse? Tie you up?" Kelly held her breath wanting to hear the answer, yet terrified of how it would make her feel.

A snort burst out of Lucy. She slapped the steering wheel as if Kelly had just told the funniest joke ever. "Good God, no."

Amused, and somewhat confused, Kelly quirked an

eyebrow. "What's so funny? I thought you loved being restrained? To the point you've tied yourself up?"

"My ex, Candy..."

Beating Kelly to the punch, Lucy waggled a finger. "No, she wasn't a porn star, far from it, unless you're talking about a star who does nothing but lay flat on her back."

"I don't mind that so much." Kelly put a hand on Lucy's thigh, loving the flex of her muscle when she stepped on the clutch and shifted down a gear.

The car slowed as they crept up a steep hill. The sea had given way to paddocks of cattle grazing, sheep on one farm, cows on the next, and the odd horse here and there.

"Right, but you like being in charge, and you give as well as take," Lucy said. "When it came to sex, Candy was all take, she'd spread her legs and say, Oh, eat me, baby, eat me."

Kelly snorted. "She didn't."

"No, not those words, but you get the point and those words were fitting considering her name."

Indeed, it certainly brought new meaning to eating

candy.

"When I suggested she restrain me, Candy chewed her lip and said, but then how are you going to please me?"

"That's sad," Kelly said, feeling Lucy's pain. Being sexually incompatible, unfulfilled, sucked.

While some didn't think sex was the be-all and end-all of a relationship, it went a long way toward making lovers just that, lovers.

"How many women have you bedded, Kelly?"

Just before Kelly replied a bug splattered against the windscreen.

When one of her father's favourite jokes sprung to mind, Kelly snickered. "What's the last thing that went through that bug's mind?"

The corner of Lucy's mouth twitched. "Its asshole." Her eye roll confirmed Kelly's joke was old and lame.

She sprayed window washer and flicked on the wipers, effectively smearing the mess. "Don't think that shit's going to stop you from answering my question either."

"Now who's being the witty one?" Kelly quirked an

eyebrow and Lucy shot her a playful smile.

"Spill."

Unable to avoid the question any longer, and not at all ashamed of her past, Kelly shrugged. "A handful," she paused before adding, "Or two, but in the words of a wise, sexy lady, who's counting?"

Even as she said the words, Kelly's brain did the maths, an average of two women a year could hardly be considered bedhopping.

When Lucy didn't reply right away, a pang of anxiety clutched Kelly's insides and short-circuited her brain. Without thought, she blurted out, "Don't worry, I'm clean. So are you."

The stunned look on Lucy's face, eyes wide, mouth open, made Kelly recoil. A sickening wave of nausea washed over her. If only she could somehow magically take back the last three words.

"See what I mean?" Lucy asked, the comment further knocking Kelly off kilter.

"No," Kelly said softly, unsure if she'd heard right and anxious to clear things up.

Lucy pointed at her face, drawing Kelly's attention

to her dark complexion.

"Like everyone else, you assume attractive means player. You could've just asked, and I would've told you I'm clean, Kelly. Perhaps I should be angry with myself for being remiss and not asking the same of you."

Bristling, Kelly clenched her jaw. Lucy's words felt like a judgement, as though she thought Kelly was diseased, which was ridiculous considering Kelly had just told her she was clean.

Nothing like having the shoe put on the other foot.

Before Kelly's mood grew any darker, Lucy chucked her under the chin.

"Cheer up, chicka. I was testing out what Jo said. Apparently, she was right."

Still not trusting herself to speak, Kelly drew her brows together.

The amused grin Lucy flashed her was downright infectious. Kelly bit the inside of her cheek, determined not to return the smile until she knew what Lucy found so funny.

"What, exactly, did my little sister say?"

"That you're easy to wind up. Relax, Kelly. You slept with someone, you didn't know who, it made sense you got tested."

Annoyed with herself for taking the bait, yet relieved that Lucy hadn't taken offense, Kelly huffed out a breath. "You're positively evil. Do you know what happens to brats?"

Lucy shot her a sassy sideways glance. "They get punished?" She turned her gaze back to the road. "Oh, fuck."

"You said it." Kelly chuckled.

"Not that." The car slowed.

Unnerved, Kelly dragged her gaze off Lucy's horror-stricken face; lips pursed, brow furrowed.

A tangle of metal filled her vision. Red, white, and blue lights flashed. An ambulance sat in the middle of the chaos. People milled around on the side of the road. Police scribbled on pads, speaking to bystanders.

The nose of a white sedan was buried in the driver's door of a red sports car, its busted radiator shooting steam into the air. The drivers of both cars had to be in a bad way.

As they drew nearer, the car inching along slowly, dread churned in Kelly's belly. Hoping against hope she was wrong, Kelly strained her eyes trying to read the licence plate. The letter's P A U 1 A confirmed her worst fears.

A vice wrapped around her heart and squeezed. Despite having entertained thoughts of doing Paula bodily harm if she hadn't backed off at Te Papa, in the bright light of day, Kelly never wanted to see her come to physical harm.

"Fuck. That's Paula's car," Lucy said, her voice a strangled whisper.

"Yay." Kelly nodded. "Pullover."

Chapter 27

The minute the car came to a stop, they jumped out, shot each other a 'this could be bad' look, and took off running.

A gurney disappeared into the back of the ambulance before Kelly could get a look at the face, or body. A medic stood with her arm draped across a woman's shoulders, body trembling, posture stooped.

The mid-thigh showy dress Kelly had glimpsed only hours ago, left no room for doubt as to the identity of the sobbing woman.

In the midst of disaster, any ill feelings Kelly harboured for Colette vanished. A potent cocktail of adrenaline, despair, and compassion flooded every cell of Kelly's being as she closed in on the macabre scene.

A traffic officer stood in the middle of the road, directing traffic around the crash site. Rubberneckers hung their heads out of windows trying to get a closer look. A perfectly normal reaction that angered Kelly nonetheless.

She wanted to hold up a curtain and tell them to stop gawking. Or better yet, to come closer and get a puncture when they ran over all the shattered glass. That'd teach them.

"Slow down." Lucy tugged on Kelly's hand.

"What if she's…." Kelly trailed off, a pain tearing through her chest. "I never wanted her dead. You have to believe me."

Lucy gave her a sad smile. "I know, hun. I know."

Not willing to step up to the rear of the ambulance, Kelly approached Colette. "Hey," she said softly, trying not to spook her.

"Kelly? Oh, thank goodness you're here."

Before Kelly could process if she'd heard right, Colette was in her arms, holding onto Kelly as if her life depended on it.

Emotion flooded Kelly, along with the overwhelming grief that had torn her apart when her father was ripped from her life.

Behind Colette, Lucy stood talking to the medic.

Kelly could make out the tone, bleak, but not the words. Lucy scrunched up her brow, nodded, glanced at the ambulance, pursed her lips and shook her head.

Getting herself under control, Colette stepped back. Black rings circled her eyes and she had a massive bruise on the left side of her head. She gave Kelly a watery smile, swiped her eyes, and wiped snot bubbles from her nose.

"Paula's a fighter. She'll make it. She has too."

When the reality of what Colette said hit home, Kelly's knees buckled with relief.

The siren whirred, and Colette jumped like she'd been shot. Her frantic gaze flicked to the medic standing nearby.

"Please, can I see her, before they take her away, just for a minute?"

"Sorry, ma'am. The elder gent, his wife, and your friend, all need urgent medical attention. We'll only get in the way."

A police officer crossed the road moving at a good clip. He nodded at Lucy and Kelly. "Ladies."

He turned to Colette. "Let's go, I'll give you a lift to

the hospital. You too, Jan."

Ah, so that was the medic's name. With her hefty bust, and mass of dark curly hair, Kelly expected her to have a name like Shirley or Curly.

The haunted look in Colette's eyes tugged at Kelly's heartstrings, and, apparently, Lucy's too.

"She can come with us," Lucy said, looking to Kelly for confirmation.

Kelly nodded.

Colette stared at the ground. "I'd like that, thank you."

Gone was the condescending rude P.A. Kelly had come to know. Funny how grief humbled a person.

The medic put a hand on Colette's shoulders and studied her face. "You still need to be checked for any internal injuries. I'll only let you go with these ladies if they are going straight to the hospital."

"We are," Lucy and Kelly replied in unison.

***

For the first ten minutes after leaving the crash site, a depressing silence hung in the air. Lucy occasionally hummed along to the radio, but the tension was so thick it was palpable.

Shocking the hell out of Kelly, Colette ended the standoff.

"Was that your sister? At Te Papa."

Unsettled by the question, Kelly glanced at Lucy. Lucy gave her a don't ask me look.

"Yes," Kelly said, not willing to give more information than necessary.

"She's very pretty."

"I love her to bits."

"I could tell, even though I was being an arse."

Squashing the urge to spit out the words, *you said it*, Kelly kept her eyes on the road. Sun glimmered off the tar seal, sending up a hazy wave.

"What about you, Colette?" Lucy said. "Any brothers or sisters? I've never heard you talk about your family."

After an agonizing pause, Colette finally replied, "I don't have any, family I mean."

Colette couldn't have been any older than Paula, possibly younger. How was it possible for someone in their early thirties to have no family?

Perhaps she didn't mean it in the literal sense, maybe she'd shunned them, or been shunned.

"By choice or design?" Lucy asked as if it wasn't one of the most invasive questions in the world.

Way to go Lucy, no sugar coating it, just cut to the chase.

"My parents were business people. They didn't want kids. When they hit their forties, they got this idea in their heads they'd need someone to look after them when they got old. A year later, along came me."

The tone of Colette's voice suggested it wasn't a happy story, or one she would've shared under normal circumstances.

"Hugs and kisses were sparse. Showing affection just wasn't done."

Lucy glanced in the rear-view mirror, but Kelly didn't dare turn around. She didn't want to feel compassion, Colette was an adult, she knew right from wrong.

"Although my parents were absent emotionally, I had the best of everything. I worked my butt off to get good grades. I left school and got a job that made my parents proud. Like any kid seeking their parent's approval, I thought that was enough. Then they died. Long story short, I resigned from a gruelling job, and secured a position working for Paula."

"And fell in love with your boss," Kelly supplied feeling like she was in the middle of a tragic love story, which would've been comical if the joke wasn't on her.

"Correct, but that's not the point I'm trying to make."

"Well, you better hurry up and make it." Lucy turned into Ruahine Street. "We'll be at the hospital soon."

Kelly wished she could see Lucy's eyes to read her emotions. She doubted Lucy felt as blasé as she sounded.

"Seeing your life flash before your eyes is an otherworldly experience." Colette sat forward in the backseat. "Having someone you've taunted rush to your side is the most humbling, slap in the face thing I've ever experienced. I'm so fucking sorry, Kelly. Can you ever forgive me?"

Hearing Miss Prissy curse made Kelly want to laugh,

but her chest was too tight.

As if sensing Kelly needed to confront Colette, the second Lucy parked she jumped out of the car.

"I'll go feed the meter. See you inside."

The door banged shut, and every slur Colette had uttered settled across Kelly's shoulders like a ten-tonne barbell.

She hated herself for caring what someone as heartless as Colette thought of her, but she wanted—needed—to make her accountable.

"Why?" Kelly asked.

For an agonizing minute, that one simple word bounced around the car like a ticking timebomb.

"I was jealous," Colette said, her voice barely above a whisper.

Hardly able to believe her ears, Kelly turned in her seat and faced Colette head on. "Of me? I'm a fucking nobody."

"You're wrong, Kelly." Colette smiled.

Kelly wanted to reach into the backseat and wipe the stupid grin off her face.

Instead, she took a deep breath and uncurled her

fists. As she calmed a little, she noticed Colette's smile held no malice, it was more one of a friend reassuring another, and that made her feel conflicted. She didn't want to like this woman.

"You're witty," Colette said. "You've got attitude, you're fiercely loyal. People flock to you." Her voice rose in pitch. "Money, a career, mean nothing when you have no one to share it with. You, Kelly…" She dared to poke Kelly in the chest. "You taught me that."

Breathing hard, Kelly didn't hold back. "It took a fuckin' car wreck for you to figure all that out? Are you sure you didn't suffer a head injury? Because I'm certain you've got a screw loose."

Colette recoiled as good as if she'd been slapped. "I deserved that."

Backing down, Kelly ran a hand through her hair, pulling on the roots, head tipping back like a wild horse being reined in.

"No, you didn't." Kelly hated that she'd lost control.

Normally, she was a bigger person than to lash out when someone was already down. Not only had Colette attempted to apologize but she'd also been through a hell of an ordeal.

Hoping some fresh air would help cool her down, Kelly shoved open the door. By the time she rounded the car Colette was halfway out.

"Truce?" Colette asked, wringing her hands together.

"I can't say we'll ever be friends, Colette, but we can be friendly." Kelly would never forget how Colette had treated her, but she could forgive.

Her mother's wise words ran through Kelly's mind. "Negative feelings are toxic, honey, let them go. You'll be a better person because of it."

God, she loved her mum. Tomorrow, Kelly's day off, she would visit. They had a lot to talk about.

The beep of a key fob made Kelly jump. She glanced around. Her heart flipped when her gaze landed on Lucy. She stood with her foot against the white hospital wall, hand high in the air, key fob pointed at her car, and a warm smile aimed at Kelly.

As soon as she was within reach, Kelly pecked Lucy on the cheek. "Thank you."

"You're welcome." Lucy squeezed her hand.

Kelly pulled her phone out. "I need to call someone." Ashleigh was going to freak. No one wanted to hear their best friend had been critically injured.

Lucy nodded, her expression grave. "I'll phone Grace."

Colette furrowed her brow as if the concept of informing friends truly was lost on her. That, in and of itself, was tragic.

Chapter 28

Once Kelly had given Ashleigh a quick rundown of events, she finally exited the hospital hand in hand with Lucy. Gone was the excitement the day had begun with. Rather than end on a happy note, it had been one of the longest, emotionally draining days of Kelly's life.

"How are you holding up?" Kelly asked Lucy as she turned into Knowles Street. Home sweet home.

"I don't know." Lucy shifted down a gear. "I haven't had time to stop and think."

Kelly hadn't wanted to see Paula, and didn't think it was a good idea for Lucy to either, but Lucy had insisted on escorting Colette to Paula's bedside.

"How was she?"

"A few broken ribs, punctured lung. It'll be slow going for a while, but she's expected to make a full recovery. Good thing she's not a smoker." Lucy chuckled but the sound lacked any humour.

"I meant how was she with you?"

Kelly hadn't heard any raised voices through the standard issue green curtain, but then again how much could someone with a punctured lung holler?

"Tearful, happy to be alive. Rambling, probably due to the morphine. She said she was no better than you, whatever that meant. She doesn't hate either of us, and that I don't have to move out in a hurry."

Well fuck, so much for silver linings. Kelly's heart sunk. Whether Paula accepted their relationship or not, she couldn't bear to see her ex and lover in the same room.

Lucy pulled up outside Kelly's block of flats. After shutting off the engine, she turned to Kelly, her expression unreadable.

"I thanked her for all she's done for me, which she interpreted as giving me a roof over my head. I told her I'd be moving anyway."

Daring to ask the question, Kelly sucked in a breath, her chest expanding. "What, exactly, did you mean by what she's done for you?"

"If Paula hadn't let me move in, I never would have

met you, Kelly. At least not in the way I did. So, for that I am thankful. I could hardly rub that in her face, though." She gave Kelly a wry smile. "Her and Colette seem smitten and I can't begrudge them that."

Still fixated on the words, "for that I am thankful," Kelly's hopes soared. "Move in with me."

Lucy opened her mouth and Kelly pressed a finger to her lips. "Please, just think about it."

"Tell me this, Kelly." Lucy's penetrating gaze held Kelly captive. "Would've you asked me the same question if today hadn't gone to shit in a handbasket?"

"No," Kelly said. "But I've…"

Lucy cut her off. "I didn't think so, and I don't want to be your charity case."

"Shut up." Kelly smiled, her confidence returning. "I've done nothing but think about what it would be like to live with you, wake up with you, come home to you, since our night out. I didn't ask before now because I didn't want to scare you. And, fuck me, Lucy."

Lucy smirked, and Kelly's heart grew wings.

"With my permission, that is. But goddamn, we're

good together. Life's fragile, there are no guarantees. Let's grab it by the balls."

This time Lucy laughed.

"Oops, bad word choice. Let's grab it by the vagina and embrace it while we can?"

A tear rolled down Lucy's cheek.

"That better be a happy tear." Kelly wiped it away with the pad of her thumb.

"It is." Lucy sniffed.

A couple walking their dog peered through the windscreen, eyeing them curiously. "Let's go inside? I can't wait to tell Nicole and Steve." Fit to burst, Kelly pushed open the car door.

"No." Lucy's arm shot out, her hand latching onto Kelly's.

Taken aback, Kelly glanced at the stranglehold Lucy had on her.

"Sorry," Lucy released her grip and Kelly wondered what had spooked her.

"What's up?"

"I need to get home, shower, pack some clothes."

"And?" Kelly asked, sensing there was more.

"Your best friends might not be as happy about the news as you are. It will be easier for them to say no if I'm not here."

"Why would they say no?" Kelly frowned. "They adore you."

"Your flat's not exactly spacious. There's barely room to swing a cat."

"Here's the thing, Lucy. As long as I've got your pussy to lick, I won't need to swing a cat." Kelly swept her arms wide. "See, no problem."

Lucy grinned. "I'm trying to be serious."

"Okay." Kelly dropped the jokes. "But I'm not getting out of this car until you promise me you'll come back here tonight."

"If you promise me you'll be honest about Nicole's reaction. I know Steve doesn't live here, but his opinion matters too."

"It does," Kelly agreed, certain Lucy was worrying about nothing, but respecting her concerns all the same.

"Deal?" Lucy fiddled with the stick shift.

"Deal. But if you're not back in an hour I'll hunt you down, tie you up, and spank your pussy."

Fanning herself, Lucy sucked in a sharp breath.

Turned on by her own declaration, Kelly leaned across the console until her face was mere millimetres from Lucy's. She inhaled deeply, breathing in Lucy's familiar scent, cocoa butter.

"Actually, that's what I'm going to do to you when you get back." She kissed Lucy hard. "After a day like today, I think we deserve a little fun."

"Hold those thoughts." Lucy fired the car to life. "I'll be as quick as I can."

Chapter 29

The second Kelly stepped inside, Nicole almost knocked her off her feet. She wrapped Kelly in a bone crushing hug. "Thank God you're home. I've been worried sick."

The comment caught Kelly off guard. There was no way Nicole could know about her shitty day. "Why? I told you where I was going."

"Because she's a worrywart." Steve waved hi from the sofa. "A friend posted on Facebook that there'd been a nasty prang on the Himatangi turnoff. Nicole put two and six together and came up with three."

"That doesn't even make sense." Kelly kicked off her shoes and slumped into her chair. Never had it felt so soft. The sides wrapped around her like a comfort blanket. Although, she liked to think it was her dad's spirit giving her a hug.

"Why didn't you reply to my text?"

"Oh, shit." Kelly dug her phone out. Three unread messages; two from Nicole, one from Jo. "I turned my phone off as soon as we arrived at the hospital."

"What the fuck?" Nicole was on her feet again.

Steve leaned forward, elbows on his knees. "Care to explain?"

Despite everything, a smile spread across Kelly's face. "Boy, have I got a story for you. Listen up, kids."

After grabbing her water bottle off the coffee table, Nicole dropped onto the sofa. Steve flung an arm across her shoulders and leaned his head on top of hers.

Warmth flooded Kelly's heart. The love they had for each other was palpable.

Mindful that Lucy would be back in less than an hour, Kelly gave them a condensed version of their trip to Te Papa. The good, Jo and Tim. The bad, Lucy being evicted. The ugly, the accident. And the rest, the hospital, Colette's attempt to make amends.

"I'm so sorry you went through all that, Kel." Nicole pursed her lips. "Lucy must be distraught. What's she going to do?"

And there it was. Kelly's chance to lay it on the

table.

"I told her she could move in here, but she insisted I ask you guys first, which I agreed is only right."

Silence.

"I know the flat's small but we're all respectful and I'm sure it would work."

Still nothing.

Panic set in and Kelly's heart raced. She hadn't expected to have to plead her case.

"Come on, guys," Kelly implored. "You're hardly here anyway."

Nicole shot Steve a look. Steve lifted a shoulder in a classic you're on your own gesture.

"Oh, for fuck's sake, spit it out, would you? I've had a day from hell, it can't get any worse. If you're against the idea, just say so. I won't break."

Liar.

Like a delicate piece of china about to shatter, Kelly barely managed to hold it together. Tears pricked her eyes, and her throat felt tight.

Nicole crossed the room and perched on the arm of the chair. "Don't get upset, honey." She stroked Kelly's hair.

"I'm so fucking tired, Nic. I don't want you to say yes because I made you feel bad. I'll text Lucy and tell her it's a no-go."

"You'll do no such thing." The chair rocked as Nicole jumped up.

If Kelly hadn't been strung so tight, she would've asked Nicole if she had ants in her pants.

With her eyes on Steve, Nicole pointed at Kelly. "Tell her."

From across the room, he locked eyes with Kelly. His expression was gentle yet serious. "We have news of our own."

Of course they did.

Kelly had been so self-absorbed she hadn't stopped to ask how their day had been.

"Nicole and I have found a place to rent." He lowered his voice, as much as a man with a deep voice could. "We want to live together." Trailing off, he mumbled, "Just the two of us."

Anguish written all over her face, Nicole dropped to the floor and hugged Kelly's knees. "Please don't hate me. It's not a done deal. I refused to sign the lease until after we talked to you. I'd never abandon you, Kel."

Finally able to breathe again, Kelly burst out laughing. Giddy with relief, she cackled like a madwoman. "Oh, my god." She swiped her eyes. "Look at us. We've been friends for over a decade, yet we're dancing around each other like delicate flowers. It's about time you two got your shit together."

If she was to be totally honest, Kelly had been expecting the news long before now.

Standing, Steve held his arms out. "Group hug?"

Ecstatic for her two best friends, Kelly leapt out of her chair and embraced them. "Love you, guys."

The top of Nicole's head tickled Kelly's chin. "The answer's yes," she said.

"Oh. Did Steve propose?" Kelly asked, only half joking.

A sharp pain shot through Kelly's backside making her flinch.

"Ow." Kelly smacked Nicole's pinching fingers away. "What was that for?"

"Because I love you. Now behave. The yes was to

Lucy moving in."

The universe, which had played a cruel trick on Kelly earlier in the day, was now forgiven. Hope flared in her chest that once again all was right in her world.

A megawatt smile lit up Steve's face. He took Nicole's hand in his.

Like a lovesick fool, Kelly pictured him dropping to his knees and proposing. That didn't happen; the next best thing did.

"Now that worrywart is no longer worried, I'm going to whisk her away. We won't be back tonight, so don't wait up."

He rubbed his chin, looking thoughtful. "Actually, after the day you've had, I suggest you head straight to bed as soon as Lucy gets here."

"Is that right, Doctor Steve? Are you prescribing some oral medication as well?"

"Kelly!" Nicole plugged her ears. "La-la-la-la." She pulled her fingers out. "Too much information."

Swooning, Steve clutched his chest. "I'm feeling sick, Nic. Can I have some of your special medicine." He waggled his tongue at her.

Nicole mocked glared at Kelly. "See what you've done."

"You can thank me tomorrow." Kelly smirked.

With a dramatic eyeroll, Nicole disappeared into her bedroom. Less than two minutes later she reappeared, overnight bag slung over her shoulder.

"Come on, you sick puppy." Nicole fisted Steve's shirt. "Let's go. I'm sure Kelly and Lucy have a lot to talk about."

"I don't think that's the kind of oral..."

Glaring, Nicole held up a finger. "Don't say it."

Laughing, Steve plucked Nicole's car keys out of her hand and exited the flat.

Suddenly serious, Nicole turned to Kelly. "You know we're only a phone call away?"

"I do." Kelly nodded. "Same goes."

"Always." Nicole shut the door on her way out.

Chapter 30

In the shower, Kelly turned the water to as hot as she could stand it, letting the heat wash away the stress of the day. Slowly, limb by limb, her muscles relaxed.

She envisioned tension draining out of her body, disappearing down the plug hole. The imagery worked.

When she no longer felt bogged down by the harrowing events of the day, Kelly shut off the water and stepped out of the shower.

While drying off, thoughts of Lucy ran through her mind. They had a lot to learn about each other, which excited and terrified her in equal measure. Kelly was optimistic that with each layer they uncovered, their bond would only deepen.

She wasn't naïve enough to think everything would be plain sailing, but if they kept the lines of communication open, they'd be fine, of that Kelly was certain.

Flopping onto her bed, Kelly fired off a quick text message. "Went better than expected, will fill you in when you get here." She glanced at her watch. "You've got fifteen minutes." She didn't add, before I hunt you down.

The words of a promise sent a jolt of desire pulsing through her body. The beep of her phone snapped her out of her erotic musings.

"Having a bite to eat with Ashleigh, Grace, and Colette. Can't wait to get out of here, but don't want to be rude."

It came as no surprise to Kelly that Colette was at the house too. Ashleigh had a heart of gold and it was just like her to take Colette under her wing. Kelly sincerely hoped Paula knew how lucky she was to have such a loyal friend.

Just as she was about to put her phone down, a message lit up the screen.

"See you in half, Miss."

A stupid grin spread across Kelly's face. The fact Lucy was going to be longer than the allocated hour gave her a good excuse to turn her threat into a promise.

If Lucy's parting word, Miss, was anything to go by, Lucy wanted to play too.

Sex wouldn't eradicate their craptacular day, but it would go a long way toward balancing out the negative.

A hunger pang tore through Kelly's insides. Even though she didn't have much of an appetite, the thought of her stomach screaming, 'feed me, feed me,' during an intimate moment, had her heading for the kitchen.

Once there, she reached for a loaf of bread, jar of vegemite, and a block of cheese.

Comfort food.

Shortly after eight, a rap on the door made Kelly's heart skip a beat. Without thought, she was on her feet.

The sudden leap out of her chair, coupled with excitement, made her heart race. Lucy was here.

God, she wanted to shout that from the rooftops.

Lucy's here! Lucy's here!

The trek across the small living room felt like five miles. Kelly couldn't get the door open fast enough.

"Hey there, sexy. Come in." She ushered Lucy inside. "Make yourself at home."

Setting her bag down, Lucy glanced around the

living room, concern etched across her features. "They didn't leave on my account, did they?"

"Oh, no. Not at all." Kelly grabbed Lucy's hands. They were warm and soft, like her smile.

"It just so happens; Nicole and Steve have found somewhere else to live. They didn't want to say anything before now, afraid I'd be upset if they left me here all alone." Kelly jutted her lip out like a baby.

"What were the chances?" Lucy asked, ignoring Kelly's theatrical pout.

"About as minuscule as running into Paula and Colette in Wellington, same time, same place, same day as us."

Finally, Lucy smiled, a beaming smile that lit up Kelly's world.

"Turns out, some clouds do have silver linings."

"That, they do." Kelly wrapped her arms around Lucy's waist, inhaling deeply. She didn't detect even the slightest hint of Lucy's signature scent, cocoa butter.

Amusement twinkled in Lucy's eyes. "You're practically drooling."

"What do you expect when you turn up here looking as edible as ever, batting your sexy green eyes, smelling all shower fresh?"

Grabbing Lucy by the hand, Kelly dragged her toward her bedroom. She wanted to forget about the day, just for a while, and sensed Lucy could do with the same.

Lucy chuckled. "What about my bag? Shouldn't I unpack?"

"Clothes are overrated," Kelly retorted.

The second they crossed the threshold to Kelly's bedroom, the atmosphere changed from casual to electric.

Without prompting, Lucy clutched her hands behind her back, opening herself up to Kelly.

"Sorry I was late, Miss Kel."

"Strip," Kelly instructed.

With fire in her eyes, Lucy pulled her thin white blouse over her head, slipped out of her jeans, and tossed both aside.

Heat pooled low in Kelly's belly as she walked a slow circle around the beautiful woman before her, clad in matching black briefs and bra.

"You're stunning, Lucy-Lou."

Back in front of her, Kelly cupped Lucy's breasts and peppered kisses all over the voluptuous mounds.

Lucy hissed when Kelly bit down on a nipple, nipping with enough pressure to draw a whimper but not hard enough to cause any lasting pain.

Although Kelly saw nothing but desire in Lucy's eyes, she wanted to remind Lucy she held the power to put a stop to anything that made her uncomfortable.

"Safe word?"

"Candyfloss."

Lucy's lip twitched, and, for a split second, Kelly wondered if there was more to Lucy's safe word than initially disclosed. Either way, if Lucy uttered the word Candy or candyfloss all play would stop.

"I'm going to take you back to a time in life when you didn't have to worry about finance, or where you were going to lay your head. Do you trust me to do that?"

Even though Kelly couldn't imagine Lucy saying no, her heart hammered in her chest.

"Yes," Lucy said, her voice sure, her eyes questioning.

There it was, that combination of confidence and vulnerability that turned Kelly on.

"Underwear off, on your back, in the middle of the bed." Kelly's voice matched how she felt, confident, in control, and hot as hell.

"Yes, Miss." With the snap of a clasp and a shimmy of her hips, Lucy's bra hit the floor, followed by her briefs.

By the time the words "holy hell, you're gorgeous" skidded through Kelly's mind, Lucy was on the bed, looking more delectable than any store-bought duvet.

This was what Kelly craved, unabashed dominance and submission. Both parties on the same page, no coercion.

The fact Lucy submitted so readily made the dance all the more intoxicating.

"You have a beautiful body, Lucy, all curves and delicious softness."

Wordlessly, Lucy tracked Kelly's movements, her gaze so intense Kelly felt it like a physical caress.

As though taunting her to get naked, her jeans suddenly felt too tight, her tank-top too small.

Emboldened by the look of rapture in Lucy's eyes, Kelly ran her hands over her breasts, down her sides, then rested them on her hips.

"I'll get naked soon enough, but by the time I do, you won't be able to see me anyway."

Rather than respond to the question swimming in Lucy's eyes, Kelly spun on her heels and snagged a blindfold off her dresser.

Lucy gave her a barely perceptible nod, her silent consent all the encouragement Kelly needed.

As she positioned the blindfold over Lucy's eyes, a shudder tore through Kelly, rocking her from head to toe. Even though the rational part of her brain knew they were alone, the thought of making love blanketed in darkness terrified her.

Shaking off the memory of that bitter-sweet night, Kelly focused on the here and now.

"You okay?"

"Yes, Miss Kel."

Lucy's softly spoken reply—the movement of her

jaw, the way her tongue lingered on her top lip when she said Kel—seduced Kelly.

Bending forward, she captured Lucy's mouth with her own. Lucy parted her lips allowing her entrance. Their tongues danced, a slow, passionate tango.

Who knew kissing could be so erotic?

Coming up for air, Kelly retrieved a long, feather duster. She trailed it over Lucy's taut nipples, swirled it across her breasts, down her abdomen, and lower.

Lucy squirmed, muscles twitching. "What's that? It tickles."

The comment delighted Kelly, she'd expected no less. Every inch of Lucy's body was incredibly responsive, her reactions exquisite.

"Feathers. Once every inch of your skin is pebbled with gooseflesh, I'm going to turn you over and bind you to the headboard."

Lucy writhed on the bed, bottom lip sucked between her teeth.

Turned on by her reactions, Kelly's pulse kicked up a notch. She teased Lucy's mons and labia with feather light touches.

Aware of how ticklish Lucy was, Kelly marvelled at her self-control when she didn't snap her legs shut to avoid the torment.

"Good girl."

Kelly tossed the implement aside and rewarded Lucy with a swipe of her tongue.

The musky scent of her arousal wrapped around Kelly. Her breathy moans filtered through the air as Kelly toyed with Lucy's labia, alternating between nipping and sucking on the succulent flesh.

"Oh, God, Miss Kel. That feels incredible."

The next thing Kelly felt was hands in her hair, gripping her head. And just like that, she was on her feet.

"You're naughty," Kelly scolded, shaking a finger even though Lucy couldn't see her.

"Did I give you permission to touch?"

"No, Miss Kel."

"Turn over. Now!" Kelly commanded.

The power she craved ramped up her excitement.

Quick as a coin toss, Lucy flipped from her back to her stomach. And there she lay, face down, arms above her head, her spankable backside swimming in Kelly's vision.

Did she just waggle her butt at me? Yeah, she did. Brat!

With no intention of doing Lucy's bidding, Kelly took her time undressing, giving Lucy time to ponder her next move.

After folding her clothes and placing them in a neat pile, Kelly crossed the room to her bedside drawer. Her heart flipped when her eyes landed on the new toy Lucy wasn't yet privy to.

"I think you deserve a good fucking, young lady."

Kelly's heart raced, excitement and nerves competing for first place. Excitement won when Lucy replied.

"Yes, please. Please fuck me." Despite her muffled reply, there was no mistaking the desperation in her tone.

"As much as I love hearing you beg, you'll have to wait."

Kelly grabbed Lucy's wrists with the intention of tying them to the headboard, then reconsidered and released them.

The thought of what she had planned made Kelly's breath hitch, but she needed to set the scene right. It would suck if she had to stop when they were both flying high because Lucy couldn't get enough air.

"Turn your head to the side, clutch your hands above your head."

The blindfold was knocked askew when Lucy did as she was told, but her eyes remained firmly shut.

That fact alone, the fact Lucy didn't try to sneak a peek, let Kelly know Lucy was in the zone. She'd turned off conscious thought, her mind attuned to Kelly.

Overwhelmed, Kelly exalted in the control Lucy had given her, because to do less would be disrespectful of the privilege she'd been given.

Certain Lucy's eyes would fly open when Kelly entered her, she adjusted the blindfold.

"Don't think I've forgotten you need to be punished. Not only were you half an hour late, but you were also topping from the bottom."

Another waggle of her bottom.

"Oh my God, you're such a brat." Like a snake

striking, Kelly's hand shot out and connected with Lucy's left butt cheek.

Three things happened at once; a loud crack echoed around the room, her palm smarted, and Lucy yelped.

"Ow. Sorry, Miss."

Kelly ran her hand over the imprint left in her wake. The contrast of pink on white made her mouth water.

"Sorry for what?"

"Sassing you."

"And being late," Kelly prompted.

"That too, Miss."

"Two transgressions earn two more blows." Kelly delivered another two short, sharp whacks.

Lucy hissed out a breath. "Thank you, Miss."

The husky timbre of her voice was music to Kelly's ears, and as much as she'd love to turn her butt a delightful shade of crimson, Kelly needed to stay on track.

The ceiling light cast a glow on Lucy's splayed body, drawing Kelly's gaze to her glistening centre. And like a star-struck lover, Kelly stared in wonder at the gorgeous woman laid bare before her.

The bed dipped under her weight, and the heat of Lucy's thighs seared into Kelly's outer arms as she positioned herself between her legs.

In one long, slow stroke, she licked the length of Lucy's slit.

A gasp tore from Lucy and her hips lifted off the bed, creating a gap between the mattress and her pelvis.

A perfect response as it gave Kelly better access to her mons.

Nostrils flaring, she circled Lucy's clit with the pad of her thumb, enticing a whimper out of her. High on lust, Kelly buried her upper body between Lucy's legs, working her to the edge with her fingers and tongue.

Once Lucy was squirming, panting, and gasping for release, Kelly backed off, not ready to grant her an orgasm just yet.

When Kelly extricated herself and stood, the bed groaned as if protesting on Lucy's behalf.

Much to her delight, Lucy didn't complain. Her submission robbed Kelly of breath. She'd played before, of course, but never with such a willing partner.

Anticipation zinged through Kelly's veins as she

retrieved the new toy out of her bedside drawer. She hiked her foot up on the edge of the bed and positioned the bulbous end at her entrance. Instantly, her arousal coated the surface, giving the smooth, blue silicon a polished appearance. Spreading her labia, Kelly slid the toy into place. It was cool but quickly warmed, matching the heat of her core.

Feeling empowered, Kelly glanced at the phallus jutting proudly from between her legs.

"Do you know what a Feeldoe is, Lucy-Lou?"

"Yes, Miss Kel."

That wasn't the reply Kelly had expected, considering the only other woman Lucy had slept with, Candy, sounded like a pillow princess.

Banishing those thoughts, Kelly asked the bigger question.

"Ever been fucked with one?"

"No, Miss."

"Would you like to be?"

A whimper. "Yes, please."

At the same time as Kelly moved to the foot of the bed, Lucy rolled onto her side.

"No! Don't move," Kelly snapped.

Lucy froze, and Kelly envisioned her eyes flying open behind the blindfold.

She put a reassuring hand on Lucy's shoulder and softened her tone. "I'm going to pin you to the bed with the weight of my body, then take you from behind."

Desire tingled under Kelly's skin. She squeezed her muscles, loving the feel of the toy lodged snuggly inside her.

Earlier, she'd considered cutting a hole in an old pair of pantyhose, wearing them over top to help hold the Feeldoe in place. But confident her vaginal muscles were strong enough, she hadn't bothered.

"Don't think, just feel. Like I said, I'm going to take you back in time. Do you trust me to do that, Lucy?"

A crease formed between Lucy's eyebrows as she, no doubt, pondered the meaning of Kelly's words.

That was all she was getting though. Having the element of surprise on her side was one of the things Kelly loved about being in control.

"Yes," Lucy said, gooseflesh pebbling her skin. "I trust you."

Kelly kissed a burning trail up the inside of Lucy's thighs.

She stopped when she reached the apex, drinking in the sight of her glistening labia.

"So wet."

Bypassing her centre, Kelly slid on top of Lucy, dragging her erect nipples over the curve of her backside, the dip of her lower back, and higher.

Kelly pushed Lucy's black hair aside and kissed her shoulder blade. "I'm going to fuck you."

A whimper tore from Lucy's throat.

It was a sound Kelly had come to know well, and it never failed to excite her.

Balancing her weight on one elbow, Kelly reached between them and lined up the phallus. Despite not being able to feel sensation in the fake cock, she could feel resistance.

For a fleeting moment, Kelly wondered if Lucy was a virgin. The thought vanished when Lucy thrust back as though trying to impale herself.

"Greedy girl." There was a smile in Kelly's voice, but unlike the first time Lucy had hinted at what she wanted, and been denied, this time, Kelly did her bidding.

After a few shallow thrusts, Kelly entered Lucy in one fluid movement.

When Lucy sucked in a sharp breath, Kelly held still, allowing her a moment to adjust to the intrusion.

"You okay, Lucy?"

"Yes, yes. Please take me, use me, abuse me."

Taken aback, yet incredibly turned on, Kelly moved her legs to the outside of Lucy's and pushed Lucy's together, effectively restraining Lucy with nothing more than her body.

"How do you feel?"

"Trapped, powerless, aroused…and embarrassed to admit that."

Titillated by Lucy's brutal honesty, yet never wanting her to feel ashamed of her kinky desires, Kelly clucked her tongue.

"Too much thinking." She thrust forward, and was rewarded when Lucy exhaled an oomph.

"Try again."

"Full."

Lucy returned her thrust. The impact of her backside on Kelly's mound set her nerve endings on fire.

Like a contortionist, Kelly arched her spine, reached back between her legs, and activated the vibrating bullet at the base of the Feeldoe.

A groan tore from Lucy the second the first pulse hit. Kelly returned it as she plastered her body to Lucy's back.

"Show me how you got off the first time you came."

Breathing hard, a shiver rocked Lucy's body. Her reaction was exquisite and exactly what Kelly had hoped for.

The feel of skin on skin, the vibrations stimulating Kelly's core, was the nearest thing to erotic torture she'd ever experienced.

Fighting back the urge to pound into Lucy, Kelly balanced her weight on her hands, silently granting Lucy permission to reposition herself.

Without a word, Lucy slid her hands under her pelvis, bunching up the sheets as she did so. She writhed beneath Kelly, humping the bedsheets and bucking against her.

The eroticism of the moment, the hitch of Lucy's breath, her half-hearted attempt to dislodge her captor, launched Kelly into ecstasy.

Although Kelly was on top, ironically, Lucy was unwittingly fucking her. With each thrust of her hips, the toy moved in and out of them simultaneously.

With each downward movement the bulbous end massaged Kelly's G-spot, hurtling her toward orgasm at lightning speed.

"Keep that up." Kelly sucked in a lungful of air. "I'm going to come."

Covered in a sheen of sweat, Lucy stilled.

Kelly's orgasm receded, leaving her frustrated and relieved at the same time.

Instinctively, Kelly shook her head. "Did I tell you to stop? Have you forgotten which one of us needs permission to come?"

As she spoke, Kelly rotated her pelvis, tormenting Lucy with slow, controlled movements.

"No, Miss Kel. But your words excited me. I didn't want to come without your consent."

Well fuck.

Love, or perhaps it was lust, bloomed in Kelly's chest. They weren't just fucking, roleplaying, scratching an itch, or whatever else fuckbuddies did. They were making love, attuned to one another's bodies, feeding off each other's arousal.

"My exact words were, 'keep that up'. Now do it, Lucy. Buck against me, struggle like your life depends on it. Or more accurately, your orgasm."

The volume of Kelly's voice increased along with her arousal.

The sharp snap of Lucy's hips caught her by surprise. She clenched her inner muscles, relieved the sudden movement didn't dislodge the Feeldoe.

After one more vigorous thrust, Lucy settled into a rhythm, rotating her pelvis in concentrated movements.

Kelly's breath hitched when the vibrating bulb slammed against her G-spot.

Lust zinging through her veins, Kelly slowly thrust in and out of Lucy, the ridges on the phallus massaging her clit.

As tempted as she was to utter dirty words in Lucy's ear, to ask if she liked being fucked from behind, Kelly didn't want to take her out of her head. Orders could be followed without thought, questions required thinking.

Losing herself in the moment, Kelly kissed the slope of Lucy's neck.

Lucy's breathy moans sent shockwaves of pleasure pulsing through Kelly.

Sweat pooled between their bodies, creating a slippery, erotic ride.

"Fuck! You're so damn sexy, Lucy-Lou."

Kelly's nipples ached, her entire body screaming for release. The vibrations assaulting her body, drove her higher and higher.

"I'm close, Lucy." Tension coiled low in her belly.

"Me...too," Lucy said, her voice pained. "Permission to come, Miss?"

At that, Kelly's arousal reached a crescendo. "Do it. Come for me."

As one, they peaked, panting and gasping, inner walls clenching and releasing the conjoined toy as they rode out their orgasms, absorbing and prolonging each other's pleasure.

Sated, and giddy beyond belief, Kelly slowly pulled

out of Lucy, removed the Feeldoe from herself and tossed it on the floor.

Clean up could wait.

Fanning herself with the sheet, Kelly blew out a breath, raising the hair off her forehead. "Damn, it's hot in here."

Face down, a sob hiccupped out of Lucy.

Stunned, Kelly's heart jumped into her throat.

Had she hurt Lucy? No, she didn't think so.

Shit, did she have sub-drop? Emotions had been running high.

Kelly panicked, she had no experience with the phenomenon. Acting on instinct, she yanked the blindfold off Lucy, dragged her up, and cradled her in her arms.

"Shhh, shhh. It's okay, I've got you."

Hot tears dripped onto Kelly's shoulder. Lucy snuggled closer, her body trembling against her side.

God, Kelly was so out of her element. She pulled the duvet up and covered them, hoping it would give Lucy comfort.

Laugh-crying Lucy flung the blanket off. "Are you

crazy, woman? It's sweltering in here."

Confused, Kelly gazed into the depths of Lucy's watery eyes, trying to get a read on her. Coming up blank, she forced a smile.

"You okay?"

"Goodness me, yes."

That smile, the one that lit up Kelly's world, spread across Lucy's face. Her hair was plastered to her forehead, tears streaked her cheeks, beads of sweat rested on her upper lip, and she'd never looked more gorgeous.

"You're doing it again." Lucy quirked an eyebrow.

Happy to be the source of Lucy's amusement, Kelly propped herself up against the pillows.

"Doing what?"

"Drooling."

"Get used to it."

Smiling, Lucy rested her head on Kelly's shoulder.

Although the atmosphere was relaxed, Kelly was still concerned. She smoothed down Lucy's hair and kissed the top of her head. "Wanna tell me what that was about?"

"You remembered," Lucy said.

The gratitude in her tone made Kelly's heart sing.

"I did," Kelly said simply.

She'd often thought back to the day Lucy had told her, so casually, that she liked being restrained, to the extent that she'd tied herself up.

"When you said you were going to take me back in time, I didn't know what you meant. I just needed to escape, to forget about the day."

Kelly cupped Lucy's chin, tilted her head back, and kissed her, hard.

A shy smile spread across Lucy's face. "You know, I always felt embarrassed about the way I got off the first time. Who the fuck humps their bedsheets?"

More people than were willing to admit it, Kelly didn't say. After all, it was a rhetorical question.

"Funny thing is, I've never told another soul, yet I just blurted it out to you." A tear rolled down her cheek. She pointed to her eyes. "These are tears of gratitude. Thank you for recreating that time for me."

A lump formed in Kelly's throat. The gamble she'd made couldn't have paid higher dividends.

Chapter 31

Cuddled up in bed after a quick shower, Kelly's post-coital bliss took a backseat as more pressing matters took forefront.

"Now what?" Lucy asked.

The sad smile Lucy gave her made Kelly's heart ache. She wished she could wrap Lucy in cotton wool and shelter her from the world. Which was ridiculous.

Wanting to offer comfort, Kelly rolled onto her side.

"Come here." She draped an arm across Lucy's waist and pulled her close. Their breasts and tummies aligned as though they were made for each other.

When their kneecaps banged, Kelly smirked. She straightened her leg, letting Lucy fling hers over top.

It was far too hot to be cuddling, but Kelly would burn in hell if it meant never letting go of Lucy.

For a minute, she lost herself in the depths of Lucy's green-eyed gaze.

"Now, you move in here," Kelly said. "We take life one day at a time, and place bets on how long you can put up with me."

When Lucy didn't so much as crack a smile, Kelly's stomach plummeted.

Couldn't she at least appear grateful, rather than look like she'd just been handed a life sentence with no possibility of parole?

"Look, Lucy. I know it's too soon for us to be moving in together…permanently." Kelly almost choked on the last word.

In the pit of her stomach, she hoped Lucy was her forever.

"I'm trying to make the best of a bad situation. If you have a better solution, I'm all ears."

A devilish smile lit up Lucy's features. Kelly didn't know whether to feel pissed off or to kiss the stupid grin off her face.

"You done?" Lucy quirked an eyebrow.

Acting her age, twenty-five, Kelly harrumphed.

Chuckling, Lucy swept her foot up the back of Kelly's legs. It was strangely comforting.

"I have a queen-sized bed, and five-piece bedroom suite." She glanced around Kelly's small bedroom. "I'd rather not have to ship them back to New Plymouth, and risk damage during transit. Although, my brothers..."

Having already thought about the issue of space, Kelly silenced Lucy with a chaste kiss.

When they broke apart, the passion burning in Lucy's eyes robbed Kelly of breath. For the second time that night, Kelly wished she could take away Lucy's worries.

"It's getting late." Kelly tapped Lucy's temple. "Shut off that brain of yours and get some sleep. Let me take care of it, of you, okay?"

Nodding, Lucy rolled onto her side.

Happy beyond belief, Kelly spooned Lucy from behind. She kissed the nape of her neck. "Goodnight, sweet lady."

***

The following morning, after seeing Lucy off to work and texting Nicole to give her an update, Kelly did something totally out of character—baked.

The end result made her chuckle. What started out as perfect dollops of cookie dough, morphed into one big cookie.

Smiling, despite her failed attempt, Kelly sliced the mass into edible sized squares. After dividing the batch in half, she put one container in the cupboard and the other in her backpack.

The morning sun bathed the flat in an orange hue, leading Kelly to believe it was another warm day. When she poked her nose outside, a cool southerly breeze whipped around her shoulders and down her neck.

Shuddering, she quickly closed the door. Who liked the cold? Not her, that was for sure.

Rather than grab her helmet, Kelly put on her sneakers and flung her backpack over her shoulders.

A brisk walk would get her blood pumping, and the thirty-minute trek would give her time to gather her thoughts.

Although her mum wasn't one to judge—she'd never been anything but supportive—surely Kelly's news would come as a shock.

Her mother was yet to meet Lucy, yet here Kelly was on her way to tell her they were moving in together. And if that wasn't enough, to top it all off, Kelly had a favour to ask.

Half an hour later, exhausted more from her mind running in circles than the hike through town, Kelly was on the home straight. The sight of her childhood home looming in the distance made her feel nostalgic.

It was a modest brick structure, built in the sixties, but it was home, always had been, always would be.

For a while after their dad died, Jo, along with Kelly, had worried their mum would put the house on the market; the memories, the absence of their father, too painful to bear. If she had, they would've understood, but all these years later, the topic was moot.

Taking time to appreciate the aroma wafting off the rosebushes her mother painstakingly tended to, Kelly paused at the foot of the driveway.

It was then that her mother's words slammed into her. "I'm rather busy these days, love. It might be best if you text from now on before you visit." Her mum had smiled as if to soften the words.

Well, Kelly was here now, so sending a text would be pointless. Besides, her mum's car in the driveway was a pretty good indication she was home.

"Hi, Ma, it's just me."

Kelly stepped inside and froze.

Her mother jumped. Mr Edwards, their neighbour, shook his hands as if they were on fire.

One second they were on her mother's hips, the next they were gone. It happened so fast, it was easy to pretend it hadn't happened at all.

"Hey, sweetheart. I wasn't expecting you today."

No kidding.

Placating her mother and feeling sorry for Mr Edwards, who looked like he wanted to bolt, Kelly smiled.

"Sorry, I should've texted first." Enjoying watching her mother squirm, Kelly asked, "I didn't interrupt anything, did I?"

Tripping over their words, Mr Edwards and her mother replied at the same time.

"Of course not."

"Don't be silly, love." Her mother's flushed cheeks said otherwise.

"You remember Jack, don't you?"

Amused, Kelly nodded. "I do." She gave him a finger wave.

"Well, I better get going. Give me a call if your pipes get blocked again."

Seriously, did he just say that?

Kelly cut her eyes from her mother's confused expression just in time to see Mr Edwards give her mum an exaggerated wink.

Ignoring the not so subtle exchange, Kelly slid her backpack down her arms and retrieved the plastic container.

By the time she looked up, the lightbulb had gone off in her mother's eyes. Figuratively and damn near literally. They were radiant, positively glowing.

"Bye, Mr Edwards." Kelly picked up the kettle, trying not to grin when she turned on the tap. "Thanks for looking out for Mum."

He tipped his head. "Any time, kiddo. That's what neighbours are for."

Clearing out blocked pipes?

Apparently, Kelly and Mr Edwards had something in common. A warped sense of humour. But the question was, did his words have the underlying meaning Kelly's had had when she'd teased Lucy, or were they innocent?

Either way, Kelly intended to have the answer before she left her childhood home.

Once they were alone, her mum kissed her on the cheek.

"It's good to see you, sweetie." She reached for two mugs and tossed a teabag in each.

Kelly quirked an eyebrow. "Tea?"

"You'll like it. Trust me."

In response to Kelly's frown, she added, "It's *berry* nice."

Overcome with love for the woman standing before her, looking delighted to see Kelly, yet jittery at the same time, Kelly kissed her on the cheek.

"Okay, I'll try it." Hopefully the berry flavour would complement her baking. "I made some cookies. Chocolate chip."

"Colour me purple, what's gotten into you?" Grinning, her mother put a hand on Kelly's forehead. "You're not sick, are you?"

Lovesick maybe, but not physically ill, unless an endless supply of butterflies whenever she thought of Lucy counted.

Batting her mother's hand away, Kelly pulled the lid off the container. "They look like crap, but taste delicious."

"I'm sure they do. Besides, it's the thought that counts." Her mother placed two steaming mugs on the dining room table, pulled out a chair, and sat opposite Kelly.

The setting made Kelly long for days gone by. It took her back to many family meals shared around the table, her father at the head, her baby sister, Jo, at the foot.

God, she missed her dad. Sure, time had eased the pain, but the ache, the sense of loss, never went away.

"Why the sad look?" Her mother, who had always been too perceptive, eyed Kelly over the rim of her mug.

Shaking off the memory, because the last thing Kelly wanted to do was guilt trip her mother if she'd started dating again, Kelly forced a smile.

"Better?"

"Much." Her mother chuckled.

Taking a gamble, Kelly went with the direct approach. "So, you and Mr Edwards?"

"Me and Mr Edwards what?"

The innocent act didn't fool Kelly.

Bristling, she held up a hand. "Don't, Mum. I'm not a child."

The air went out of her mother. "No, you're not. Yes, me and Jack."

"How long?" Kelly asked, feeling detached.

"Six, almost seven months."

A snapshot of images flashed through Kelly's mind. Mr Edwards popping in for a drink last Christmas. Mr Edwards mowing her mum's lawns. Mr Edwards smiling for the first time in months. And further back, the perpetual dark cloud that had hung around him when he moved in five years ago.

Kelly had left home by then so on the odd occasion

she'd seen him looking miserable, she'd just assumed he was a grumpy neighbour.

It wasn't until much later her mother had revealed Mr Edwards was a widower.

"That long, and you're only just telling me now?" As hard as she tried to keep the conversation light, Kelly's question came out as an accusation.

"Oh, Kelly." Her mum put her hands on the table, palm up.

With her mind in turmoil, Kelly placed her hands in her mothers. The gentle stroke of her thumbs comforted Kelly, the same as it had when she was a child.

"For the first few months, I struggled with being disloyal to your father. I prayed for his forgiveness, that he'd understand."

"That had to be tough."

"Yes, sweetie, it was—still is—but I'm getting there."

"And that's why you didn't tell me, because of your own feelings of guilt?" Kelly asked, trying to process what she was hearing without coming across as judgemental.

"No." With a sad smile, her mum shook her head. "Because I was terrified of what you'd think of me."

"Me?" Kelly asked, unable to keep the incredulity out of her voice.

All she'd ever wanted was for her mother to be happy. God knew, she'd grieved long enough. Why she was worried what Kelly thought was beyond her.

A wistful look glimmered in her mother's eyes, her gaze focused on something Kelly couldn't see. A memory?

"You were so fiercely loyal to your dad." Her mother smiled warmly. "You followed him everywhere."

"I did," Kelly said, her chest tight.

She'd been his little shadow, and even though her parents would never admit to having favourites, Kelly was her father's girl, and Jo her mothers. Sweet, sweet Jo, who loved to play dress-ups, go shopping, and help her mother bake. While Kelly preferred to be outside, pushing her toy mower alongside her dad, and tinkering in the garage any chance she got.

"Dad wouldn't want you to be old and lonely,

Mum."

"Hey." Her mother playfully slapped Kelly's shoulder. "Watch who you're calling old. Forty-nine's the new twenty-nine, I'll have you know."

"Same age as Lucy," Kelly mused out loud.

For several seconds, her mum held Kelly's gaze.

Kelly didn't bother filling the silence, her mother was able to read her like a fortune teller.

"Girlfriend?"

"Yeah."

"Serious?"

"I'd like to think so, she's pretty great."

"That look suits you."

"You too, Mum. Give love a second chance."

"I am."

Simultaneously, chair legs screeched as Kelly and her mother rose to their feet. Kelly rounded the table first, falling into her mother's embrace.

"I'm happy for you, Mum." A lump formed in Kelly's throat. "Dad would understand."

"I know, honey. I know." A tear ran down her mum's cheek.

Fighting to hold her own emotions in check, Kelly hugged her mother tighter.

"Jack has been honourable, taking his time…"

Deciding it was time to lighten the mood, Kelly stepped out of her mother's arms.

"Honourable!" She feigned outrage. "He cleaned your pipes out."

"Oh dear." Chuckling, her mother turned crimson. "Even old people need loving."

"La-la-la-la." Kelly plugged her ears and screwed her eyes shut.

Despite being happy for her mother, she didn't want to think about her doing the dirty.

Elbowing her playfully, her mum picked up their mugs and put them in the sink.

"Enough about me. When do I get to meet…Lucy, is it? The woman you've mentioned on and off for the past few weeks. Or are you going to continue to keep her all to yourself?"

Suddenly feeling nervous, Kelly bit her lip. "Mum, I need a favour."

Her mother narrowed her eyes. "Go on."

"Lucy and I are moving in together, we need somewhere to store her furniture. I wondered if it'd be okay to put it in the garage." Kelly knew she was rambling, but she couldn't stop. "There's plenty of room, and hopefully it'll only be for a few months. Until Lucy buys a house."

An oppressive silence hung in the air. Kelly squirmed like a child about to be reprimanded.

Way to go, Kel. Perhaps you should've started at the beginning.

Looking Kelly dead in the eye, her mother calmly, too calmly, replied, "Let me see if I've got this right. You've met a woman who's so wonderful, you're shacking up with her like a pair of lovebirds, yet you haven't found the time to introduce her to your own mother?"

"Yes. No. Dammit, I'm making a mess of things."

Kelly smacked her forehead, an attempt to align her head with her heart.

The last thing she wanted to do was hurt her mother's feelings.

"Relax, honey." She gave Kelly a meaningful smile,

"Everyone has their secrets, and reasons for them."

Wasn't that the truth.

***

An hour later, after giving her mother the censored version of her whirlwind romance, Kelly strolled down the driveway feeling lighter than she had in days.

With her mother's blessing and Mr Edwards' help, offered via her mother, they would move Lucy's furniture after work that night.

Sheltering under a tree, out of the wind, Kelly pulled out her phone and tapped out a quick message to Lucy. "We can store your stuff at Mums. She's invited us for dinner too, if you're free?"

Kelly didn't want to assume Lucy hadn't made other plans. Perhaps she went to the gym on Monday nights. Although, Kelly doubted it. Lucy kept in shape, but she didn't have the ripped body of someone who pumped weights. She had a body Kelly couldn't wait to fall asleep next to every night.

The ping of her phone snapped Kelly out of her musings. "Thanks, that's a load off my mind. Can't wait to meet your mum. Cheers to new beginnings." She ended the message with an icon of glasses clinking and a smiley face.

Grinning like an idiot, Kelly practically floated home. For the first time in longer than she could remember, if ever, she looked forward to spending her days, her nights, her hopes, her fears, her passions, her life, with the woman who'd stolen her heart.

Epilogue

Nine months later…

Kelly awoke to a crisp spring morning, alone in bed. Cracking an eye open, she squinted against the glare of the bedside clock 6:00am. Ugh, far too early to be awake on a Sunday.

The sound of Lucy's sweet laughter coming from the kitchen, made Kelly break out in a jaw busting grin.

Hell, for the last six months she'd woken with a smile on her face. At times, she pinched herself to make sure she wasn't dreaming, because being a proud home owner felt surreal.

The bank owned a big chunk of the two-bedroom villa, but Lucy and Kelly had paid the deposit and their names were on the title.

Considering Lucy contributed significantly more than Kelly, Kelly had insisted on writing up something like a prenup, but Lucy wouldn't hear of it.

When Kelly had asked, "Aren't you worried I'll take you for a ride if, God forbid, we break up?" Lucy had kissed her on the lips and replied, "Nope"

Kelly's heart had soared knowing the trust Lucy had in her extended beyond the bedroom.

Yawning, Kelly climbed out of bed and slipped her robe on. Until meeting Lucy, Kelly had rarely slept naked, now though, she couldn't get enough of the feel of Lucy's body nuzzled against hers. The skin on skin contact, knowing Lucy was by her side, never failed to lull Kelly into a peaceful sleep.

The innocent act of tying the belt on her robe had her mind racing back to the first time they were intimate. It wasn't an experience Kelly ever wanted to repeat, nor would she change it. Thankfully, her horror story had a happy ending.

The past year hadn't been all smooth sailing. Buying a house was stressful shit, throw-in rambunctious twins and life couldn't be more chaotic, or rewarding.

After a quick pitstop, Kelly padded from the bathroom to the kitchen. The hardwood floor was cool beneath her feet.

"Hey," she said softly. "What are you doing up so early?"

"Look at them." Lucy's face lit up like a proud parent. "They're so cute. I just wanna snuggle them all day."

She slid down the wall and patted her thigh. A drop of kitten milk dripped off Tabitha's tabby grey chin as she climbed into Lucy's lap, and plonked her furry backside down.

Possum, who had the bushiest tail Kelly had ever seen, took a playful swipe at his sister.

"Hey, play nice." Kelly scooped him up and kissed his cute little nose. He responded with a high-pitched meow.

Kelly chuckled. "Don't sass your mamma. You should be looking after your sister, not tormenting her."

Out of the corner of her eye, Kelly saw Lucy grinning. It was hard not to; her smile was so big it almost split her face in two.

Unsure why she was being laughed at, Kelly harrumphed. "What's so funny?"

"Do you realize what you just said?"

"What?" Kelly asked, unsure what part of her sentence Lucy found amusing.

After putting Tabitha in the basket beside her, Lucy stood. Her sheer nighty clung to her curves, making Kelly want to drag her down the hall, toss her on the bed, and ravish her like a woman possessed.

"Up here." Lucy pointed to her eyes drawing Kelly's gaze from her voluptuous breasts to her smiling face. Eyes twinkling, she slipped her hands inside Kelly's robe.

"You're playing with fire." Kelly growled, a deep rumble rising in her chest.

Two pudgy kittens eyed her curiously, heads tilted to the side.

"So, Miss-I-don't-get-it-when-pet-owners-call-themselves-mum-or-dad. What changed?"

Kelly was finding it hard to concentrate on anything other than Lucy's soft, warm hands resting innocently on her hips. "Huh?"

"You referred to yourself as mamma."

"Oh shit, I did, didn't I? It just felt right." Kelly

shrugged. "Like your hands on me." She pushed a thigh between Lucy's legs.

Looking the picture of innocence, Lucy bit her lip and batted her beautiful green eyes. "Am I in trouble, Miss?"

In the corner of the kitchen, Possum and Tabitha had fallen asleep, a tangle of grey and white forming one big fur ball.

Love for the woman before her, their home, and, yes, their fur-babies, bloomed in Kelly's chest. Overcome with emotion, she put a lid on her libido.

"I love you, Lucy-Lou." Kelly swallowed the lump in her throat, and thumped her chest. "So much, that at times it hurts, like my heart is so full it's going to burst."

"I love you too, Kel. You're my world, my life, my anchor." Lucy swiped a tear, her lip kicking up. "My mistress."

"Forever and for always," Kelly said.

Intending to show Lucy exactly how much she loved her, every inch of her, Kelly led the way back to bed.

Also by Donna Jay

Finding Love Down Under - https://tinyurl.com/y8cfke7b

When Claire discovers her fiancée has abused her trust in the most heinous way possible, she severs all ties.

A year down the track, she couldn't be happier living a life of solitude on a vineyard. That is, until a quick trip into town changes everything.

Suddenly on her own in New Zealand, and on the edge of despair, Zoe never expected to find her salvation in the form of a beautiful and complex woman.

The following months are fraught with highs and lows as Claire and Zoe learn to navigate their way around each other. Both women need to overcome huge trust issues if they have any hope of forging a relationship.

Printed in Great Britain
by Amazon